I0671039

JOY RIDE

DESIREE HOLT

❧

Decadent Publishing Company
www.decadentpublishing.com

This book is a work of fiction. Names, characters, places, and incidents are the products of the author's imagination or used fictitiously. Any resemblance to actual events, locales or persons, living or dead, is entirely coincidental.

Joy Ride
Copyright 2011 by Desiree Holt
ISBN: 978-1-61333-136-1
Cover design by DZR Images and Cribley Designs

All rights reserved. Except for use in any review, the reproduction or utilization of this work, in whole or in part, in any form by any electronic, mechanical or other means now known or hereafter invented, is forbidden without the written permission of the publisher.

Published by Decadent Publishing Company

Look for us online at:
www.decadentpublishing.com

Printed in the United States of America

"What the Critics are saying..."

"When the books opens you meet Emma Blake who has had enough of her humdrum boring life. After suddenly breaking up with her boyfriend she decides to head to the last place on earth she would ever go. Aftershock is a bar where great bands perform and people drink beer. As Emma pulls up outside she knows that this is a place she has to check out. Once inside she orders her first beer ever and heads to the stage to watch the band. Mark is the bass guitarist of the band and Emma is drawn to him like lighting. Which is the name of the band Marc is in. They make eye contact and that evening they make sweet music together. Emma gives herself a fake name Music Lady which is what she wants to become.

The rest of the story is Emma coming to terms with the new person she is becoming and her learning to trust Marc. She feels that all he is, is the bass guitarist that she met at the club however Marc has a much deeper side. He spends much of the book trying to learn more about the real Emma and not that girl he met at the bar. He knows if he is patient enough she'll come around!

I highly recommend this book. It was fun to read and it made me think a little about myself. I would love to shed my quiet personality and go meet a guy in a band and Emma shows me that he can be everything I'm looking for! Wonderful job, Desiree!" ~ *Got Romance Reviews*

"Emma has never had a night of recklessness, abandonment until now. Moreover, Marc Malone is not your usual rock star, but instead, an average man looking for the right one. One night is all it takes for these two to know their wait is over.

In one word *Joy Ride* by Desiree Holt is AWESOME. I loved

how you have Emma who just wants one night of anyone except good ole' Emma. Hence, JoyRide is definitely the perfect title for this tale of mystery, passion and love in an unusual place and time.

In my opinion, *Joy Ride* by far is Desiree Holt's best book. The story grabbed my attention right from the beginning and I couldn't put it down. Although Emma and Marc are so opposite from each other, they do have one thing in common, love. *Joy Ride*, which consists of rock music and unadulterated passion, outshines Desiree Holt's other stories."

~ Rated 5 Ravens and a Recommended Read
by Lena of Black *Raven Reviews*

~DEDICATION~

To Jackie Joyride, the real Marc Malone who inspired me and made me fall in love with the music all over again. You rock, Guitar Man.

Chapter One

"*I* can't do this any more."

Emma Blake pushed herself up from the couch, stared at the man focused intently on the television, and wondered why she didn't run screaming into the night. All week she'd been restless, almost dreading their usual Saturday night. Pizza, an old movie, and obligatory sex. The lingering aroma of the oh-so-boring cheese and pepperoni still drifted in the air, but an unexpected feeling of nausea grabbed her. As if she'd finally reached her limit.

Andrew Fielder put the movie they were watching on pause and looked at her, puzzled. "Do what?"

"This." She waved her hands to encompass the room. The television. Him sprawled into a corner of the couch. "What we're doing."

"You mean the movie?" He frowned and started to uncoil himself from the couch. "No problem. I'll put in another one."

"No, Andrew." She wanted to stomp her foot. "I don't just mean the movie." She had an instant sensation of suffocating, of the room—maybe her entire life—closing in on her. A feeling that had been creeping up on her the past few days. "I mean *everything*. All of it. This routine. This...this...nothing. Everything."

He stared at her as if she'd spoken in a foreign language. "Emma, I don't know what the hell you're talking about."

"I know, I know." She began pacing, frustration threatening to explode inside her. "That's the problem. You. Just. Don't. Know."

Six days ago her college roommate, Jacie Monroe, blew into town on her way to a conference, blooming with the happiness of an exciting marriage, a wonderful child, and a more than fulfilling career. Her satisfaction with life shimmered around her. And just like that, Emma had gone from the flavorless acceptance of her own simple, uneventful life—a life she hadn't even realized she was dissatisfied with—to a case of raging discontent.

She'd stewed about it all week, hoping it would dissipate when Saturday night rolled around. But instead it only underscored her colorless existence. One minute she'd been happy with the gray she'd always known, then she wanted the bright flashes of color that seemed to sizzle from Jacie.

He leaned forward, a perplexed look on his face and, when he spoke, his voice was pitched in the patient tone of someone speaking to a child. It occurred to her that he often took that tone with her.

"You're making me nervous, Emma. Please just sit down and tell me what seems to be the problem. Just straight out."

Tell him? How could she put into words what had been rattling around in her mind all week, ever since she had lunch with her college roommate and saw the glow in the woman's face, the enthusiasm in her eyes when she talked about her husband and her job and her child? Emma was startled by the awareness that she had none of that. Nothing about her life sparkled. Although up until now, she'd been perfectly content. Or so she thought. But that day, she had the sensation of a veil lifting, showing her a world she could have if she'd just grab on to it.

Andrew would never understand. He was too satisfied with the way things were. Too comfortable. This was what he wanted.

And all Emma had wanted *until now.*

"Okay. Okay, okay." She stopped pacing, took a deep breath, and faced him. "Here's the thing, Andrew. In a couple of weeks I'm going to be thirty. *Thirty!* And my life is about as exciting as boiled water. I'm bored out of my skull. Is that straight out enough for you?"

"Bored?" He looked stunned. "Emma, how could you possibly be bored? We have a very good life. You know that. Right?"

She laughed, hearing the edge of hysteria in the sound. "A good life. Oh, yes. Right. Of course. We work all week. Have dinner with my folks on Friday night or brunch on Sunday. On Saturday I come over here, we order in pizza, watch an old movie then go to bed and have sex." She threw up her hands. "What more could a girl possibly want?"

"Emma, what in the hell has gotten into you?" He rubbed his jaw and blinked, as if he'd missed some important clue and didn't know what it was.

"Something. Everything." The sense of being suffocated or choked squeezed her again. "Tell me, Andrew. When we have sex, don't you ever want me to be on top? Don't you ever want to fuck me from behind?"

"What? For God's sake, Emma."

She wasn't sure if he was shocked at what she suggested or the fact that she said *fuck*. It certainly stunned *her* to hear the words coming out of her mouth. Here was poor sensible, unexciting, dependable Andrew—wearing her parents' stamp of approval along with his tailored slacks and collared polo shirt—looking as if someone had pulled the rug out from under him, and he'd landed on his ass.

It was just more than she wanted to deal with. It was like drinking flat champagne while everyone else got the bubbles. And she realized with unexpected clarity just how unsatisfied she'd been with the absence of bubbles all her life.

"I can't do this now. If you don't understand, nothing I say will make a difference."

She grabbed her purse from the table next to the couch and headed for the front door. If she didn't get out of this house right away, she was afraid she might choke to death. How could she explain to Andrew what the problem was when she wasn't quite sure herself? How could she tell him that sitting on that couch, watching a movie she hated, she suddenly saw a vision of herself fifty years in the future doing exactly the same things in exactly the same way, and life would have passed her by? She had to get away.

Andrew followed her onto the little porch, his fingers closing on her arm before she could make an escape. "Wait a minute. Emma, hold on. Come back here. Let's talk. Please."

Talk? About what? There was no way he'd ever understand the sudden need for excitement that was raging inside her. She saw clearly that it wasn't in his makeup.

"No, I can't." She moved away. "I have to get out of here. Sorry, sorry, sorry. I'll call you."

She hurried down the steps before he could try to stop her again, pressed the button on the fob to unlock her car, and jumped into the driver's seat. Andrew was still standing on the porch beneath the overhead light, staring. Bewilderment in every line of his body.

"Emma?"

She slammed the car door, cranked the engine, and quickly backed out of the driveway. She had no idea where she was going except away from here.

Poor Andrew. This wasn't even his fault. It was hers. She had no one to blame but herself for wearing blinders all these years. The good girl who never colored outside the lines. If her roommate hadn't been passing through town, if they hadn't met for lunch, she might have still been content and never hungered for something else. She drove through the quiet residential streets, wondering how she'd let this happen. How she'd managed to be satisfied with a life so defined. So confining. Constricting. So much that she felt suffocated.

She stopped at a red light at a busy intersection and tapped her thumb impatiently on the wheel until the light changed.

All these years she'd seen nothing wrong with the pattern of living her parents had established for her. They were truly wonderful people, but she saw now that they led a life you could set clocks and calendars by. She'd accepted the same for herself. Dating boys then men they considered appropriate and acceptable. She was comfortable with a conservative style of dress—plain, unadorned jeans, an undistinguished tailored blouse. In a pale blue.

The way good girls dress.

Her only rebellion had been one time in high school, when she and three of her "proper" friends had taken Sandy Piper's father's car for a joy ride. The thrill of the forbidden had lingered in the back of her mind all this time, buried but apparently still bubbling. Waiting for something to let it loose.

Turning right at the end of the street, she blended into the traffic on the four-lane thoroughfare lined with stores and other businesses. She passed a restaurant with sidewalk tables under outdoor lights, happy couples laughing and chatting. She'd never done that. Not with Andrew or any of her other dates. They all hated eating outside. Too many bugs. Too much exposure.

She drove aimlessly up one street and down the other, thoughts chasing each other around in her brain. Her birthday was closing in, and she was frightened that a life she'd never thought about or even known existed was passing her by.

She lost track of time and direction as she drifted toward no particular destination, so it was with some shock that she found herself on a street at the opposite end of town in front of a cement block building. The sign over the doorway read "Aftershock", and even with the car windows rolled up, she could hear the heavy sounds of a rock band bleeding out into the night.

I've never been to a rock club.

Because the men she dated didn't hang out in places like that. Or even listen to that kind of music.

But now, without thinking about it, she pulled into the crowded parking lot, climbed out of her car, and headed for the entrance as if on autopilot. The sign next to the door read "Now Appearing - Lightning." An appropriate name for a band playing in a club named Aftershock. The moment she opened the club's door, she was assaulted by the sheer volume of sound, the noises of the crowd mixed with the blast of the music.

Someone was shouting in her ear. "Ten bucks."

She stared at the large muscular man blocking her way, intimidating in black jeans and a long-sleeved black shirt, his hand outstretched.

She frowned. "What?"

He leaned closer to her ear. "Ten bucks. Cover. No money, you don't get in."

Emma fumbled in her tiny purse and found a ten-dollar bill. When she passed it to the man, he grabbed her arm and pressed a rubber stamp to her wrist—a stamp in the shape of a lightning bolt. She gawked at it, fascinated. She'd never been to a place where they stamped hands.

She looked up at the man. "What's this for?"

"So you can get in and out," he explained. "You never had a cover stamp before?"

Not that I'll admit to anyone.

"Oh. Of course. Thanks."

The place was so dark, she had trouble adjusting her eyes. Blackness shredded by the molecules of light illuminated the stage from the booth located high on one wall. Red and yellow mingled diffusely with the darkness, creating a surreal atmosphere for the four bodies totally immersed in the music they were creating. The room was packed with people screaming their approval at the band, bodies so jammed together caught up in the heavy beat filling the room that Emma had trouble inching her way in. Feverish energy crackled in the air, sizzling all around her. So palpable she felt it scorching her skin, and she realized just how appropriate the band's name was.

Emma stared at the crowd, at the bodies moving

suggestively, almost as if they were having sex to music. She'd never seen anything like it and it shocked her to the core. Then a strange heat surged through her own body, and she had trouble catching her breath. Not the suffocating feeling from earlier but something new, something that stimulated every one of her senses. For a moment, she wondered if she had wandered into an alternate universe, one where the outside world ceased to exist.

A drink, that's what I need. Something to calm her jittery nerves. Wriggling her way to the bar, she ordered a beer. Although she seldom drank, it seemed the easiest thing to order in all the chaos. Anyway, tonight was a night for new experiences, and she didn't think many of the people in here were drinking diet sodas.

Hardly anyone was seated. Instead, they were all moving their hips, raising their arms as they kept time to the thundering beat of the sound, and focusing on the band cranking out another high-energy song. The melody poured out into the darkened room, each member adding his own chemistry to the mix. Unsure what to do, Emma stood uncomfortably by the bar, holding her drink and listening to the seductive blend of instruments.

She was peripherally aware of the lead guitar's wail, the husky voice of the lead singer, and the heavy syncopation of the drums. But what captured her attention, sent her pulse pounding, was the heavy *thump, thump, thump* of the bass vibrating up through her body.

Well, she'd wanted something different. Something a little wild. She'd definitely found it here.

She needed to be closer to the stage, to see who was sending out that beat that echoed from her throbbing core to her breasts, but people were jammed together, filling every inch of space and blocking her view. At five-foot-two and in flat-heeled shoes, there was no way she could see over anyone's shoulders.

Clutching the cold beer bottle in her hand, she wedged her way between gyrating bodies, hypnotized by the music, until she reached the front of the crowd...and stopped at the edge of the stage, mesmerized. The bass guitarist stood with one foot balanced on the monitor in front of him, his body leaning into the sound. His head was thrown back, dark hair flying around his face as he pounded out the rhythm of the song they were playing. He was wild, uninhibited, totally immersed in his music. He moved with an incredible grace to the accented beat, hips thrusting as his clever fingers plucked the strings and slid on the neck of the guitar.

For one incredible moment, Emma had the feeling he was playing only for her and she realized she really *had* been struck by "Lightnin'." Permanently electrified by it.

A surge of heat raced through her, and it wasn't the kind that emanated from the tightly packed sweaty bodies. Instead, an electric excitement gripped her, sending a charge of unfamiliar sexual thrill to every nerve. Her breasts tingled and between her thighs, she felt a throbbing as deep as the sound of the bass. At first she stood stiffly, clutching her drink. People jostled and shoved her as they kept time to the beat. She took two quick swallows of the beer, grimacing at the bitter taste. But as the alcohol eased her tension, she found herself catching the rhythm of the music and trying to mimic the movements of the bass player—totally caught up in the seductive lure of the song. For one crazy moment, she was gripped by an uncontrollable urge to jump up on the stage, and bump and grind with him. Her! Emma, the good girl!

Clumsily juggling the beer bottle, she slipped the thin strap of her purse over her head so it lay crosswise between her breasts. Her focus still on the bass player, she swayed to the beat, hips moving, rocking. When the song ended, the bass guitarist threw back his head on a final note and then looked out into the crowd, peering beyond the glare of the stage lights.

His eyes seemed to find hers as if pulled by a magnet, and a fist slammed through her.

Ohmigod!

She couldn't have torn her gaze away from his if someone

had paid her. The look on his face was so intense; it was as if a hand had reached out and touched her. Her heart rate sped up, stuttering erratically. In the next moment, the lead guitar laid down the opening bars of the next song, the bass player came in on cue, then the drummer, before the singer belted out the first lines. Again the bass pulsated through her, sending sensual shock waves into every part of her body. There was a raw, untamed feeling to the sound that made inhibitions disappear and excitement rage like an uncontrolled storm. The bass player finally dragged his eyes away from her, but she couldn't stop staring at him. The way he threw his head back and his hair flew wildly like a thick curtain around his face. His body moved sensually, making love to the music, so caught up in its rhythm that he and his instrument were one.

Emma finished her beer and stuck the empty bottle on the little shelf around one of the support pillars. Barely aware of what she was doing, she undid the clip holding her hair and shook her head, letting the waves cascade past her shoulders. Her hands yanked her blouse out of the waistband of her jeans and she knotted the tails just beneath her breasts, leaving her midriff bare—something she never did in public.

But tonight all bets were off. Tonight, Emma Blake was throwing off the restricting mantle of her life and finding out what was on the other side.

The band finished the song, launched immediately into another one, and Emma continued to gyrate with the crowd, hips thrusting, feet moving, throwing back her head the way her bass player did.

Her bass player?

But that was how she viewed him—this man on stage who was sex personified. She would have imagined doing all kinds of wicked things with him, if she'd know enough wicked things to do. She danced in place, arms waving, tossing her head, and wiggling her hips in a suggestive fashion. The Emma she knew disappeared, left behind in the erotic atmosphere of the dark club and the pulse-pounding music.

By the time the last song of the last set ended, she was both exhausted and exhilarated, her body vibrating with arousal. Her gaze had locked with the bass player's each time he'd stared out into the audience. Now, as the band broke down the stage and put away their instruments, she saw him snap his guitar case shut and unexpectedly turn to face her. The coil of lust unwinding in her belly was so intense it shocked her.

She should follow the rest of the crowd out of the club, but she wanted to watch him until the last possible moment and store every image into her mind. At last reluctantly realizing she was the only person left, she walked slowly out into the parking lot. She could still hear the music in her head, still feel that *thump thump thump* that throbbed in all her erogenous zones. Still see the come-fuck-me look in the bass player's eyes.

Emma dragged her feet as she headed toward her car, not wanting the magic of the night to end, and nearly screamed when a hand touched her shoulder.

"It's me." The voice was low, almost a soft growl.

She turned and there he was, scant inches away from her, his masculinity almost overpowering her, the sound of his voice still echoing through her, mesmerizing her. The light in the parking lot cast a halo around him; the glow reflected in the dark irises of his eyes.

"Oh!" was all she could think to say.

"I saw you watching me." The words were like a caress sliding over her skin.

"I-I like your music."

His smile was almost feral. "Maybe you'll like this, too."

His hands slid up to cup her face and when his mouth touched hers, it seemed the most natural thing in the world to respond. He licked the closed seam of her lips with the tip of his tongue, a feathery touch that sent shivers skating along her spine. Her legs wobbled and she wrapped her fingers around his wrists to hang on, feeling the hard muscle and sinew beneath her fingertips.

He kissed her slowly, a languid movement as if he'd devoted

himself to nothing else but seducing her mouth. And the rest of her along with it. His tongue moved back and forth in soft, gentle strokes, finally pressing a little harder until she opened for him. When he thrust inside, the effect was like an electric shock through her system. Her mind blanked, her only focus on the reactions stirring inside her body. He licked and plunged and savored, all the while holding her face in the warmth of his palms. The beating pulse in her womb ratcheted up, and her breasts felt full and swollen.

She had a sudden sensation the world was spinning in slow motion before it stopped dead on its axis. Fire raged instantly to life between them.

When he lifted his head, she was dizzy with sensation. Those dark coffee eyes locked with hers, sending her silent, erotic messages.

He touched his lips to her ear. "Come home with me."

A shiver of delicious anticipation shimmied over her skin and without a moment of hesitation, she said, "Okay."

Chapter Two

Marc Malone couldn't believe his luck. This kind of thing never happened to him before. Despite the perception people had of musicians, women weren't exactly dropping into his lap. At least not like this one. Not that he was celibate or anything, just a lot pickier than others. And this one was something special. He knew it from the moment he spotted her. There was a freshness to her, a unique appeal that he didn't see in most of the women who came to Aftershock.

Which was why he passed on most of them.

When this one caught his eye, she had the look of a fish out of water, stiff and self-conscious, not quite sure what to do with herself. Brand new to the club, or he definitely would have noticed her before. He could tell the moment the music captured her, visibly loosening a constricting coil wound inside her. First her feet began to move, tentatively, as if she was unsure what to do. Then the hips bumped a little from side to side. When she shook her hair free and knotted her blouse beneath the breasts, he couldn't stop staring. He had to shift to stand with his foot on the monitor again until his sudden hard-on cooled down.

He kept expecting her to leave after each song ended, but she stayed hemmed in by the crowd, hips gyrating, head thrown back. Those sizzling moments when their gazes locked, he had the feeling she was looking directly into his soul. His entire body went on full alert, and his heart turned over. He felt like a sugar junkie lusting after candy. The need to see her and talk to her grabbed him like a giant fist. He had to find out who she was. How she'd happened to show up at Aftershock when he'd never seen her there before.

Following her into the parking lot had been a real risk. She could have slapped his face or worse yet, called the cops. The invitation to come home with him had been issued impulsively, just like the kiss. He could hardly believe she'd accepted both, her response shocking him. Bad girls were only too willing to acquire what he thought of as a badge of honor fuck. Good girls usually ran as if they'd been courted by the devil. But it seemed the magic had reached out to this woman as it had to him.

He kept glancing in his rear view mirror to make sure she was still behind him. Yeah, those were her headlights.

For the first time in a long time, he was nervous. He tried to remember if his place—the little house he'd bought last year—was clean. Were there dirty clothes lying around? Dirty dishes? Did he have fresh sheets on the bed? Should he offer her wine first? Did he even have any?

And then he was turning the corner onto his street.

Okay, buddy boy. Here we go. Don't fuck this up.

I'm doing it! I'm really doing it! Going home with this man who rocked my world.

God! I can't believe this!

It wasn't the beer. It wasn't even the spurt of rebellion, or the choking frustration of her existence that had her following the black Jeep Cherokee through the quiet streets of the city. She could have gone into that club, listened to the music, tasted a new and different slice of life and gone home, hugging it to her like a treasured secret. No, it was the bass player. He'd looked out at her with his stormy eyes and an invisible but powerful connection had been forged.

This was the most daring thing she'd ever done.

All kinds of possibilities ran through her mind. She wasn't dumb. Only an idiot would be completely unaware of what he had in mind. He was a musician, right? Her knowledge of his world was limited but she read all the gossip magazines. She was torn between a desire to step off a ledge into the unknown and fear that the fall would be more than she could handle. If she was smart she'd get away. Run back to her safe little world.

Yet she couldn't make herself do it. The electricity that zapped between them the moment their eyes connected was bad enough. But the instant collision of senses when they'd kissed in the parking lot had invaded every nerve and muscle. No way could she have just gotten in her car and driven home. Not when temptation beckoned so strongly.

Wait. Are you crazy? What if he's some kind of mad rapist? Or had a load of drugs stashed in his house? Or...Or what? He calls to you like no other man you've ever been with. You secretly wanted this the moment you felt that connection. And remember. You can always leave. Any time.

She was startled to realize they were driving in her neighborhood. But the street he turned into wasn't a familiar one. Small bungalows lined both sides of a roadway guarded by ancient oaks. He pulled into a wide driveway, leaving room for her to park next to him. She climbed out of the car on legs not quite steady. This was the first time she'd ever followed a man home in her life, one she barely knew. Was she really about to step into the unknown with him? The thought both excited and terrified her. The same thrill she'd felt taking Mr. Piper's car for a joy ride all those years ago surfaced now and sparked through her body.

Suddenly seized by an attack of nerves, she looked down to see her hands shaking as she turned off the ignition and dropped her keys into her purse. This was so far outside her comfort zone. What if he wanted more than she could give? What if she said yes to him and wasn't any good at it? Her experience, especially for someone her age, was embarrassingly limited. Good, safe Andrew was only the third man she'd slept with, and she was pretty sure none of that had prepared her for whatever would happen tonight.

Oh, Andrew. He'd been the furthest thing from her mind. After tonight there was no going back, even if he wanted her. He was part of the Emma who had run from his house. Now she was filled with the desire to test her wings and her exhilaration was mixed with fear and guilt. For a very brief moment, she was tempted to turn the engine back on, back out into the street, and drive away like a bat out of hell.

What am I doing here?

Emma Blake didn't go to rock clubs. Didn't kiss strange men, especially rock musicians. Didn't go home with them almost the moment after they met. Emma was the quintessential good girl who never did anything the least bit daring.

She quaked at the thought of what might happen if she went inside but she was sick and tired of her life that suddenly looked dull gray. Even though her anticipation was mixed with fear and guilt, she wanted to be a little wild and crazy. Push the envelope. Take a chance on what came next tonight. Whatever that was.

If I get hit by a car tomorrow, I'll never know what might have been. She paused to take in a steadying breath and let it out.

Okay, Emma. You wanted some excitement. Here it is, so don't screw it up. Take a chance.

He waited for her to walk around the car and catch up to him, looking dark and mysterious in the ambient light from a street lamp. Emma put her hand into the one he was holding out to her, and he led her up the steps to the front door. Tiny sparks of electricity danced through her, heat suffusing her.

"I don't even know your name," he said as he fished one-handed for his house key.

"I don't know yours, either," she told him.

"It's Marc. Marc Malone." He opened the door and gestured for her to step inside. "What's yours?"

"It's...um...." Her voice faded off. Tell him her name? Good girls didn't give their names to sexy men they went home with from a bar. Besides, anonymity was her cloak in this wild exhilarating joy ride, and she wrapped it tightly around herself.

He stood there, an expectant look on his face.

Tell him something, dummy.

She opened her mouth but nothing came out.

"Not a hard question," he prompted. "You gotta have a name. Everyone does." When she still didn't answer him, he said, "Okay, I'll call you Music Lady, because you danced to the music. ML for short. How's that?"

She giggled nervously, her purse sliding from her hand. "Okay. Maybe I'll call you Guitar Man."

"Call me whatever you want." His voice was low, seductive.

Kiss me again. Please. Then I don't have to worry about things like names.

As if he'd heard the silent message, he turned her toward him, cradled her head in his warm palms, and lightly pressed his mouth to hers. His lips were as warm and sensuous as she remembered, and the feel of them sent sparks flying through her. The male scent of him surrounded her, invading her like an addictive drug. Her nipples stiffened again and between her thighs, she felt a low throb deep inside her body. She clung to his wrists again, anchoring herself.

His fingers gripped her skull and he slanted his lips this way and that, finding a better angle before thrusting his tongue deeper inside her mouth. His touch was firm. Possessive.

Ohmigod!

Kissing had never, ever been like this, so arousing that every nerve screamed for his touch. He was tall enough that she had to reach up to him but not so tall he towered over her. Lean but not skinny. Muscular. And their bodies fit together as if made for each other. For the first time in her life, she wanted a man inside her more than she wanted her next breath.

I want him to fuck me.

Lordy, where had that come from? Andrew would have been shocked into a state of performance anxiety if she used it with him. She swallowed a laugh, seized by a hysterical desire to show up naked at Andrew's front door and scream *"Fuck! Fuck! Fuck!"* at him.

But in the next moment, all she could think about was the scorching flame of Guitar Man's tongue searing her every place it touched, seducing her, coaxing her. Wiping away the attack of nerves that had invaded her. He moved his hands slowly down her neck and shoulders to her breasts. She moaned into his mouth as his palms cupped her, and his thumbs rubbed her nipples through the fabric of her shirt and her bra. More cream flooded her core and the throbbing in its walls intensified. Every pulse point pounded as wildness surged through her.

And still his tongue danced with hers, coaxing more and more of a response. She thrust boldly into his mouth, loving the purely male essence of him, wanting to drink him in so she could hold the taste forever.

The shock of it slammed into her. This was what she'd been looking for her entire life without even knowing it. This! This feeling. This man. And even while it terrified her, she welcomed it.

When he lifted his head, they were both gasping for air. Marc stared hard into her eyes as if searching for an answer to a silent question, then backwalked her into the house. He reached out a hand and in a moment, soft light from a small lamp illuminated the space.

Now she could see the strong line of his jaw, the clear dark blue of his eyes framed with thick eyelashes, the strong nose and the high cheekbones. There was something so totally masculine about him. She felt it sizzling straight to her sex.

She stared at him, flashing hot and cold.

"Yeah, that's right, keeping looking at me. Don't look around," he whispered and laughed, a low, rusty sound. "I'm not sure what the place looks like. Bachelor pad, you know."

"I don't care." She sighed. "You're the only thing I want to see."

When had she ever been so bold? Colored outside the lines?

But with this man she was someone else, someone ready to fly into hyperspace.

"And I want to see you. Every bit of you. You are just so damn beautiful."

Beautiful? Had anyone, even Andrew ever told her that? And in a way that made her think it might be true?

She stared at Marc's face, trying to read his expression. His smile was warm and genuine, lighting him from within. It was soothing and at the same time stimulating. And he smelled completely delicious. Time seemed to slow down as his gaze took in every inch of her. Finally, he threaded his fingers through her hair and tilted her head back slightly.

"I could get lost in these hazel eyes. I bet they change with whatever you're feeling. And I want to see them change." He kissed each eyelid. "A perfect nose." Another kiss on the tip, and his lips trailed down her cheek to her chin and then the column of her neck. His tongue slid along her jawline then down the column of her neck, and shivers skimmed the length of her spine. "So soft," he murmured. "Like satin."

He pressed his lips against the hollow of her throat, and she was sure he could feel her pulse pounding erratically. She clutched at him, her knees weak and the crotch of her panties already soaked.

He raised his head to look into her eyes and, even in the semi-darkness, she could see a wealth of emotion there. When he took her hand and led her down a short hallway into an unlit room, she wanted to tell him, *Hurry, hurry.* A flick of a wall switch and light bloomed from a small bedside lamp. Emma saw what seemed to be like acres of dark blue on a king-sized bed, covered with a dark blue comforter. An image of the two of them naked rolling around on it made heat creep to her cheeks and an unfamiliar hunger gripped her.

Marc lifted her hands to his mouth and kissed her knuckles. "You're shaking." He studied her expression. "We don't have to do this if you don't want to. We can stop right now."

She trembled with need, not fear. Her gaze skimmed his

face, dark hair falling around it like a silk cloak, stubble shadowing his strong jaw, stormy blue eyes flashing with fire. Not do this? Was he crazy?

"Don't stop," she told him in a soft voice. "I want this."

"Me, too." His voice was a low, sexy growl.

She wet her lips. "I-I never do this. I want you to know that."

He grinned at her. "Have sex?" he teased.

Her face heated. "Go home with someone I've just met."

She expected arrogance, male pride, self-satisfaction but what she got was a look of such tenderness, it made her heart clench.

"I figured that out already, babe. It's okay. We'll just take things easy."

"No." She shook her head. "I don't want that. I want you. Everything. All of it."

All the things I've heard whispered about but never experienced. I want what put that look in Jacie's eyes.

He brushed his mouth over hers. "Then that's what you'll get."

He untied the tails of her blouse and popped each button slowly, pushing the fabric down her arms until the garment fell to the floor. In the next instant the bra followed it. The heat of his gaze raked over her breasts. He took her nipples between thumb and forefinger of each hand and squeezed gently.

"Jesus, you have the most gorgeous breasts." He sounded almost reverent. "Your nipples are so rosy, so firm."

Bending his head, he took one firm bud into his mouth and sucked deeply, flicking his tongue over the pebbled surface. His lips and tongue were so soft, she melted beneath them. The sensation was almost unbearable, and she moaned in response.

His warm palms cupped her breasts. His palms holding the weight of them as he worshipped first one nipple then the other. The slightly rough surface of his tongue sent jolts of heat through her. Emma stood there feeling truly desirable for the first time in her life. This was no obligatory action. This man actually wanted her. *Her!* And she wanted him just as badly.

She lifted her hands and stroked along his jawline, loving the rough texture of his late night growth of beard. She moved her fingers upward to the thick shock of hair that was so soft and smooth as she touched it, still wild from his movements on stage. Her breathing hitched as he pulled harder first on one nipple then the other before tracing a line down the valley between her breasts with his tongue.

Marc moved down her rib cage to the waistband of her jeans, and she heard the pop as the snap opened and the hiss of the zipper being lowered. He pushed her jeans and panties down past her hips before urging her down to the bed, lowering her to the edge of the mattress. His gaze never left hers as he tugged the garments off the rest of the way. Then he put his lean fingers on her thighs and spread them wide.

At first, Emma felt self-consciously exposed, his eyes drinking in the sight of her pubic curls and the pink flesh of her sex. The men she'd been with before this always did everything in the dark. Now she wondered if Marc liked what he saw. If she was as sexy as the other women he'd been with.

As if he knew what she was thinking, he murmured, "Beautiful."

When he knelt on the floor in front of her and she realized what he was about to do, she tried to push him away.

"You—you don't have to do that," she stammered.

He looked up at her. "I don't *have* to do anything. I *want* to. Hasn't any man ever wanted to eat this sweet pussy before?"

The word shocked her. It wasn't one she used in conversations with girlfriends. Not even with Annie, her best friend. And certainly none of the pitifully few men she'd been with used blunt sexual language. Sometimes Andrew seemed almost embarrassed to acknowledge they were having sex.

While she was still trying to form an answer to his question, he bent his head and traced a line down the length of her slit with his tongue.

The blast of heat that surged through her was shocking. Every nerve fired and her...*pussy*...clenched! Just that one caress nearly did her in.

He made a humming noise of satisfaction. "And delicious, too," he murmured against her flesh.

His words made her shiver, made her pulse ratchet up and erotic hunger clutch at her. Without thinking she widened her legs even more, and he groaned in pleasure against her flesh. Another lick. Another stroke with his tongue. Then a flick against the throbbing bud of her clit, and another jolt of sensation speared her so powerful it gripped her like an iron fist.

He nudged her back on the bed until she was lying flat and draped her legs over his shoulders. Dropping to his knees, he opened the lips of her sex with those lean talented fingers, stroking her as if he was playing his guitar, and thrust his tongue deep inside her.

"Ohhhhh." A moan slipped past her lips.

Then he did it again. And again. Moving his fingers so he could rub and tease her clit as he fucked her with his tongue, coaxing her to a higher plane of arousal.

Emma lay there wrapped in a cloud of pleasure that drifted over every inch of her skin, giving herself over to responses that were new and startling. She wanted this to go on forever—that glide and plunge of his tongue, the flick and rub of his fingers. But the coil of need wound so tightly inside her began to unfurl itself and spiral up through her body.

She tensed for a moment when Marc used his fingers to scoop some of the cream from her soaking vagina. Aware that she was wetter than she ever remembered, she jumped when he slid lower and lower until he reached the tight ring of the anal sphincter. No one had ever touched her *there* before. But then her lips parted, her breathing hitched, and she lifted to him.

His fingers, calloused from playing the bass, rasped against her tender skin and slid to her pussy again, sending frissons of excitement skittering along every nerve. He worked three of them into her as his mouth sucked hard on her clit. The orgasm hit without warning.

"Oh, oh, oh." The sounds of pleasure rippled from her

mouth. Body shaking, her own whimpers and cries echoed in her ears.

She jerked her hips, arching toward him as she shook with spasm after spasm. Deep inside, every muscle clenched in response. Marc's tongue continued stroking and lapping until the tremors subsided, and she became a limp mass. He licked the last drop of juice from her pussy, humming his appreciation.

He rose to his feet and leaned over her, the liquid of her arousal gleaming on his face. When they kissed she tasted herself on his lips, a taste that was shockingly pleasurable.

"You are incredible," he murmured. "A goddess. I want to worship your body forever."

She smiled at him, spent, but unbelievably feeling a response growing again at his words. And wondering how it was even possible.

But now she was hungry to see every lean, muscular inch of *him*.

"I want you naked," she told him, the words spilling from her mouth with a new boldness.

Marc grinned but when he spoke, his voiced was ragged and uneven. "I thought you'd never ask."

He rose and pulled his T-shirt over his head, tossing it to the floor on top of her clothes. His jeans and boxers followed, and then he stood before her in his wonderful lean nakedness, dark hair curling on his chest and arrowing down to his groin where his magnificent cock rose proudly from its thick nest of curls. A beautiful tattoo sleeve covered one arm, unlike anything Emma had ever seen before. The only ones she was familiar with some actor had sported on television. But the beauty of the colors of this one, the scrollwork and unique characters and the delicate tracery of the design fascinated her. The hues were vivid, the lines scrolls and sweeps, each blending into the next, some more powerful than the others. Like his music, she thought. She could spend hours just studying it, artwork worthy of display in a museum.

Tentatively she reached out a finger and ran it over the

intricate design. The feel of it somehow excited her.

He was the most beautiful man she had ever laid eyes on. Not just his body, but the strong set of his jaw, the straight nose, the dark eyes fringed with thick lashes. The same electric shock of excitement that had grabbed her when she first saw him in the bar seized her now.

And she'd never felt so totally and completely connected to another person.

Marc saw the heat flare in her eyes as she took in every inch of his nudity and if it was possible, his cock hardened even more. Jesus, he wanted this woman. Wanted to bury himself deep inside her and stay there forever. He could hardly believe she was actually here. With him. In his house. Naked in his room. He was afraid if he pinched himself she'd disappear. He'd been with a fair amount of women—all kinds—but it didn't take a genius to know this one was special. The real deal.

This was no groupie going from musician to musician, or some barfly stimulated by alcohol. No, she'd radiated such nervousness at first he was afraid she'd bolt and run. Music Lady was pure, clean woman, sensual and shy at the same time. A combination that made him so hot he had to grit his teeth to find the edge of control.

All his adult life, he'd looked for a woman like this. A woman who, despite the fact that she'd come home with him after one scorching kiss, definitely did not seem the type to fall into anyone's bed. A woman whose mannerisms, lack of experience, whose every action and reaction with him set her apart from the other women he'd been with.

His dream, only now forming, was to find someone who could become a real part of his life. One he could share things with. A very special woman who understood the demands of the music business and the soul of an artist. Someone who could adapt to him working nights, rehearsing days, needing quiet time to write his music. Someone who could live with the volatile environment of his career.

Just that quickly, he knew he wanted it with Music Lady.

The question was, did she desire it with him? And would she really turn out to be what he thought or was it just wishful thinking?

He had a hunger to learn everything about her. What she liked to eat. What movies appealed to her. What her favorite color was. Anything and everything that could unlock the secret of his Music Lady—why she'd come to Aftershock tonight, and more importantly, why she'd agreed to come home with him. But first he had to fuck her every way possible so he could completely imprint himself on her body inside and out.

Aroused to the point of desperation, he lifted ML in his arms, yanked back the covers on the bed, and placed her carefully on the sheets. His eyes roamed over every inch of the perfect oval of a face and hazel eyes fringed with heavy lashes. Her body was flushed a soft shade of pink, cream still glistening on the soft blonde curls covering her mound. He ran the tip of one finger through them, stroking the silken folds, and was rewarded with the sight of a delicious shiver racing over delicate skin. His breath caught at the wonder of this woman.

She lifted her arms to him and he knelt between creamy thighs, trailing soft kisses over her breasts, stomach, hips. Pressing his face to her tummy, he inhaled deeply, loving the scent that drifted up his nostrils, a heady mixture of light floral and feminine musk. His balls tightened and his swollen cock flexed.

He ran his palms down the length of silken skin from hip to ankle and back again, memorizing the dips and swells of her body. Bending her legs at the knees, he pressed his palms against soft inner flesh, spreading them wide and giving him a view that nearly made him come right then. He stared, looking his fill of the glistening pink pussy flesh darkened from the rush of the recent orgasm, the bud of the swollen clit peeking out at him from its protective hood, the graceful curve of ass where it met thighs....

Jesus!

Marc swallowed, a difficult feat since his mouth was almost totally dry, and allowed himself the pleasure of covering her from neck to mound with a trail of kisses. Now he understood the meaning of that phrase, "I could eat you up with a spoon." Her skin made satin seem rough, and the scent of it filled his system more intoxicatingly that any whiskey he'd ever had. He lost himself in the dizzying taste of her, the seductive feel of her. This woman was the treat he'd been looking for all his life, and he wanted to make a permanent feast of her.

The little cries of pleasure she made as his mouth traveled over her only turned him on even more until he knew he couldn't wait another moment to be inside of her. Reaching into the nightstand drawer, he pulled out a condom, tore away the foil wrapper, and sheathed himself. Wrapping his fingers around his cock, he touched it to her opening, rubbing it against her cream to lubricate it.

"Get ready, darlin'." His voice was thick with raw hunger.

He pressed into her slowly, gaze locked with hers, reading there an answering need. The tight walls of her cunt stretched around him as he filled her, gripping him like a hot, wet fist. For sure.

Holy sweet Jesus!

He'd died and gone to heaven. When he was fully inside her, the rush of pleasure was so perfect he wanted to weep. He looked into her beautiful eyes, the connection between them so profound it scored his very soul. He could stay buried in this woman for the rest of his life.

This is what I always wanted. Not that I have that many notches on my bed post, thank the Lord. Pure sweetness.

Better make it damn good for her, buddy boy.

Marc closed his eyes and drew in a deep breath, fighting for the control that was rapidly slipping away from him. Then he began to move, slowly at first, then faster as her body answered his, until they were moving in a rhythm that had its own music. In. Out. In. Out. Faster now. Her legs wrapped around him and pulled him deeper into her wet heat. He felt the trembling inside her surging and intensifying, his eyes watching hers for the signal she was up on that erotic cliff with him.

Yes! There! Panting, she parted her lips slightly, her legs tightening around him, her hips arching up to him. He pumped into her, driving her to the edge with him. More, harder, faster.

"Come on, babe," he rasped. "You're gonna take me with you. Just let it go."

And she did, shattering beneath him.

The tumble into space shocked him with its intensity. He wasn't aware of anything except a back velvet void, the grip of her pussy around him, and an orgasm that shook every muscle in his body. He couldn't breathe, and his heart raced madly as he poured himself into the latex reservoir. For the first time since he'd started having sex, he hated the thin barrier that kept him from feeling her skin to skin.

At last, spent, he fell forward, catching his weight on his forearms, dragging air into his lungs. His heart was pounding ferociously, or maybe it was hers. He kissed her—a soft kiss no longer ravenous with hunger—loving the velvet surface of her lips and the electric glide of her tongue against his.

He barely had strength to ease himself from her body and dispose of the condom. Then he was beside her, turning off the lamp, tugging the covers over them, and wrapping his arms around her. He brushed her hair back from her cheek and kissed the soft skin as she snuggled back against him. The curve of her buttocks fitted nicely against his groin.

"Sleep," he murmured, and closed his eyes.

Emma didn't remember falling asleep, and when she opened her eyes at first she couldn't figure out where she was. A warm male body was curled around her, a muscular arm thrown across her hip.

Andrew.

But not sleeping on his stomach, his skin her barely touching as usual.

She shifted slightly and realized she was sore in places she didn't even know she could feel.

What time is it?

She lifted her wrist with the watch on it, but the room was dark so it was impossible to see. Turning her head slightly, her eye caught a bedside clock. Red numerals told her it was just after five.

Wait! Andrew doesn't have a clock like that.

Tentatively she touched the arm wrapped around her, trying to ease out from beneath. And her heart nearly stopped. This was not Andrew's arm. She was familiar enough with it that she could tell the difference in how it felt.

Turning on the bedside lamp, she looked at the man lying beside her. A man with a tattooed arm. And for a moment she wanted to scream. Where was she and who was this person?

But then it all came back to her with startling clarity.

Andrew!

The argument.

Frustration with the entire situation. With her *life!*

Running from his house.

The club, Aftershock.

The bass player whose eyes seemed to see into her very soul.

And the magic of their erotic coupling.

Ohmigod!

I have to get out of here. Right now. I have to get home.

She wasn't brave enough to face her joy ride in the light of day. At least not at that moment, not with her hands shaking and her heart racing a mile a minute. What on earth had she been thinking about?

That Emma was tired of being a good girl.

Well, guess what? She's not a good girl anymore.

Thankful that the light hadn't woken Marc, she slid carefully from the bed, got down on her knees, and felt around on the floor for her clothes. Silently pulling them on, she picked up her sandals and tiptoed out of the room toward the front of the house.

Purse. Where's my purse?

Oh, yeah. Living room.

She had just unlocked the front door with a soft click, when she heard him behind her.

"Music Lady?" His voice was hoarse with the remnants of sleep.

She turned and nearly swallowed her tongue. He was standing not two feet away from her gloriously naked, his cock semi-erect, his hair in that sexy tangle. He pushed it back from his face and squinted at her.

"Where are you going?"

"I-I have to leave," she stammered.

In seconds he was beside her, his hands on her shoulders. "Don't go. Please. We didn't even get a chance to talk."

"Talk?" she squeaked. All she could remember was the intense physical and emotional connection. There hadn't been any room for words.

"Please," he repeated. "I want to get to know you."

"I-I-I...." She shook her head. "I have to go. I'm sorry." Panic, guilt, embarrassment all swirled in a volatile emotional cocktail. She had to leave, to get some perspective on the very impulsive act of hers. Get away before he could start asking questions she didn't want to answer. She trembled with an anxiety attack.

What have I done?

His hands slid up to cup her cheeks. "I want to see you again."

"I don't know." She chewed her bottom lip. She wanted to stay but the intensity of her emotions and the reality of what she'd done frightened her. How could she care about someone so quickly? Someone so completely opposite everything else in her life?

"Then will you at least come to the club? Next week? We play Tuesday through Saturday."

"Maybe. I...maybe."

"Here's something to remember while you're trying to decide."

He lowered his mouth to hers, rubbing his lips against hers very softly before pressing his tongue against the seam. She opened for him without thought and welcomed his intrusion into the hot well of her mouth. She melted, excited by his touch. Her own small tongue slipped past his lips and danced with his while her body quivered, and the throbbing in her sex reminded her of how he made her feel.

His thumbs caressed her cheekbones while he fed from her, the kiss invading her senses. Gasping she broke away.

"I-I really, really have to go. Now."

Yanking the door open, she raced down the three steps to her car, pressing the fob to unlock it, and leapt into it as if she were in a footrace with the devil. She backed quickly out into the street, but then she glanced toward the house and saw him standing in the doorway, unabashedly naked, haloed by the street lamp next to the house.

Ohmigod.

He lifted his hand to wave and she pulled quickly away, her body sending her messages but her mind scattered to the winds.

How had she let herself do this?

Because she'd wanted a change. Excitement. She'd certainly gotten it. But she'd also gotten something else she hadn't counted on—an emotional awakening that suddenly made Marc Malone very important to her.

So now what the hell did she do now?

Chapter Three

Marc stood on his back porch watching the blossoming sunrise and the lifting of the night, drinking a cup of strong instant coffee. He couldn't believe she'd actually left, his Music Lady. Just...put on her clothes, got in her car, and drove away. One minute they were asleep, exhausted by the most incredibly fulfilling sex. The next, she was tiptoeing around his room, gathering her clothes, and trying to sneak away.

He'd already been entertaining thoughts of waking up with her wrapped in his arms. Showering with him. His cock hardened as he imagined all the things they could do in the shower.

Then he'd take her out to breakfast. Talk to her. See what kind of things she liked to eat. Find out what had brought her to Aftershock last night. Why she'd gone home with him. How he could convince her to do it again and again.

Well, that idea had run down the shithole in a hurry. She'd taken off like a cat with its tail on fire.

He carried his mug into the bedroom, shucked off the jeans he'd pulled on and sat on the bed. With the mug in one hand, he grabbed a fistful of sheet with the other and lifted it to his nose. Inhaled deeply. Her scent was still so strong on the fabric, a light floral essence that teased at his nostrils and jacked up his hormones.

Had he said or done something wrong? Frightened her in some way? He replayed every word they'd exchanged over and over, easy because they hadn't talked all that much. He'd felt such an instant powerful connection at the club. He hadn't been wrong about that. He was sure she sensed it, too, or she wouldn't have come home with him.

But she was skittish, like a newborn colt going through the process of imprinting, eager for it but sidestepping as if afraid to like it too much. He'd already guessed her trip to Aftershock fell somewhere in that kind of thing. Where did she come from? What had brought her there?

He swallowed the rest of the coffee, set the mug on the bedside table, and leaned back on the pillows, still clutching the sheet. In his mind he went over every single thing they'd done, the memories scorching his skin. Being inside her was the closest to heaven he'd ever come, and he wanted more of that.

More of her.

The ring of the phone on the nightstand shattered his reverie. He snatched up the receiver, hoping it was *she* before he realized she didn't have his number. Maybe she didn't even remember his name.

God, he hoped he was wrong about that.

"Yeah?"

"Get up on the wrong side of the bed?" Rick Trajean, the lead guitar player and the band's leader chuckled on the other end of the connection.

Marc shook himself mentally. "Sorry. Didn't get much sleep last night."

"I hope it was in a good cause," Rick teased.

Maybe Rick knew who she was. Could help him find her.

"Listen, did you happen to notice someone new in the club last night? A blonde, tiny, drinking a beer?"

Now Rick's laugh was full and loud. "Are you shitting me? That could describe half the women who come into Aftershock. What's with you?"

Being an idiot. Rick's right. Why would he even notice one woman from another in a crowd like that, unless she came onto him?

"Sorry. Stupid question. Forget I asked. What's up?"

"Rehearsal at one o'clock tomorrow." The club was closed on Mondays, which meant they could work straight through into the evening. Other days, they had to squeeze it in before five then go home, change, and psych themselves up for the night. "I want to work on those two new numbers."

"Okay, okay. I'll be there."

"See you then," Rick told him before hanging up.

Marc dragged his fingers through his hair. Maybe Nico, the bouncer could tell him something about her. Except if she'd been to the club before, he was damn sure he'd have noticed her. She wasn't just another good-looking female. She was special. Very special. And if he didn't see her again, he might drive himself nuts.

What could she possibly be hiding that made her refuse to give him her name? Or run away like that? Was she married? Living with a jealous boyfriend? Somehow he didn't think that was her style. She didn't look or act like a cheater.

Quit driving yourself crazy. Get up and do something.

Wanting her scent and the imprint of her body to linger as long as possible, he left the bed just as it was, unmade. He needed to do normal things to get his brain back on track. Shower. Get dressed. Eat. But the remnants of whatever in his fridge were enough to take away his appetite.

Good thing I didn't try to feed her. Okay. Shower then hit the grocery.

Very few people knew that he often relaxed by cooking. He came from a family where food and cooking were a traditional pastime. His father was an accomplished chef and he'd passed the love of cooking and the talent on to him. In the early days of his career when he was still living at home, sometimes on the weekends he'd wake up totally drained from the performance the night before, needing something to smooth out the edges.

He'd sit at the kitchen table drinking coffee while his father made culinary magic with his fingers. It fascinated him, drew him to try his hand at it. Now he found that working in the kitchen was a great counterbalance to the frenetic atmosphere of a rock club.

In the bathroom he stared at his face in the mirror, flinching when he spotted the thick beard stubble on his jaw.

I should have shaved last night. She probably has whisker burns all over her.

Damn! Where was my head? I was in such a fucking hurry I didn't think of half the things I should have. Strike two. No wonder she ran off the way she did.

As if doing it after the fact would somehow absolve him, he took the time to shave very closely. Then he showered and washed his hair, and spent time taming it so he didn't look like a wild man. A clean pair of jeans and a collared shirt with the sleeves rolled down and buttoned at the cuffs, one of the vests he loved to wear, and he was ready.

Marc the hot rock star was gone for the day, replaced by Marc, the nice guy next door.

Emma still couldn't believe she'd actually done it. Not just running out of Andrew's house in the grip of frustration that was choking her. Not even the daring visit to Aftershock where she'd been so seduced by the music. No, what shocked her was going home with a man she'd just met and having wild sex beyond anything she could have imagined.

And ohmigod! She'd cheated on Andrew.

Where was the guilt? Didn't good girls feel guilty when they did something like this? Except in her mind it wasn't really cheating. The minute she left Andrew's house, it'd been over. Finished. She just had to make sure he knew it. Even without Marc that relationship was dead.

What would people think if they knew?

She actually smiled to herself.

Right now? Who cares!

She should take a shower, but she hated to wash away the remnants of his touch on her skin. Safe in the shelter of her own home, she alternated between wild exhilaration and the terrifying feeling she was swimming in water over her head. She curled up in the big armchair in her living room, eyes closed, and just relived every moment of the night with her bass player.

Yes, **her** bass player. She couldn't stop thinking of him that way.

Guitar Man.

Leaning back in the chair, she let torrent of sensations and emotions Marc had stirred within her cascade over her once more, hugging each detail to herself like a precious jewel. The image of Marc in the club flashed across her brain like an instant video, his body limned by the stage lights, wild with the beat of his music, the sound of his bass humming through the darkened room. In her mind she saw the image of him in the dim light of his bedroom, magnificently naked, his cock jutting proudly from its thick nest of curls.

She shivered remembering his talented hands on her body as he coaxed responses from her she hadn't even known she was capable of. Stroked her as he did his guitar. If she tried hard enough, she could evoke the impression of his mouth on her nipples, pulling and sucking on them. Feel his fingers sliding into her, reaching for her sweet spot. His thick shaft filling her.

Emma squirmed in the chair, her sex throbbing with residual sensation. He'd put his lips *there*, right on her clit, sending heat rocketing through her. Oral sex had never been something Andrew enjoyed, either giving or receiving. Her other experiments in that area had been less than fulfilling, and she had resigned herself to a sex life without that special thrill.

One night with Marc and she discovered she not only loved it, but craved it. His every touch had been an all-out assault on every one of her nerve endings. And the sensations were still there, reminding her of a pleasure more deep and satisfying than anything she could have imagined.

It wasn't just the act of sex that lingered with her. He'd been so tender, caring, attentive. Focusing on her satisfaction before taking his own pleasure.

Without realizing it, her hand crept down between her thighs and she began stroking herself through her jeans.

Ohmigod!

She yanked her hand back as if fire had scorched it. What was she doing?

Get your act together, Emma. Make breakfast. Read the paper.

All her usual Sunday things—things that could lock last night away in her mind where it belonged. One walk on the wild side was enough.

Wasn't it?

Or had the hours with Marc released a side of her that refused to be hidden away again?

She glanced at her watch. After seven. She'd been sitting here caught up in an erotic reverie for more than an hour. Sighing, she pushed herself out of the chair and headed for the bedroom. A blinking red light caught her eye, and she realized there were messages on her answering machine. Almost resentfully and reluctant to let the real world return, she pressed the playback button.

"*Emma?*" Andrew's voice. "*Emma, where are you? Where did you go? What's the matter? Call me.*"

"*Emma? Me again. Pick up the phone. I want to talk to you.*"

"*Okay, damn it. I know you're there. Answer the phone.*"

And the last one, Andrew's anger evident.

"*Emma, where the hell are you? I want to talk to you? I drove over to your house and it's all dark. Where did you go? We have to talk. Call me at once.*"

Emma's stomach knotted. He drove to her house?

A confrontation with Andrew was the last thing she wanted this morning. He'd demand an explanation, and she wasn't nearly ready to give him one. She needed more time to get her mind to function. No way could she tell him what she'd done. He'd never understand. And he'd tattle on her to her folks as if she were some errant teenager who'd broken the rules.

Okay, so he deserved an explanation. Some reason why she was basically going to tell him she'd thrown away the last few years of her life. *His* life. For a reason he'd never in this world understand. She just had to find the right words and at the moment, her brain couldn't piece them together.

Well, maybe she had, in a manner of speaking. She'd gone along to get along for so many years that anything out of the ordinary was sure to shock everyone. But she'd do it again in a heartbeat.

Again? Really? Go back to that club? Let the music take hold of her body?

Go to bed again with Marc?

In a hot New York minute.

Get your act together, Emma. Next time you see him, he probably won't even remember who you are.

Next time?

Emma shook her head. Time to shower and change and get on with her day. Somewhere she had to find the courage to see Andrew and try to make him understand. It was time to step back into the real world.

Marc wandered up and down the aisles in the grocery store at a leisurely pace with his shopping cart, not really sure what he was looking for. Maybe he'd make a good marinara sauce. He loved blending the spices until he got the taste just right. Or he might try out the recipe he'd found for a chicken and vegetable casserole with wine. He stood at the meat counter for a long time, thinking barbecue could be the answer. Combining for the sauce to him was like putting together the notes of a song.

But nothing really appealed to him. All he could think about was his Music Lady—the blush of pleasure on her skin as she slowly came down from the grip of an orgasm, the sweet taste of her cream, the feel of her hard nipples on his tongue.

Jesus, Marc! Quit it. You'll be walking around the store with the mother of all boners.

He meandered into the produce section. Maybe the fixings for a salad would inspire him. Yeah, that would do it. A big salad. He'd mix up his own dressing. Fix a steak. Maybe even a loaf of that sweet bread his mother always made.

He almost laughed out loud. What would all those people at Aftershock think if they could see him walking around the grocery store thinking about baking bread?

In the produce area he stopped short, his breath caught in his throat. He had to blink twice to make sure he knew what he was seeing. But yes, there she was. His Music Lady! Right here in his grocery store.

Wait. Did that mean she lived around here? In his neighborhood? Could he find out her address somehow, someway?

Yeah, right. Just paste "stalker" on my forehead.

She looked so different today, in dark jeans and a pretty blue top, her blonde hair gathered up high in a ponytail that bounced as she walked. Her feet encased in neat little tennis shoes. She was holding a melon in both hands, staring at it as if the secrets of the universe were printed on the skin.

He finally unstuck his feet and moved forward, walking up to her slowly.

"Hi!"

She turned, startled, and a tiny frown creased her forehead.

"Hello?" It was a question, not a greeting. She blinked, a bewildered expression on her face as if she'd never seen him.

He reached out a hand to touch her, but she flinched so he quickly drew it back. What the hell was this all about?

"ML? It's me." He gave her what everyone told him was his most appealing smile, hoping that would put her at ease.

Instead she took a step away. "I'm sorry. I don't know you. I think you have me confused with someone else."

He felt his smile slipping. "You forgot me already? I thought I made a better impression than that."

I sure tried my damndest.

She stepped further away, dropped the melon into the bin. "Excuse me. I have to finish my shopping."

Grabbing the handle of her shopping cart, she skittered past the rows of produce and hurried the corner into the frozen food section.

Marc stood there, staring after her. She didn't *know* him? What was going on here?

Had he done something wrong?

Had she regretted it all this morning and was trying to pretend it never happened?

What do you think, asshole? A nice girl like her was probably just taking a quick walk on the wild side.

But they'd connected. He knew it. Felt it. It was more than just sex. A lot more.

Okay, so she'd only seen him in the weird lights from the bar and the little glow of the bedside lamp at his house, but did he really look that different? Should he have rolled up the long sleeves of his shirt so she could see the tatt? She'd been so fascinated by it, running her finger over it. Would that have jogged her memory or as she deliberately burying it? He'd been all too aware last night wasn't a usual event for her, and he'd tried to take as much care with her as possible. Make sure she was completely satisfied.

Blow it off. There are a lot more out there just like her.

But the fact of the matter was, that wasn't exactly true. His Music Lady was one of a kind.

And he'd have to figure out how to find her again.

The anticipation of preparing food dissipated. With rapid strides he pushed his cart up and down the aisles, tossing in the bare essentials he needed.

Hoping to see her again.

And trying to convince himself that he was imagining the

hurt burning in his heart.

Emma hurried to the farthest corner of the store, as far away as she could get. She huddled in the soft drink aisle, hand pressed to her chest, heart pounding. She was more mortified than anything else. A stranger walked up to her and she panicked? What could possibly happen in the grocery store? Was she so freaked out moving passed her boundaries last night that strangers frightened her? Could she have acted any more like an immature teenager? Or worse yet, a prickly spinster?

She had to admit good-looking men didn't usually come on to her in the grocery store. Or any place else. Probably because for years, she'd walked around with that "Keep Away" sign all but plastered on her forehead. There had been something familiar about him, but at the moment she was still wrestling with her late night joy ride. She couldn't handle another strange guy stepping into her life.

Of course, she could have handled it better. Right? Instead, she'd just made an ass of herself and the guy was really cute. Sexy. Neatly combed mink brown hair. Lean body in jeans and a long-sleeved, collared shirt. A vest. Clean shaven with the scent of something fresh and outdoorsy tickling her nostrils. Stormy blue eyes.

Stormy blue eyes?
Really?
Ohmigod!
Was it him?
Shit, shit, shit.

Discomfiture crept over her like a thermal blanket. How could she not have recognized him? After the incredibly intimate hours she'd spent with him? Bad enough she was still trying to straighten out the maelstrom her emotions had become. Now she had embarrassment to add to the mix.

Okay, so she wasn't expecting him to look like Nick Next Door when she saw him again. But that was no excuse. You didn't have incredible erotic sex with a man one night and then not know who he was the next day, even if he wasn't wearing his rock star persona. No wonder hurt had flashed in his eyes.

Dork—that was the word for her.

Emma was torn between wanting to find him again and hiding until she was sure he'd left the store. What if someone saw them together? Told Andrew? Okay, told him...what? That she was talking to a strange man in the grocery?

A hysterical laugh bubbled up in her throat.

What if Andrew himself showed up here? He shopped here sometimes. He was already angry at being unable to reach her. Just one question about the man she was talking to and her face would give her away. She had never been a very good liar.

And then, of course, Andrew would immediately be on his cell talking to her parents.

More fun.

Emma, Emma, Emma. You wanted to experience life. Okay, here it is.

But give her a break. Who expected a rock musician to be wandering the aisles in a grocery store? In her limited, distorted view she never associated them with mundane, every day activities. Big mistake.

Sliding open the door to the cooler, she pulled out a can of soda and rolled the cool aluminum against her hot cheeks while she tried to pull together the fragments of her brain. She waited in the corner as long as she could before venturing down the aisles again. She moved slowly, keeping an eye out for her Guitar Man, wanting to apologize yet afraid to face him again. Finally, she made it to the front of the store without running into him. Her grocery shopping was done for the day. She couldn't look at melons and tomatoes when all she could see was the hurt in Marc's eyes.

Way to go, Emma. You can kiss sexy boy goodbye.

No, wait. She wouldn't be able to kiss him at all now.

Disgusted with herself, she shoved her grocery cart back into place at the front of the store and hurried out to her car. She'd lost any desire to prepare food, anyway. She drove home in a fog, cursing herself and wondering if she'd be able to scrape up the courage to go back to Aftershock and see if he'd give her another chance or just blow her off. But the club, just like Marc, was forbidden fruit that good girls should stay away from.

Her life was changing in a dramatic way. She wanted to embrace this change, wanted to be the person hidden inside her all this time. There was a freedom waiting for her and an exploration of her own sensuality if she could just come to terms with it. There was no way she could make any kind of decision until she figured out how to deal with it. She had a lot of thinking to do.

But then she turned onto her street and her stomach clenched. As if things weren't bad enough, Andrew's car was parked in front of her house and he was sitting on her steps. He didn't look happy either.

Oh, God. Just what I don't need right now.

Chapter Four

*E*mma pulled into her driveway, shut off the engine, and drew in a deep breath. As she got out of the car, Andrew rose from the steps, his forehead creased in a scowl.

He folded his arms and glared at her. "Where have you been?"

"What?" She started to answer him then clamped her mouth shut, irritated by his attitude. "Andrew, I can't talk to you right now."

"Now that's where we disagree. You definitely need to explain what last night was all about." He glanced at her front door. "I think we should take this inside, don't you? We don't need the neighbors listening in on our conversation."

Emma wondered if she could vaporize into the air, but she had to talk to him and give him some kind of explanation. After all, she was the one who had an emotional fit and raced out of his house. Poor stuffy Andrew didn't even know yet that they'd broken up. She certainly couldn't tell him that she'd practically gone from his bed to that of a total stranger. Good girls didn't do things like that.

You've made a real mess, Emma. A big stinking mess.

But she needed some time and space to process the upheaval in her life before she could have a conversation with Andrew.

"I wasn't aware I had invited you in." And wasn't she just being rude on top of everything else?

His entire body tensed into one rigid mass of muscle. The frown on his forehead could have cut grooves into his skin and his mouth tightened into a straight line. At his sides his fingers curled tightly into his palms.

"I didn't think I needed a special invitation. I never did before."

"Things have changed. Listen, Andrew." She sighed. He had every right to be angry, but please not now. "I know we need to talk but I can't right this minute. Okay? Please? Just call me." She started up the stairs to the porch.

"I would," he snapped, "except you don't seem to answer your phone. Where the hell were you last night?"

Emma glanced over her shoulder at him, spotted her neighbor across the street standing on her porch blatantly staring, and she sighed.

"Come in," she told him, resigned to the confrontation.

She unlocked the door and left it open for Andrew to follow her. In the kitchen, she popped a K-Cup of hazelnut coffee into her Keurig machine, stuck a mug under the spout, and pressed the button.

"Would you like some coffee?" she asked, ingrained courtesy getting the best of her.

"Yes. I would."

The hostility simmering in his voice reached out and blanketed her. She couldn't blame him. This was not going to be easy no matter what she did. He had every right to be furious with her and any explanation she'd gave him would just confuse him. How could she tell him that the conservative good girl he was used to had an overnight epiphany and a new woman stood in her place? She accepted the fact that she and Andrew were a dead issue. Now to convince him....

To make matters worse, the new Emma was already wondering if she had another chance with Marc.

Suck it up, Emma. Get your head screwed on straight. You

owe this man something and whether he understands or not you have to give him an explanation.

Pulling another mug from the cupboard, she filled it from the same K-cup, handed it to Andrew and leaned against the counter, sipping her own drink. She studied him, standing in front of her so stiffly in his trademark khakis and golf shirt, hair combed back from his forehead, and brown eyes dark with a level of anger that vibrated in the air. She swallowed a sigh.

Just yesterday she'd been more than ready to settle for the routine of a life with this man. And routine definitely described their situation. But that was before her friend blew into town and gave her a wakeup call on how much she was really missing out. Jacie, whose eyes sparkled with life and excitement, who spoke of her husband as if describing a hot lover whose bed she'd just left.

"He makes my life complete and my body sing." Jacie had smiled as if she alone had a special secret and described her marriage, her five-year-old daughter, and her career with equal parts of excitement and satisfaction.

Emma's job with a textbook publishing house had suddenly seemed embarrassingly dull. What she really wanted was to write books, not edit them. And definitely not dull textbooks. And the only song she heard with Andrew was a Sousa march that kept the rhythm of her life in perfect ordinary time.

Last night it had all boiled over, making her all too aware that she'd *settled*. She'd done what everyone expected of her—in her choice of career as well as her choice of men. And she'd understood with startling clarity that she was just damn tired of it. Finally. She wanted to grab life the way Jacie had.

Still, she owed it to Andrew to make him understand, even if she thought the task next to impossible.

She gestured toward the kitchen table. "If we're going to have this discussion, why don't we sit down?"

"No, thanks. I'll stand."

"Fine. Whatever." She took a sip of the hot liquid in her mug. "I'm sorry I didn't return your phone calls but...I wasn't sure what to say to you yet."

Or ever.

"You didn't think you owed me an explanation for running out the way you did? In the middle of the evening?" He glared at her over the rim of his mug.

She bit back another sigh. "I...just needed some time to get my thoughts together."

And figure out how to tell you it's over. Finished. And how to make my well-meaning parents understand that I'm not a teenager anymore and can make my own choices. Even if people won't like them.

"I'll take them any way you deliver them," he told her. "But I want to know what I did to make you leave the way you did. One minute we're watching a movie and I'm looking forward to going to bed with you, the next you run out like a crazy person. What's up, Emma? This is just not like you."

No kidding.

She moved to the little bay window that looked out into her backyard, staring outside but not really seeing anything.

"No matter what I say, Andrew, I don't think you'll understand. I'm afraid you'll be hurt and there's nothing I can do about it." She tried to swallow but the strain of the situation made her mouth too dry. She was all too aware she should have thought of this earlier, but when she fled his house, the only thing on her mind was escaping a suffocating situation. And didn't that just say something about her feelings for this man that she hadn't even given one thought to his reactions?

Yes, Emma. Something you should have done before racing out of his house as if your pants were on fire. Or when you tried to blow him off a while ago. He might be dull and stuffy but you were with him a long time and he's still a human being.

"Hurt? Damn straight I will." His anger rolled through the room in waves. It was the most emotion Emma had ever seen from him. "But there's certainly something you can do about it. You can forget all this nonsense." He smoothed his hand over his hair. "Emma, we've been together for two years. I thought we had plans. I just assumed...."

"Yes." She whirled around, coffee sloshing onto her hand. The liquid burned and she grabbed a paper towel from the counter to blot it. "You assumed. And that's as much my fault as yours. I know you love me, in your own way, but my feelings for you have changed."

"In my own way?" He frowned. "What's that supposed to mean? My way was good enough for two years."

"Andrew, I can't think of another way to say this except we aren't going to be seeing each other any more."

Hurt and confusion were etched on his face. "You're breaking up with me? Why? I thought...expected...."

"And that's part of the problem." She set her mug on the table, guilt and irritation waging a battle inside her. "We met, everyone thought we were perfect for each other, including my folks. I was convinced everyone was right. Except...." She turned away, unwilling to deal with what she knew she'd seen in his eyes. It was so clear to her now he'd never understand her motivation—her desperate need for change.

"Except what, Emma? *You* didn't think so? Then what was the past two years all about? We're comfortable with each other, for God's sake."

"But that's just it," she cried. "I'm tired of being comfortable. Tired of doing what everyone expects of me. Tired of being the poster child for the typical good girl. I want more out of life. A lot more."

He stared at her for a long time, a mixture of emotions shifting across his face. "You're bored with me." He said the words as if each one was a poison pellet.

"Not just you." She held out her hands, palms open, as if pleading with him. "With my *life*, Andrew. All of it." She bit her lip. "Try to understand. I like you a lot but I don't think I've ever really been in love with you." God, she was such a coward. And selfish. She just wanted this conversation to be over with. "I don't think I've ever been in love with *anyone*."

Until now. And I've probably screwed that up good and

tight. Serves me right, I guess.

"Not even me?"

He stood there clutching his coffee mug, a muscle working in his jaw, anger sparking in his eyes. It was hard for Emma not to make comparisons. Where Andrew was all smooth edges and precise, like the clean lines on an architectural drawing, Marc was...well...the joy ride. Excitement. Dark fantasies. Visceral emotions. Oh, yes, plenty of emotion.

"Emma?" Andrew's voice was sharp.

She jerked back to reality. "Yes?"

"Where did you just go? We're having a conversation here. Or at least *I'm* trying to."

She rubbed her palms on her thighs. "Sorry, sorry, sorry."

"You keep saying that. So let me try to make sense of this. The past two years have meant nothing to you, right?"

"Not true." She had to leave him with some dignity. And it hadn't all been bad. "I enjoyed your company, Andrew. It's been very, um, pleasant."

"Pleasant," he repeated. "A word to make a man's heart beat faster."

She shoved her hands into her pockets, not knowing what to do with them. "I don't know what else to say except I wish things could be different but they aren't. I regret ending it this way."

"I wish you hadn't ended it at all," he spat out. "There's more to this than you're saying. How about telling me where you went last night? I know you weren't home." He glared at her. "When you didn't answer my calls, I drove over here. The house was dark and you didn't answer the door. I knocked so loud I was afraid the neighbors would come out and chase me away."

"I heard what you said on the answering machine. I suppose you were worried about me. I'm sorry."

"Stop saying that." He raked his fingers through his hair. "You didn't think I was just going to sit around and wait for you to give me some kind of explanation, did you? Or did you think at all?"

No, she hadn't, and that was one of the worst of her sins.

She'd been thinking of no one but herself.

His anger still shimmered in the air along with a healthy dose of bruised ego. He wasn't letting this go, and Emma just wanted it to be over. Done. So she could be alone and figure out what to tell her parents who were sure to be all over her like a plague of locusts.

"I don't really want to discuss where I went or what I did. That's my business now. I'm very sorry, Andrew, but it definitely *is* over. And it would be better for both of us if you would leave. Now."

Andrew was gripping the coffee mug so hard Emma was afraid for a minute it might shatter. Then he set it deliberately on the table and walked out of the room, Emma on his heels. At the front door he turned toward her, resentment still outlining his features.

"Just so you know, I'm not giving up. Whatever little brain fart you had last night will work its way out and then life can get back to normal." He opened the door. "And I'll forgive you."

Emma stared after him, open-mouthed.

He'd forgive her?

How truly magnanimous of him.

If the door hadn't already been closed, she would have slammed it.

Finally, she went back into the kitchen and rinsed out the mugs. Too bad she'd already taken her shower. That was the place where she did some of her best thinking.

And where I can conjure up Marc again, pretend my hands on my body are his. Pretend—

Crap, Emma. Get a grip.

Marc was jittery and unsettled. The episode at the grocery store had really put him off his game. After scarfing down a sandwich from the deli, he changed into old, faded jeans and a ratty T-shirt. Now he couldn't figure out what to do with the rest of the day. He'd thought about going over to his parents' house and immersing himself in the environment there. Being with his family always centered him. Maybe his brothers would be home from college for the weekend, and he could hang out with them. Sitting here alone was only driving him crazy.

He was aware most people didn't think of rock musicians as having families. Someone once said to him, "I'm sure they just think we were hatched." And truly, too many of the musicians he knew had no family support at all. Marc never took his for granted. They'd encouraged him with his music right from the beginning, and he always let them know how important they were to him.

But maybe today wasn't such a good time to head over there. One of his brothers was sure to figure out why he was so fidgety, and he wasn't at all ready to tell them about Music Lady. He didn't even know her name, for God's sake. Or have any idea how to find her. Get in touch with her.

Try explaining to my brothers I had mind-blowing sex with a woman who wouldn't even tell me her name. And that the next day she acted as if she'd never met me. What's that all about?

Why does her attitude hurt so badly? Why am I even thinking about her if she can blow me off this way, treat me like a stranger?

He didn't like feeling unsettled. It had never happened to him with any other woman and he wasn't sure how to handle it. One night with Music Lady and his emotions were all over the place.

He shook himself mentally, cursing himself for acting like an idiot. Finally, after wandering around his house, he thumped himself down on the couch. But try as he might, he couldn't get his Music Lady out of his mind. Thinking about her now made his cock hard as a steel pole, and he shifted to a more comfortable position. When he closed his eyes, he could see her again gloriously naked in his bed, her satin, soft skin flushed with pleasure, eyes glazed, streaky blonde hair falling around her like a cape. His hands fisted convulsively remembering the feel of her breasts, the stiff pebbled nipples, the beat of her heart against his fingers.

He wished she were here, right next to him, so he could pull those luscious buds into his mouth again. Nip them with his teeth and soothe them with his tongue. Lick her body all over and plunge his tongue deep into her wet pussy. Taste that sweet pink flesh and suck the hot bud of her clit.

He wanted her to sit on his face and—

Marc jerked himself into awareness. What the hell was he doing? He wasn't sixteen anymore, having wet dreams about the cutest girl in class. No, he was thinking about a woman he'd probably never see again. He checked his watch. Four o'clock. Where the hell had the afternoon disappeared to while he'd been sitting here daydreaming like a fool?

It occurred to him that he'd spent most of the day alternately nursing his hurt feelings and dreaming erotic fantasies about a woman he'd spent one night with.

Stupid, stupid, stupid.

Yeah, but there's something else at play here. Something I can't put a name to. Yet.

He knew only one cure for what ailed him. Fishing a bottle of beer out of the fridge, he grabbed his acoustic guitar and carried everything out onto his back porch. Slouching into one of the Adirondack chairs he'd recently repainted, he took a healthy swallow of his beer, set the bottle down, and cradled the guitar in his lap. Maybe he could put all this energy into something constructive.

Like a new song.

About Music Lady.

"Coming, coming, coming. Hold your horses."

Emma hit save on her computer and hurried to the front door. Someone was ringing the bell and not too patiently. If it was Andrew again, she'd have to do more than just tell him to get lost. The more she thought about him and his attitude, the more irritated she became. With herself as much as him, at the last two years she'd wasted in an oatmeal relationship.

The doorbell rang again and Emma jerked the door open, ready to read her erstwhile ex-boyfriend the riot act. *God! Did you call a man your ex-boyfriend when you're almost thirty?* But she froze in place when she saw her mother standing there, hair perfectly upswept, tailored blouse and slacks perfectly creased.

A stray thought burrowed its way into her brain. *I wonder if the woman ever perspires.*

She sucked in a breath and dug out a smile. "Hi, Mom. What brings you around today?"

Angela Blake stepped across the threshold. "Can't I stop by to visit my daughter without an invitation?"

Emma peered around her but saw only her mother's car in the driveway. She was alone, thank heavens. Of worse yet, Andrew could be skulking in the bushes.

"Of course, of course. Come on into the kitchen. I made some sweet tea earlier."

When they were settled at the kitchen table with filled glasses, Emma looked at her mother expectantly. She could feel a lecture coming, and there was nothing she could do but to get through it.

Angela trailed a finger down the sweating glass. "It occurred to me that you have your thirtieth birthday coming up in a couple of weeks."

"That's right." Emma sipped tea and waited. With Angela that was the best course of action, something she'd learned well over the years.

"That's an important event in a woman's life. I was just thinking we could celebrate with a small birthday dinner. That might be a good time for you and Andrew to announce your engagement."

Emma wanted to bang her head on the table. Her mother

was so transparent. Before last night, she would have dutifully agreed with the woman and pulled a notepad to begin making a list. Maybe even confessed her sins, thrown herself on her parent's mercy, and begged forgiveness before regressing into Andrew's little mouse.

But not the new Emma.

"You did?" She might have turned a corner in her personal life but her relationship with her parents wasn't about to change that fast. "And should I ask if Andrew had anything to do with this suggestion?"

This was exactly the thing she was afraid of and it was so very Andrew—just like him to do an end run around her with her parents. Her mother often thought he should have been their son, and her, the odd woman out. He was perfectly suited for them. Emma laced her fingers together to keep her hands from trembling.

Angela touched her perfectly arranged hair and then took a ladylike sip of her tea. "He did happen to drop by and say he was a little worried about you."

"Worried about me," Emma repeated. Her stomach pitched at the thought of the discussion they probably had.

"He said the two of you had a little tiff last night, and he thought maybe if the two of you finally nailed down your plans, it would settle you down."

"Settle me down." Emma couldn't stop herself from repeating everything, as if stuck in a bad rerun of parts of her life. She believed she and her mother had a good relationship, but it was all a sham. As long as she behaved like a clone of Angela Blake things were fine. But the minute she colored outside the lines, the disapproval rating was off the charts.

Oh, Mom, why can't you listen to me? See me for who I am? Even more, for who I want to be.

"Well, honey, you've been together for two years. And in case you hadn't noticed, you're going to be thirty before you blink your eyes."

Exactly the thought that had pushed her to rebel.

"And thank you so much for reminding me."

Emma stood up and wandered to the little bay window where she'd stood when Andrew had been there. Two birds were dipping into the tiny birdbath she'd set up. Watching them gave her the opportunity to center herself, gather her frayed thoughts, and some measure of courage.

"Emma, it's just the truth. There's no getting around it."

Poor Emma. Thirty and unmarried and on the outs with her boyfriend.

"Mom, what's this really all about? I can't remember the last time you *dropped in* on me to dig into my personal life."

"That's because your personal life has always been nicely predictable. And appropriate. As it should be."

Predictable. Appropriate. Two of the very reasons I ran from Andrew's house last night.

She searched for something to say.

"Emma." She heard the clink as her mother set her glass on the table. "I don't know what this disagreement you had with Andrew is about, but I'm sure it's something that can be fixed. And then," her voice brightened, "you can announce your engagement."

Emma turned slowly, quaking inside. She was about to take another big leap in her life and she didn't know which would be worse—saying the words or facing the wrath of her mother. She swallowed hard and wet her lips.

"I think this will probably come as a shock to you, but I'm not going to marry Andrew. Not this year. Not any year." *Courage, Emma.* "If you want to know the truth, he bores me."

If Angela's jaw hadn't been attached to her skull, Emma was sure it would have clunked on the table.

"Did I just hear you right? He *bores* you? Are you out of your mind?"

"No. As a matter of fact, I think I've probably just found it." She shoved her hands into the pockets of her jeans. Her heart was beating erratically with the knowledge she was taking another step off that unseen ledge, but she just couldn't stop herself. The joy ride was just beginning but already she found it exhilarating. She wanted her mother to be happy for her but that may be a very long time coming. "As you were so kind to point out, I'm almost thirty and my life is predictable. Appropriate. I've never done one exciting thing in my life."

Well, okay. One thing.

"Exciting?"

"Yes." She wanted to wring her hands. "Can't you try to understand?" she pleaded. "I want something more than I have right now. Is that so hard for you to comprehend? Look at me, Mom. Really look at me and listen."

"I have no idea what you're talking about." Angela sounded truly bewildered. "What kind of exciting things do you want? You have a good job, a steady boyfriend. A settled life ahead of you. What is it you're looking for?"

Emma could tell this whole conversation was pointless. There was no way she could explain what was happening with her when she was still coming to terms with it herself. She wanted empathy from her mother and instead she got platitudes. If she looked back over the years, she should have expected nothing else. Everything in Angela's life had always been well-planned and well-ordered. It was her security. And she wanted the same thing for her daughter.

But that's not me any more. How can I make her see that?

Emma let out a slow breath, clenching her fists in her pockets.

"Andrew is a very nice man, Mom, but he doesn't, well, ring my chimes. And I really, really want to hear bells. Lots of them."

"So let me get this straight." Angela's body was set in rigid lines, her eyes flashing disapproval. "You're willing to throw away a good solid relationship at a time in your life when you should be married, for...for...what? Some unknown man?" She narrowed her eyes. "Or have you already met him? Is that what this is all about?"

Emma turned away again, afraid her expression might give something away and her mother would poke and prod until she got it out of her. That was a conversation she was hardly prepared for at the moment.

"Do you remember Jacie Caldwell? My college roommate?"

"Well, of course, darling. A really nice girl. But what does she have to do with this?"

"She's Jacie Monroe now. Married, with a great husband that she obviously adores and a really cute kid. And a job she loves."

Angela frowned. "That's nice. But I still don't understand. Wait. Did she call you? Say something to set you off on this?"

"No, Mom. But she came through town last week on her way to a business conference. And you know what?" Emma wanted to cry, thinking about it. Wishing Angela could understand what she was trying to tell her. "She had a sparkle in her eyes when she talked about her husband that I never get when I think of Andrew. And I want that sparkle. Is that so terrible?"

The silence in the room was so loud they might have been shouting.

Finally, Angela rose very slowly from the table, her face set in lines of disapproval. "I swear, Emma, I don't know what to do here."

"Nothing, Mom," she cried. "There's nothing for you to do except tell me you want me to be happy."

"I thought you were. Apparently I was mistaken, and I don't understand how."

"Can't you just let me be? Maybe you haven't noticed but I'm no longer a kid who needs monitoring, for heaven's sake."

"We planned a good life for you, Emma, one that would give you security," her mother pointed out. "You've been fine with it up to now. You should be smart enough to know that what make's Jacie's life good for her won't necessarily work for you,"

Emma had to curl her hands into fists to maintain her control. She wasn't getting her message across at all. "Didn't you ever just want to take a chance? Do something that was wild and different? Shake up your life?"

"I have no idea what you mean, Emma."

That was certainly the truth. Emma felt as if they were conversing in two different languages. She huffed in frustration. "Mom."

"Why ever would I want to do that?" Puzzled, Angela shook her head. "Maybe it wasn't such a good thing that Jacie came through and visited with you."

"Look, I appreciate all that you and Dad have done for me. Really. But maybe I've realized there might be more to life than what I know and I want a chance to find it. To explore what else is out there."

Angela studied her for a long moment then sighed. "Just be aware of the fact that when you're through doing...whatever it is you're doing, Andrew might not still be waiting."

"I know you won't understand this, but I hope he won't be. I hope he moves on. Finds someone who really appreciates him."

"Well." Angela gathered up her purse and keys and headed for the door. "It's obvious you don't. Your father will have a fit. He really likes Andrew."

"Then maybe he should be the one to marry him," Emma snapped, and instantly regretted the words.

Her mother opened the door and never looked back, just walked out onto the porch and closed the door firmly.

Emma wanted to cry, not because things were over with Andrew but because she realized how impossible it was for her parents to understand her after all these years. Of course, she was just beginning to understand herself. To realize the deep sensuality begging to be fully released. The awareness of self. The need to explore new opportunities. Maybe in every area of her existence. So how could she blame them for not sensing any of this?

Two weeks ago, she had no idea she'd be reliving the thrill of a joy ride and loving it. That she'd discover a world of sensuality previously unknown to her. That the new feelings would crowd out the old ones. Now she didn't know what to do with them or have any idea where to go from here.

She dumped the remains of the tea in both glasses and stuck

them in the dishwasher, then walked outside onto her back porch. Looking up at the sky, she wondered when the first stars would come out. And if wishing on one would help her get what she wanted.

Guitar Man.

Chapter Five

"Could you possibly get your head out of your ass and pay attention?"

"Huh?" Marc looked up to see Rick glaring at him.

"Exactly. We're all here. Where are you? Obviously not with the rest of us."

It was Monday and the band was rehearsing at Aftershock. Or at least three of them were. Marc couldn't seem to get in sync with the others. His mind kept wandering back to the scene the day before in the grocery store. Why had Music Lady refused to recognize him? He'd spent a fruitless Sunday afternoon and evening trying to come up with answers, which totally shot his efforts to write a new song. He couldn't remember the last time a woman had screwed with his head like this.

"Gotta be a female." Garrett Barnes, the drummer did a soft rim shot. "Only a female could get his balls in a twist like this."

"Yeah?" Rick was in his face. "I thought you were the guy who could take 'em or leave 'em. Isn't that right, Marco Polo?"

Marc took a step back, putting space between the two of them. He hated it when Rick called him that stupid name. The guy only did it when he was angry or wanted to get a rise out of him. Right now Marc was sure it was both.

"Yeah, right," he agreed, barely concealing his irritation. He picked a few low notes on the bass. "Okay, I'm in it. Let's go."

But everyone on the stage was well aware his mind was not one hundred percent on the rehearsal.

After another lackluster hour of work, Rick put down his guitar. "Okay, let's pack it in. Guys, tomorrow at one. We can get in three good hours before we have to go home and get ready for the evening. Marc, hang back a little, will you?"

Marc knew he was going to get the third degree. Well, it was his own damn fault for letting his mind wander when he should have been concentrating on the material. He put his guitar away, carefully snapped the locks on the case, and shoved his hands in his pockets, waiting. Garret and the lead singer, Danny Chavez, left and it was just Marc and Rick. And the elephant in the room between them.

"Okay, guy." Rick hitched his butt onto the stool at one side of the stage and folded his arms across his chest. "Let's have it. I'm guessing this has something to do with the blonde you asked me about yesterday."

Marc sighed, picked up the bottle of water next to his guitar case, and took a long drink from it. He capped the bottle with a slow, deliberate movement, trying to figure out how to explain this to Rick.

"I didn't think the question was so hard," his friend commented.

"No, it's not." Marc exhaled heavily. "It's just...this will sound so stupid."

Rick laughed. "No more stupid than half the things I've done myself. Come on. Let me have it."

"Okay, okay." Marc stuck his hands in his pockets and stared at the floor. "Usually all you can see from the stage is the mass of bodies in the crowd. You know? The lights get in your eyes and everything's distorted.

"But sometimes when they shift, you can zero in on someone, right?"

"Right. Just as we were finishing *Hard Lovin' Man*, I glanced down and there she was. Practically shoved up against the stage from the force of the crowd behind her."

"And?" Rick prompted.

"I swear, it was like being hit by lightning. I know how corny that sounds but it's the damn truth. The rest of the night, I felt like I was playing just for her."

And getting her out of his mind since then had been next to impossible. She was so different than the others women, with a rare freshness to her. How could he not be so fascinated by her?

"Okay." Rick nodded. "I get it. So you're all twisted up about some female you saw in the crowd? That's not like you."

"Oh, I *met her* all right." Marc looked down at his feet then back up at his friend. "She stayed until the end of the last set. And then she came home with me."

Rick's jaw dropped. "Just like that?"

"Just like that."

"A little swift even for you, isn't it?"

Marc pulled his hands out of his pockets and ran his fingers through his hair. "I never expected it. Honest to God. I followed her into the parking lot because I just had to meet her, touch her...kiss her. I was afraid she'd either smack me good or call the cops."

He was only comfortable discussing this with Rick. Their friendship went back so many years and they knew most of each other's secrets. He'd never open up this way to the other guys but usually Rick was able to give him perspective.

One corner of Rick's mouth lifted in a smile. "I'm guessing she didn't do either of those."

"She kissed me back." Marc was still stunned by the whole thing. "Then she came home with me. And Rick? I had the best sex I've ever had in my life. Even better than sex." He paused. "Am I making sense to you?"

"In a strange sort of way. So what's the problem? Call her. See her again. It's not like you haven't had the hots for someone before." Rick chuckled. "Although this is the first time I've ever seen you with your shorts in such a twist about it."

"It's not so simple." Marc raked his fingers through his hair again. "I can't call her because I don't know her number. Or her name."

"What?" Rick stood up from the stool. "Are you shitting me? I might expect something like this from Garrett but not from you. How come you didn't get her name?"

"Believe it or not, she wouldn't give it to me." His voice was laced with simmering frustration. What could Music Lady possibly be hiding? She'd certainly hauled ass out of his house as if her tail were on fire. This was an experience he had no *experience* with.

"That's not good." Rick frowned. "She has to be hiding something. Is she married? You never mess with married women, Marc. None of us do. You know that."

"No." He shook his head. "I'm sure she's single. I think...."

"Think what?"

"I think Saturday night is the first time she's ever done anything like this. Even been to a rock club. *Any* club. And I think she was scared."

"But obviously willing enough to go home with you and have wild monkey sex," Rick pointed out.

"Hey." Marc tensed. "It was a hell of a lot more than bedroom acrobatics."

Rick got right up in front of him. "Then why didn't she give you her name? Or her phone number?"

Marc turned away. "It gets worse." He explained about the episode in the grocery store.

"Fuckin' A." Rick's voice held a stunned tone. "And you still can't get past her? What's wrong with your head?"

Marc spread his hands in a helpless gesture. He'd been struggling with his emotions from the moment Music Lady refused to acknowledge him in the grocery store. How could he explain to his friend how he was feeling when he couldn't even explain it to himself? "What can I tell you?"

He had different objectives for his future than many of his friends. Unlike a lot of musicians he knew, including a couple in his own band, he was pretty selective about the women he took home with him. Especially now that his goal was something permanent. He might start work at nine at night rather than nine in the morning, but he wanted the kind of solid situation for himself like his parents had. A relationship where the people were two halves of a whole and fit together perfectly, no matter what life threw at them.

He'd always expected when he did find his special lady that it would be a slow and steady process to a permanent relationship. Could he build it with Music Lady, connect with her emotionally as well as physically? He sensed the beginning of something special, just after one night. The incident at the grocery store still hurt, but he hoped she'd come back to Aftershock. Explain why she acted the way she did. Let him know if he'd done something wrong. Then maybe they could start over.

If she came back.

Rick studied him for a moment. Silence stretched out uncomfortably.

"Say something," Marc said.

"What can I say? You're acting like a stupid schmuck. Forget her. Get your head out of your ass. You know something big might be happening for us any day now. It's in the works. We have to be ready. We've got a lot of work to do, and this afternoon's rehearsal was damn near worthless."

Marc knew his friend was right. "I'm sorry."

"You need to be more than sorry, Marco Polo."

He ground his teeth. "I hear you."

"Go home." Rick picked up his guitar case. "Focus on the script for the new video we're doing. We're going to shoot it this week, and I've lined up some folks to take a look at it."

When the band first got together, Marc discovered writing came as naturally to him as creating and playing music. He'd then become the *de facto* scriptwriter for every video they did. This would be the fifth one they shot, and it would feature a new song. And if things worked out right, it could bring them the big break they'd been working toward for so long.

"Okay." He picked up his own instrument. "I'll call you later."

"You bet you will. I want a progress report. At least we'll get something out of today."

They were seated at a high pub table in Hot Salsa, their favorite place to meet. The sounds of Happy Hour swirled around them. Emma stirred her drink with the hot pink swizzle stick and stared into the slush of a frozen margarita. No salt.

"The drink isn't going to change no matter how long you stare at it." Annie Fletcher's voice was colored with humor. "Nor is it going to reveal the secrets of the world."

Emma looked up at her closest friend and sighed. "I know, I know."

"So you want to tell me what's got you so tied up in knots? You hardly ever obsess about anything."

"Isn't that just the truth?" She dipped a warm tortilla chip into the bowl of salsa, the special recipe for which the place was named.

"So give. You've hardly said two words from the minute we got here."

Emma had known Annie for ten years, since the day they'd both moved into the same apartment building. Their friendship had grown and strengthened over the years, as they hung out together after work and on weekends, shopped together, and shared secrets about their lives. No one understood her more than this woman. So why was she so reluctant to tell her what was going on? Surely Annie of all people wouldn't censure her.

Emma nibbled on the chip and swallowed it, then took a deep breath. "I've met someone."

Annie's eyebrows lifted almost to her hairline. "*Met* someone? But you already have someone. What happened to Andrew?"

"Nothing." She took another chip, crumbled it into pieces on the little cocktail napkin. "That's the problem. He's...nothing.

We broke up." She was almost afraid to see the expression on her friend's face. "Do you think I'm terrible? For doing this?"

"You broke up with Andrew? Isn't it a little...out of the norm for you?"

"Maybe my norm needs a little shaking up." *Maybe it has for a long time and I just didn't know it.*

Annie frowned. "I'll admit Andrew is a little, well, bland. Maybe not my taste, but you and him seem so suited to each other."

Emma sucked down a gulp of her margarita. "Yeah. And what does this say about me? My whole life can be summed up in one word. Bland."

"Sorry, kitten. I only meant it in a...nice way." Annie picked up her own drink and sipped at it. "So you say you met someone. Who? Where?"

"Okay, don't leap off your chair and screech, but last Saturday night I went to a rock club." She took another fortifying sip of her drink, waiting for a reaction.

Annie's jaw dropped and she almost spilled the contents of her glass. "A rock club? You?"

At least she didn't screech her disapproval. Not yet, anyway.

"Uh huh." She stared into her glass, remembering the scene last Saturday. She couldn't believe it'd only been a week ago. "I think I nearly gave Andrew a heart attack because I jumped up in the middle of watching *Full Metal Jacket* for the third time, said I couldn't do this any more, and ran out of the house."

Annie burst out laughing. "Good for you, girlfriend. It's about time."

"About time?" She raised her eyes, startled. "Annie, if you thought I was making a mistake with him, why didn't you ever say something before this? We're not exactly strangers, you know."

Her friend's face sobered. "Emma, you were so content with your life, everything comfortably planned out. So secure in it. Who was I to rock the boat? I thought that was what you wanted."

Until she had an epiphany and took a good look inside herself. For the first time in her life, she figured out she didn't really know she was. That what she wanted wasn't at all what she had. What she was 'settling' for.

"So did I. Until it struck me in a couple of weeks I'm going to be thirty and the most exciting thing I've ever done was a joy ride I took when I was seventeen."

"So what did you do? How'd you end up at the club?" Annie's mouth curved in a wicked grin. "Come on. I want details."

By the time Emma had given her the entire story, she'd nearly finished her drink. She didn't know why she needed the liquid courage to confess everything to Annie, her best friend. It just eased the edges of her anxiety at bringing it all out into the open.

"So there you have it." She shoved away the empty glass. "All the grubby details."

Annie had a shocked expression in her eyes. "I can't believe I'm hearing you right. Are you kidding me or what?"

"Which part are you having the most trouble with? Running out on Andrew? Going to a rock club? Going home with a man I just met?"

"Everything. All of it." Annie gave Emma a penetrating look. "First of all, Aftershock is the primo rock club in the city, although I'm sure you didn't know that." She crunched a chip. "I've been there a few of times myself, as a matter of fact."

"You have?" For a moment Emma was hurt. As close as she and Annie were, as easily as they'd connected and as much as they shared, apparently there were more secrets the woman kept locked away. But then she realized some things were hard for people to tell someone else. If she didn't need Annie's help to straighten out her head, would she even have said anything about Marc?

"Uh huh. When there is a particular band I'm dying to see."

"How come you never mentioned any of that stuff?"

"Emma." Annie put a hand on her arm. "Rock clubs weren't exactly part of our conversations. Or even part of your world.

You hate the music I listen to, always wanting to change the radio station when we go someplace and I'm driving. You couldn't even stand the CDs I wanted to play for you."

"Yeah, yeah, yeah. I know. Can I help it if I've been fed a steady diet of soft rock and pop?" Emma sighed. "Explaining it just sounds so stupid. The beat's too heavy, too thumping. The guitars screeched." She waved her hands in frustration. "What can I say? But Annie, the band I saw was different. The sound was—I don't know—smoother? More emotional? I can't explain it."

"Yeah? So tell me. Who's this wonder band playing there now?"

She picked up another chip and swirled it in the salsa. "Some band called Lightnin'. I think."

"You think?" Annie nearly dropped her drink. "Holy shit. Emma. They're one of the hottest bands around. Everyone says they're about to really break out."

"Break out?" Emma frowned, puzzled. There must be an entire segment of the English language she was unfamiliar with. And then her heartbeat stuttered. How much did Annie know about her bass player? "Break out of what?"

"You know. The club scene. Small local concert gigs. I hear they're about to get a chance at the big time. You should Google them and check out their website. Learn a thing or two. Holy shit, mama. When you decide to do something, you don't mess around."

Annie was right. Emma Blake was morphing by the minute into someone she had yet to figure out. She looked at her friend helplessly. "How was I supposed to know all that? I only ended up there by mistake."

"And you went home with their bass player? I should make such mistakes."

Emma had to ask. "Do you know him? Have you met him? Do you know anything about him?"

"Honey, no. I just know the buzz about their music. But I've seen them perform and he's definitely sex on the hoof."

Emma bit her lips, wondering if the night had been less special for Marc than it was for her. If he slept with strangers on a regular basis. She pushed the thought away as soon as it popped into her head, not wanting to diminish the importance of what had happened.

"So you don't think I'm weird?"

"Going home with a man you've never met? Weird for you, maybe. My God, when you do it you really do it." Annie bit into a chip, crunching on it thoughtfully. "But I do know this. From everything I read he's not a big player. Doesn't get into the groupie thing."

Relief swept through Emma. "So then you don't think I made a big mistake?"

Annie laughed and shook her head. "It's not like I'm promoting indiscriminate sex, but I think it's about time you did something a little on the naughty side. But I have to say I'm amazed." Humor sparkled in her eyes. "You are probably the last person I'd expect to do this, but I say good for you."

For a moment Annie's words stung. Then she realized apparently she'd kept the real Emma bottled up so tightly even her best friend didn't see her.

What a bore I must have been. I should thank Annie for liking me in spite of myself.

"You make it sound like I've been living in a closet." Annoyance crept in again.

"Honey, in a way you have. But there's definitely hope for you now. Just don't let yourself get consumed with regrets and run back to that closet. Let yourself live."

I'm trying to.

Annie leaned a little closer across the small tabletop. "Tell me, Emma. Was it good? Are musicians as good as they're cracked up to be?"

Heat rose in her cheeks as she remembered details of the night—her incredible and caring lover, the things they'd done together. "This one was. He's spectacular." She bit her bottom lip. "Annie, I swear. I never thought sex could be half so good."

Her friend grinned. "Now you know why I always have a smile on my face after a sleepover." She sobered. "I bet Andrew had a shit fit."

"You have no idea." Emma picked another chip out of the baskets, feeling a surge of anger at Andrew's overbearing and demanding attitude. Yes, she had to admit she'd hurt him. And yes, she expected some sort of reaction. But not the one she'd gotten. Not from Andrew. She crumbled the chip onto her little napkin. "And of course, he ran to my folks and complained about it."

"Honey, don't take offense at this but I think Andrew's closer to your folks than you are."

"I think you're probably right." The knowledge made her sad.

Annie studied her. "So tell me. Did the Ice Queen want to give you a time out for bad behavior?"

"My mother's not as bad as you make her out to be." The past couple of days had been a real eye opener for her. One thing became clear to her. She didn't know her parents as well as she thought or was nearly as close to them as she thought. Still, Emma felt a need to defend her mother, even though Annie was probably right. "She's just...comfortable with rules."

But she wasn't sure she believed that herself. The unpleasant conversation they'd had wouldn't leave her brain.

"Which is the way she's always wanted you to live your life, sweet cheeks. I bet she went into shock when she found out what you've done."

Emma ducked her head. "She doesn't know."

Annie choked on her drink. "She doesn't know? You didn't tell her?"

"How could I? Or Andrew, either." She squirmed on her high stool. "After the way they all reacted to my walking out and breaking up with him, they'd probably have me committed. The worst part is I feel like a teenager afraid to confess she's sneaked out of the house."

"Holy shit, Emma. What excuse did you give them?"

"I said I'm going to be thirty, and I can't stand my life any more." Emma waved at the waitress for another.

"You'd better slow down there," Annie warned. "One is usually your limit, and we're not even halfway through Happy Hour."

"Maybe my limits need changing. I feel as if everything in my life needs a do-over so why not my drinking habits?"

"Wow. Pinch me. Where is Emma Blake and what have you done with her?"

"Turning her into someone different. I hope. Anyway I'm good. I'll eat a lot of chips."

"Yeah? You seem to be pulverizing more than you're eating." She shifted on her stool. "So want happens now?"

Emma shrugged. "I don't know. Probably nothing."

The thought ate at her. She carried a lot of guilt at the way she'd reacted in the grocery store, especially after the fantastic night together and the tenderness he'd shown her. Painfully aware she'd been more than a quick fuck for him, she never felt so stupid. Why hadn't she apologized as soon as she realized her mistake?

Because I'm a scared idiot.

Now she needed to find a way to correct the situation. Hopefully, Annie could give her good advice.

She could always just walk into the club again, but did she have the courage? She wanted to see him again so badly.

"Nothing? You meet this great guy at a rock club, have off-the-charts sex with him, and it's already over? I don't get it. Did he blow you off in the morning? He may be Mr. Dark and Smoldering but from what I've read he doesn't have the rep as that type of guy."

Okay, that made her feel better.

Emma took a long swallow of her third drink. "No, it's worse." Staring down at her hands Emma spilled out what happened at the grocery store.

She expected Annie to be shocked, but instead her friend burst out laughing again.

"Hell, Emma. Only you could fail to recognize a guy you slept with because he cleaned himself up."

"What? Why? I don't understand what you mean."

"You compartmentalize things, honey. And you had this Marc stuck in one place in your mind. You never expected to see him as part of your world. Come on. Confess. I'm right, aren't I?"

Emma frowned. "So what do I do now? It's been a week since this all happened. Maybe I've let it go too long and he's just written me off as a rude idiot."

The crowd had swelled in size and the noise level rose accordingly. Emma had to lean closer to hear her friend.

"Depends on you. Do you want to see him again?"

She thought about this for a long minute and the answer was very clear. Yes, absolutely. Without a doubt. "More than I can possibly tell you."

Annie grinned. "Hooked you good, did he?"

"Uh huh. Is that terrible of me?"

"Not a bit, sweet cheeks. I like seeing you embrace life a little. Has he called you?"

Emma shook her head. "He can't."

Annie frowned. "Can't? Why not? Doesn't he have a phone?"

If she called him out of the blue and he had Caller ID.... No, she couldn't do that. She needed to keep her anonymity in case it all turned into disaster. God, what a weak-kneed idiot she was. She wanted to be with him again but couldn't expose who she was to him. Just in case. Was she being stupid or smart?

She looked down at her hands and blurted out, "I didn't give him my name."

"What?" Annie froze in shock. "Didn't give him your name? What's the matter with you?"

"I...was afraid to. What if I could only do this once? We're so different. I don't even know if we have anything else in common."

"Well, you'll never find out if he doesn't know who you are. Anyway, the first thing you have to do is go back to Aftershock. Find a way to talk to him. You probably hurt this guy's feelings. You have to make it right."

Emma tore little pieces off her cocktail napkin, squirming as she recalled the way she'd run from his house like a frightened mouse, barely saying a word to him except she had to go. And then that incident in the grocery store. He probably thought she was a real nutcase. An image flashed in her mind of all the screaming females in the club who she was sure wanted him as badly as she did. And weren't as stupid about it. Had she damaged her chances permanently?

"What if I hurt him to the point he doesn't want to see me again? Or be with me?"

"You won't know unless you go to the club and make an effort to patch this up. Go for it."

"What if you're wrong in your opinion of him and he's just another horny musician?"

"I may not know him personally but if that's the kind if guy he is, the buzz would have made him for it."

Emma fiddled with her glass, staring into the remnants of her drink. "Would you go with me?"

"Go with you?" Annie repeated.

"Yes." Emma pulled out her swizzle stick and licked the edges of it.

"You're keeping him a big secret but you want to drag me along with you?"

"I'm not hiding him from you. Come on, Annie. I don't think I have your kind of courage. I can't do this by myself. You know your way around this scene and besides, I need you for moral support. If you'll take pity on me, I'll be your slave for life."

"Be careful I don't hold you to it." Annie sighed. "Okay, okay. And what am I supposed to do while you send hot signals back and forth with this guy?"

"Just make sure I don't pass out from anxiety and humiliation." She sipped the rest of her drink. "Oh, and one other thing?"

"Yes?" Annie's lips curved in a smile as if she knew what was coming.

"Would you mind if we drove in separate cars?"

Chapter Six

"*I* can't believe I'm here."

Emma took in the parking lot at Aftershock, jammed even on a Tuesday night.

"Well, you are." Annie grinned. "Ready?"

Drawing in a deep breath, she let it out. "As I'll ever be."

Annie, who knew what she was doing, had called Aftershock to find out what times Lightnin' played. Emma didn't want to arrive too early but she didn't want to wait until the end of the evening, either. The band had just started their third set, which meant she had an entire hour to listen and watch Marc before trying to catch him before the last set of the evening.

"This is one of the few bands I've heard of capable of pulling in a crowd like this in the middle of the week," Annie noted.

"You've heard *of* them but never heard them?"

Her friend shrugged. "The few times I've tried the place where they were playing was too packed and my so-called dates didn't like standing in line."

"Well, then. Wait until you hear them. I never thought I'd fall in love with music like this."

Annie chuckled. "I don't think you've been in love with any*one* or any*thing* before now. It's about damn time, you know."

Emma paused at the door, a wave of anxiety gripping her. *What if he ignores me? Or doesn't want to talk to me? What if he won't give me a chance?*

Annie nudged her. "Go on. I'm not letting you chicken out now."

Her hand trembled as she pulled the club door open. When she walked in, it was just like Saturday night. The sound of the music blasted out at them. The same man was at the door and leaned closer so she could hear him when he spoke.

"I see you came back again. And brought a friend."

"Yes." She handed him the cover charge, then was surprised when he held out change to her.

"Only five bucks Tuesday and Wednesday," he explained.

"Then keep the whole thing. I'll pay for my friend." It was the least she could do for dragging Annie into this.

She clutched Annie's arm and tugged her along as they worked their way into the main room, the intensity of the music and excitement of the crowd surrounding them.

"Wow." She took in the scene as they edged their way through the mass of moving bodies. "I go to a lot of clubs, girlfriend, but they're never packed like this on weeknights. No wonder people say this band is hot, hot, hot."

Emma leaned her head toward Annie in an attempt to be heard over the din. "Let's get a beer, and you can judge them for yourself."

"A beer?" Annie stared at her. "I didn't think you drank beer."

Emma gave her a tentative smile, aware so much about her was changing. Things like the lure of the rock music, the way her body moved to it. Even to what she drank. All of it was new, both to herself and to her friend. "I guess I'm doing a lot of things I never did before. Come on."

She had yet to look directly at the stage but the heavy sound of the bass guitar vibrated through the room and shimmied up through her body. While they were waiting for their drinks at the bar, Annie punched her in the arm and pointed at the wall over the array of bottles. Displayed in a glass case was a T-shirt, dark blue with a lightning bolt on it and the word *Lightnin'* in script below it.

"You should get one," Annie yelled over the noise.

"We'll see." But she could already imagine herself in it. Maybe she could wear it at Marc's. Maybe with nothing underneath.

First you have to make eye contact with him and see if he'll even talk to you.

They grabbed their drinks and slithered and wriggled their way to the front of the crowd. Only then did Emma allow herself to glance at the stage, and a bolt of what surely was real lightning shot through her. She nearly dropped her beer. Marc was standing there with one foot on the monitor just like when she'd first seen him, talented fingers moving along the neck of his instrument, hair wild and sexy. Dress jeans clung to his lean form, and he wore one of the band's signature T-shirt like the one on the wall. The muscles in his arms flexed and rippled as he worked the strings of the guitar.

She closed her eyes for a moment and recalled the image of Marc gloriously naked in his bedroom. Feel again his mouth on hers, on her nipples, on the moist heat of her sex. The sensation of his cock sliding into her, filling her, stretching her. Shocked at the desire gripping her, she forced her eyes open.

And discovered Marc watching her.

Her stomach knotted, the butterflies hibernating in there exploding in a triple-time dance. The pulse in her womb hammered like a jungle drum and every part of her body suddenly turned to liquid heat. She couldn't breathe and her chest was too tight. Was he glad to see her? Angry? Did he wish she would just go away?

Someone's fingers pressed reassuringly on her arm and she heard Annie shouting over the crowd and the music.

"Holy shit, Emma. I'd go home with him myself."

Emma grinned nervously.

"Just hang tight here," Annie said, her mouth close to Emma's ear. "Whatever it takes. He's worth it."

She looked directly at Annie, hoping her friend could read her lips because the sound was deafening. "What if I crash and burn?"

What if he ignores me or my courage fails at the last minute? What if I make the effort and he shuts me out?

Annie drew closer. "Better than not taking the ride at all."

Maybe.

Emma couldn't ever remember being this nervous, not even on the dreaded first day of school, or on her first real date. She rolled the chilled bottle of beer against her forehead, trying to take the edge off the heat blasting through her. Her eyes were glued to the stage, to Marc, to the fluid actions of his lean, muscular body, and the way his hair flew around his face with the movement of his head.

He wasn't watching her now, instead lost in his music and the sexy rhythm of the bass. The song was high energy. Its throbbing tempo rocking the crowd. When Marc did a solo on the bass and everyone clapped in time to it, every nerve in her body vibrated in response. At the end of the song, the mass of people cheered and screamed for more and Emma found herself screaming right along with them.

Glancing over at Annie, she saw her friend was as caught up in the ambience and the energy as everyone else. Her body twisted and swayed, and her eyes were alight with excitement. She bumped her hip against Emma's, grinned, and made an okay sign with her thumb and forefinger.

The crowd was already into the next song, and when Emma looked to the stage, she saw Marc focusing on her again. Every part of her body heated beneath his gaze, her core throbbed with an unfamiliar hunger, and her breasts felt heavy and aching. The memory of his hands and his mouth arousing her, his thick cock inside her, filling her, sent a surge of lust through her so strong it nearly brought her to her knees.

Ohmigod!

What was happening to her? And what would she do if he turned his back on her? She was anxious for the set to end yet at the same time she wanted it go on so she wouldn't have to face her Guitar Man.

As if reading her thoughts, Annie squeezed her arm again and leaned sideways until her mouth was close to Emma's ear.

"It will be all right. You'll see."

Marc was in the middle of a particularly complicated riff when Music Lady walked in. He was focused on his bass yet something intangible reached out to him. He chanced a peek at the crowd, and there she was. Just as delicious and tempting as she'd been Saturday night. He nearly lost his concentration, but he was a disciplined musician. He pulled himself right back into the music. Tonight she had a friend with her, similar in looks but as dark as Music Lady was fair. A woman who appeared wiser, harder, as if she'd learned the score a long time ago.

Then as they swung into the ending of the song, he risked another glance into the audience again.

At first the lingering hurt from the incident at the grocery store swept over him, shreds of anger still clinging to him and he was tempted to just blow her off. Then he brushed it aside as his mind ran in all directions, remnants of his conversation with Rick flashing in his brain. Why had she come here tonight? Had she finally remembered him or did she just want a hot fuck like Saturday night?

No. He was pretty sure that wasn't her style. So why was she here?

Get with the music, buddy, or you'll make an ass of yourself. Worry about her later.

But it took every ounce of his self-control to do so. The band swung into its final song. At last the set ended, and Marc decided to see what the hell she was doing here after a week had passed. Surely she hadn't shown up just to blow him off again. He didn't know her well but his conscience told him otherwise. He settled his guitar in the stand behind him and hopped down from the stage. Music Lady was at the front of the crowd, wetting her lips and twisting her hands in an obviously nervous gesture, uncertainty plain on her face.

Okay, this was a good sign, right? If she was worried about his reaction?

He tried to push his way through the crowd to her but then that piece-of-work Lacey was all over him the minute he cleared the stage.

"Hey, Marc," she crooned, tossing her long, red hair. "Were you playing for me tonight?"

He eased his arm away from her grip. "For everyone, Lacey. Always everyone."

She grabbed his arm again. "If you played just for me I could be really grateful."

This time he deliberately lifted her fingers from his skin. "We've been through this before. Chill. Find someone else. It's not happening between us."

His eyes kept straying to ML who was watching him carefully. To someone new to this scene, he had an idea how this would look and he shook his head, hoping to signal her it meant nothing. More people came up to him, yakking about the music, talking about the band. At least they surged between him and Lacey, saving him from more contact. But he had to get to ML. By the time he got loose, he'd lost sight of her and was afraid she'd decided to leave.

No! He calmed when he spotted her against the wall by the back door. He pushed his way over, nodded and smiled at her friend, then took her by the arm.

"Sorry, it took me a minute to get to you."

She shrugged. "I could see you were held up. By one of your *fans*."

He almost smiled at the way she spit the word out. "Hey. That's just Lacey, Queen of the Groupies. I think she's trying to work her way through the band. I'm nobody special to her."

ML looked over his shoulder and bit her lip. "She seems to

think differently."

He turned and followed her gaze. Lacey stood with her hands on her hips, glaring at them through the crowd. "Her problem. Like I said, no one for you to worry about. Believe me."

"I-it's okay. Really."

He studied her face. "You came back. Why? What's the deal with you, anyway?"

"C-can we talk someplace for a minute?"

Okay, tonight she knows who I am. What's changed?

"Definitely." He glanced at her friend, wondering if the woman had something to do with ML being there. What and how?

Well, at least she cared enough to show up and make the effort no matter what got her here. A promising sign.

"Don't worry about me," Annie said. "I'm good."

"Come on, then." He tugged Music Lady along with him out the back door into the small area behind the club. A few people were wandering around taking a quick smoke. Marc pulled Music Lady to a quiet area and stopped, drinking in the sight of her. When he started to say something, she held up her hand.

"Me first. If I don't get it out now, I'll lose my courage.'

"Okay. Go." He really wanted to haul her into his arms and kiss her to death but he forced himself not to move until she got out whatever she'd come to say. If he offended *her*, or hurt *her* in some way and that was why she acted the way she did in the grocery store, then he needed to know. In only one night, this woman had stirred him emotionally as no other woman ever had and he wanted somehow to make this right without scaring her off again.

She twisted her hands together, drew in a breath. "I'm sorry."

Surprised but pleased by the apology, he waited to see if she'd say anything else.

"I'm stupid. That's my only excuse." She lowered her gaze. "I...um...I mean. Oh, crap." She sighed. "I'm so stupid I never expected to see you dressed the way you were, and you caught me off guard and...and...."

Marc paused. "Is there some reason you don't think of musicians as normal people?" he asked in a flat voice."

"Yes. No." Her words were so soft he had to lean forward to hear her. "I apologize for my stupidity." She twisted her hands again. "I've...never been to a rock club before. Or any place like it. I...I...."

A whole new perspective opened for him, giving him a better understanding of her. There was no mistaking the sincerity in her words. Threading his fingers through her hair, he tipped her face and kissed her with all the pent-up heat he'd been dealing with since she'd run from his house early Sunday morning. She hesitated just briefly before opening her mouth and accepting the hard thrust of his tongue. When she wound her arms around his neck, he pulled her tight against his body, his rock-hard erection pressing into the soft flesh of her tummy.

He heard the soft gasp as he molded to her to him, and he drank more deeply from her, sliding his tongue across hers, enjoying the soft pressure of her lips touching his. His balls ached and his cock throbbed, and he wanted to strip off her clothes and plunge himself into her right then and there. Reaching for his sanity, he broke the kiss and cupped her cheeks.

Her eyes were filled with unanswered questions: anxiety, hope, desire. The color shifted from grey to smoky green in the haloed light of the parking lot.

"Do you forgive me?" she whispered.

"If you tell me your name."

Her entire body tightened and she started to pull away. "I shouldn't have come here. It was a big mistake."

Big mistake, buddy boy.

He was going to lose her unless he accepted her on her terms. She had some specific reason for this, whatever it was. Maybe she's so out of her element. Needs to wait until she feels safe and secure with you. Trusts you.

And she was so ingrained in his system in just a short time he didn't think he could survive it.

"No. Wait." He brushed his lips against hers, the kiss a soft breeze against her skin. "It's okay. I just thought since you brought your friend with you everything would be okay."

"You mean I'd tell you who I was? Please, Marc." Her voice was pleading. "Can't I just be your Music Lady and you can be my Guitar Man?"

Could he move forward under this circumstance? He wanted her so badly and not just to take to bed. Somehow he'd find a way to resolve this problem. Swallowing his misgivings, he brushed his knuckles against her cheek and forced himself to relax.

"Okay. For now." He glanced back at the club. "Can you come home with me again? What about your friend?"

"She brought her own car." Music Lady licked her bottom lip, nervously casting her eyes around the parking lot as if expecting someone to jump out at her.

"She did?"

"Uh huh. I just needed her to come in with me for moral support. I drove my own car so she could leave if we...um...if you...you know. Let me apologize."

He studied her, trying to tamp down his annoyance. She was obviously willing to go home with him but for what? Just sex? This was a new feeling for him and not a pleasant one. He'd never treated sex as casually as his friends. Sure he'd brought ML home impulsively but there was an instant connection he'd never felt before. And he was convinced it hadn't diminished.

"I get the feeling you weren't planning to tell anyone about this. Us. Whatever. Pardon me if I'm confused, but you brought your friend to the club and you won't tell me your name? What's up with that?"

She nibbled her lower lip. "Annie and I have been friends for years. And I needed someone to keep me from falling apart." She was trembling. "Marc, listen to me. This is all so new to me. I hardly know you. I might not be your style."

"Listen to me, babe." He tilted her chin up so her eyes met his. "Whoever or whatever you are, you are most definitely my style. One of these times I might even get you to believe it." He touched his mouth to hers briefly.

He wanted her. Badly. And not just her body. He and this woman had the beginning of something very special here. But if she wasn't ready to tell him her name, they had a long road ahead of them. Right now he was just so damn glad to see her under any circumstances. He'd have to work to get her to trust him as much as she did her friend.

He studied her face as if there was some secret answer written there. "Okay, then, Music Lady. We'll do things your way. For now." He smiled. "But one of these days, I'm going to get you to trust me enough to tell me about the real you."

She rubbed her hands nervously on her jeans and lowered her eyes. "You might not like the real me, Guitar Man."

"I bet I will." He tucked a strand of hair behind her ear. "Now. We have one more set to play then we're done for the night. Will you stay until the end? Come home with me again?"

He held his breath, waiting for her answer. When she nodded wordlessly, he smiled for the first time in days.

"Good. Let's go back inside. I'll get you a drink, and I can get ready for the last set. But first...."

He pulled her hard against him and touched his mouth to hers, the feel of her soft lips so arousing, her light floral scent filling his nostrils, her taste intoxicating. When he licked her lower lip with his tongue, she opened for him and he swept inside, gliding over every wet surface. She moaned into his mouth, wound her arms around his neck again, and pressed her body to his. The soft feel of her breasts with their hard little nipples were driving him crazy. He thrust his hips slightly, letting her know how swollen his cock was and knowing he'd need to find a way to hide his gigantic boner when he went back into the club.

Marc broke the kiss before it reached the point of no return and took a step back, reaching for her hand.

"Let's go back inside. If you stay near where I found you, close to where I stand on the stage, we can slide right out this same door as soon as I'm finished for the night. You good with that?"

"Yes. And I want to tell my friend she can leave."

"Okay. Good. Come on." People were jammed everywhere but he got them both inside and handed her off to her friend, who was standing in the same place. Putting his mouth to her ear he whispered, "Later."

When she nodded and gave him a shy smile, his heart turned over. Forcing himself to focus on what he had to do, he leaped onto the stage and picked up his guitar. He winked at ML before checking the song list for the final set. It couldn't be over soon enough for him.

I must be crazy. Genuinely nuts. I cannot believe I'm doing this.

She'd been a bundle of nerves wondering if he'd turn her away. But she wanted him—needed him—more than she thought it possible to desire another human being.

Annie had just grinned at her when she came back inside with Marc, gave her a quick hug, and said, "I wouldn't walk away from him, either. And don't worry; my lips are sealed. I won't blab to Andrew or your folks. And you can tell him your name, you know."

"I can't explain it," she said, feeling helpless in her own insecurities. "But when I'm with him, I'm not Emma but someone else. I *feel* like someone else. And right now I need that. You think I'm crazy to act this way, don't you?" She grimaced. "I probably am."

Annie shrugged. "It doesn't much matter what I think. This is your life. You have to do whatever you're comfortable with. I'm just glad to see you break out of your tight-ass mold."

"Tight-ass?" Emma stared at her. "Is that how you saw me?"

"Only in the nicest possible way. Now I'm going to slide out of here. You go have a good time."

So here she was, following Marc again through the quiet, nearly deserted streets. Emma, the quintessential good girl, going home for a second time with a man she wouldn't even tell her name to.

Well, Toto, we're not in Kansas anymore.

Shut up! You're almost at his house. Get your act together.

Marc pulled into his driveway while Emma parked in front of the house. He waited while she locked her car and came up the walkway, holding out his hand to her. When she took it, she noted his skin was warm against hers and she could feel the callouses on his fingers from years of playing the guitar. She trembled, whether from nerves or anticipation she wasn't sure. She remembered the last time she'd been here to his house and thought about what was going to happen next. As soon as Marc unlocked the door and tugged her inside, he pulled her around to face him and smiled. God, his smile could melt her panties.

It also took the edge off her nerves.

"Relax." He brought his free hand up and caressed her cheek, his eyes locked with hers. "Everything's fine, ML. Just like the other night. There's nothing to worry about." He bent his head and brushed his lips against hers. "I promise."

When he touched her, she couldn't think about anything except being with him. She inhaled the scent uniquely his—the earthy aroma of a man who'd worked hard on stage blended with his cologne that reminded her of the outdoors. His body felt so good pressed lightly to hers. His lips were firm yet gentle, his taste intoxicating. Their tongues glided against each other in a kiss that speared through her like lightning. He was a pure sexual animal, and she knew she was already addicted to him.

She had one brief moment to give thanks that he'd forgiven her stupidity on Sunday before falling into the sensuous web he was weaving around her. None of the erotic romances she read quite prepared her for how powerful the real thing was.

The kiss was light. Gentle. A brief touching of mouths. Then he lifted his head.

"Are you hungry?" he asked her.

"No." Her laugh was tremulous. "Annie wanted me to get an early dinner with her at Hot Salsa but I was too nervous to eat."

"So you like Mexican food." When she nodded he said, "Me, too. I've been to Hot Salsa. Casual place. Quality food."

"It's one of our favorite hangouts."

"Maybe I could take you there sometime."

Emma hesitated. "Maybe." She spotted a stack of DVDs on top of his television and went to check them out. The one on top, *The Blind Side*, was one of her favorites. She picked up the case. "This is such a great story. I could watch this movie again and again."

His eyes lit up. "Me, too. Seems like we have similar taste in movies and food. Good to know."

Her stomach did a funny little flip.

No old war movies for this guy. And I'll bet he'd ask me what I like to watch and what kind of pizza I like, too.

"Maybe some time we could watch a movie together?" he asked.

Do something normal? Something besides share incredible sex?

She just didn't know where she fit into the scheme of things with him, another reason she hugged her identity so closely—her protection against the moment things turned upside down. At least she'd have a life to go back to without him. A place where she could shut him out of her mind and continue to dwell in a grey world.

She needed to get past her Emma hang-ups and really let herself enjoy this man. Be his Music Lady. See if the connection sizzling between them was really what she hoped. A relationship needed more than just sex. Even spectacular sex. It stunned her he was willing to offer the possibility under the circumstances. Inside she was shaky and excited at the same time.

"Maybe," she said, wondering if they would really get to that stage.

"Meanwhile I need to shower. Come on, babe. I want us to shower together."

"Shower?" She blinked. "Together?"

He grinned. "Yeah. You know, like standing under water and using soap? I'll bet you do it every day, right?"

"Um, yes, but I've never...."

"Showered with anyone? What a lot of things you've never done. You have no idea what you've been missing." He kissed her cheek, his tongue feathering over her skin. "You'll love it." His voice dropped lower. "As long as I'm the only one you ever shower with."

Ever? Was he implying something here? She kept trying to wrap her mind around the fact she was way out of her comfort zone and actually enjoying herself. Besides, Andrew—like the few other men she'd been with—insisted on his privacy when he showered. He didn't consider it a couples' activity.

Exactly what *did* Marc consider a couples' activity, now that she thought about it? What an alien world she'd walked into, almost as if she'd been living in her closet all these years for as much as she knew about anything. Sexual and otherwise.

"Come on." He led her down the little hallway to his bedroom and into the bathroom connected to it, flicking on lights as he moved.

Emma was surprised at what she saw. The floor and walls were covered in matte finish tiles in two colors arranged in a diamond-shaped pattern. A gleaming stall shower stood next to a deep Jacuzzi tub. The vanity counter was a pebbled chocolate and everything on it was amazingly neat. She couldn't help staring as she looked around.

Marc laughed, a deep, warm rich sound. "Cleaner than you expected, right? I straightened up in the hope I'd have special company tonight."

She gaped at him wondering just who he meant.

"You, Music Lady. I was hoping for you."

The tiny knot of apprehension gripping her unwound and disappeared. She ran her fingers over the vanity. "This is just beautiful."

He waved his hand at the room. "The bathroom was in pretty

bad shape when I bought the house. My dad and brothers helped me do all the improvements."

"I can't get over the fact you actually own a house. I guess I expected...I don't know *what* I expected."

"An apartment filled with beer cans and dirty underwear?" He laughed again and cupped her cheeks, brushing his thumbs across her cheekbones. "I want roots. The music business is unsettling enough. I needed someplace to really call my own. Maybe tonight you'll actually get to see more of it." He paused. "After."

And there was a wealth of meaning in that word.

She knew what he meant and a thrill of anticipation ran through her. But what he said chased itself around in her mind. She thought she had solid roots with Andrew but they turned out to be gray, until she discovered colors. She still had the same goals, but suddenly she had other options. Could she have them with Marc? Did she want to? The idea trickled through her like melted chocolate.

She laughed, slightly breathless. "Maybe."

Marc pulled the edges of her pretty short-sleeved sweater upward, urging her to lift her arms so he could tug it over her head. His eyes darkened when they took in her breasts in the satin and lace bra she'd chosen to wear. He ran the tip of a finger over each plump swell, and her nipples tightened against the restraint of the fabric. He skimmed the same finger over the hard points, a hungry look etched on his face.

"I could just eat you up with a spoon." The rusty sound of his voice sent shivers skating along her spin.

No one had ever said those words to her before or anything like them.

Is he going to do the same thing again with his mouth? Please? Please?

She stood there, breath hitching unevenly, as he lowered his head and closed his lips over one nipple, taking it in fabric and all. The heat of his mouth burned through her, igniting her blood and soaking her panties with the liquid of her arousal. His warms hands slid up the length of her arms, caressing her skin, coasting over her shoulders and down her back. He spent so much time on each nipple, Emma wasn't sure she'd be able to remain standing, but at last he opened the clasp of her bra, slipped the straps down her arms, and dropped the garment on the counter.

He took a great deal of care removing her jeans and panties, pausing to lick the skin of her inner thighs and place kisses on her ankles, a place she'd never considered an erogenous zone before this.

She wanted him naked, too. Her heartbeat stuttered when he pulled off his T-shirt, boxers, and jeans. He was just as magnificent as she remembered, hard chest covered with the soft matte of dark hair arrowing down past the flat stomach to the very erect cock making her mouth water. His arms and legs were roped with sculpted muscles and dusted lightly with the same dark hair. A totally sensuous male. *Talk about eating someone up with a spoon.*

Giving her a definitely predatory smile, he reached in to turn on the shower, holding one hand under the spray. When he was satisfied with the temperature, he took her hand again.

"Come on, Music Lady. Time for another new experience for you." He gave her earlobe a gentle nip. "One I promise you'll love every minute of."

Chapter Seven

Marc had to dig deep for his control. Having Music Lady with him again, naked, in his shower was more than he had hoped for. After Sunday's incident, he wasn't sure he'd see her again. He wasn't sure if he should be pissed off she didn't think musicians could clean up good or ecstatic because she was here in his house again. He decided ecstatic had a lot more going for it.

He let his eyes roam over her skin, so smooth beneath the water beading on it, then he threaded his fingers through her wet hair and took her mouth in a hungry kiss. God, she tasted so good. Her flavor so sweet and unique. Her lips lush and tempting. She opened for him at once and his tongue dove in, licking every surface, feasting on her like a starving man. Tonight she was a little bolder, thrusting her own tongue into his mouth, savoring him as he was doing to her.

His cock was so hard he was afraid if he bumped against something it would break off, and his balls ached with a fierce need. No woman had ever gotten to him the way this one did.

He lifted his head only when he needed to drag air into his oxygen-starved lungs and stared into her eyes. They were more blue than green, the shifting hazel a reflection of her mood. Blue for passion—his Music Lady had a passionate soul. He sensed a zest for life welling within her, and he wanted to tap into it if he could breach that final barrier she kept so firmly in place.

Reaching out with one hand, he grabbed the bottle of plain shower gel on the built-in shelf, squirted some into his palm, and worked it into a rich lather. Still holding her gaze, he began to smooth it into her skin, swirling the foam in a circular pattern. Her wonderful slender neck first. A stop at the hollow of her throat where her pulse beat rapidly. The line of her collarbone. Each arm, from shoulder to wrist then gently rubbing every finger.

He massaged each area slowly, feeling her muscles relax incrementally as the motion of his hands soothed her.

More gel, more lather.

He drew circles along the swell of her breasts and underneath the plump mounds. Around and around, just the lightest touch. She trembled as his hands went up the sides of her breasts to those puckered rosy nipples, pinching them lightly, rasping them with his soapy thumbs. Loving the pebbled texture of them.

And all the while she stood there, hands at her sides, her eyes never leaving his. So much emotion, he thought, he could drown in them.

Jesus, could I keep this up without losing it?

More gel, again, and more lather.

He knelt in front of her and began with her feet, applying the suds even to her toes, then her ankles and up the length of each slender leg. But when he got to her pussy he stopped, saving it for last.

"Turn around," he told her, barely recognizing his own voice, and urged her with his hands.

He trailed his palms over the slope of her shoulders, the graceful line of her spine, touching each indentation until he reached the swell of her ass. He curved his hand over each cheek in turn, caressing it, cupping it. Tentatively, he drew one lather-covered finger down the length of the hot crevice, pausing only briefly to circle the tight puckered ring before moving on.

She tensed but didn't pull away from him and little whimpers of pleasure burst from her mouth. Anal sex, to Marc, was the most personal joining of two people. The fact Music Lady reacted the way she did was a sign she trusted him with her body.

But not her name?

He brushed the thought away as quickly as it came. When the time was right she'd tell him. And he'd work hard to get there.

His hand drifted away from her ass to her waist.

Later. That's for another time.

She was like a gentle flower just beginning to blossom. And he wanted her to be *his* blossom. *His* flower. To be a part of his life almost more than he craved his music. He was tired of the lonely nights, of the hours when he had no one to share his success or soften his failures. Even as little as he knew about her, there was something growing so tenuously between them. He was going to do whatever it took to nurture it. Just like in the songs he wrote when he hit the perfect combination of notes, when the magic was plucked out of the air with no rhyme or reason. His heart told him this woman could be the one for him.

Gently he turned her to face him again, brushing his mouth over hers and skating his tongue over her lips.

"God, you're so special," he murmured.

"Really?" Her lips moved against his as she leaned into him. "Special? You think so?"

"Oh, yeah. Trust me on that." He continued to massage her shoulders with his soapy hands until she was loose and pliable beneath his touch. "Relax. I promised you'd enjoy this. Wasn't I right?"

"Yes. You did. And you are." Her voice was musical. Sensual. Her fingers resting on his hips sent sparks through him. As if he even needed them.

"And it's going to get even better."

He skimmed the swell of her breasts before dropping to his knees in front of her. Taking her hands, he placed them flat against the wall behind her and lifted one of her legs to rest on his shoulder. It brought her pussy directly to him at eye level, and the sight made his blood pump and his pulse beat harder. It was so pink and soft and covered with silky dark blonde curls. Inhaling her fragrance, he touched her clit with one soapy finger, then outlined the wet, glistening, plump lips.

Emma pressed herself back against the wall, and a low moan escaped from her mouth.

Marc traced a line along her folds, swirled soapy lather into her nest of curls, and brushed back and forth over her swollen nub before sliding first one and then two fingers inside her.

Oh, Jesus.

She was so slick and wet, and the inner walls of her cunt pulsed around his touch. He wanted to fuck her right then and there, in the shower, with the warm water sluicing down over them, her hair wet and slicked back. But he couldn't do her justice here. And his Music Lady wasn't yet to where he could take her anywhere—in the shower, against the wall, on the dining room table. But soon. When she trusted him completely. When she realized it was a hell of a lot more than just sex.

She was moaning and whimpering, and he had to force himself to pull out of her tight grasp and stand up.

"My turn," he said in a low voice.

Her eyes opened wide. "Yours?"

"Uh huh. Showering together is a two way street, babe. Hold out your hands."

He poured gel into her palms and watched her work it into a rich lather. Almost tentatively, she reached up to his shoulders and began to spread the suds over his chest. She seemed fascinated by the matte of hair, rubbing it over and over. When her fingers found his flat nipples, they both sucked in a gasp.

"Do you like this?" She was watching his face as she brushed across pebbled flesh, and she scraped her nails across hard tips, as if mesmerized by the sight.

Like it? Was she kidding?

"Oh, yeah. You bet." He had to curl his hands into fists to

grab the edges of control.

For one fleeting moment, he wondered what kind of assholes she'd been with that the simple pleasures of making love were so unfamiliar to her. And he was eternally grateful she was discovering them with him.

Eventually she added more gel, worked up more lather and stroked the suds down the flat plane of his abdomen. When she reached his cock, her touch almost hesitant, he dug his nails into his palms to keep from grabbing her, lifting her up, and plunging into her. But he let her explore him, her small fingers so soft yet so strong on his throbbing shaft.

Her eyes locked with his as if searching for some sort of signal. She then slid her hand between his thighs to cup his balls, squeezing them gently. He couldn't hold back the groan that rumbled from his throat or prevent his hips from thrusting forward at her. He closed his eyes for a moment, letting a myriad of sensations wash over him. When he opened them, Music Lady had a tiny, self-satisfied smile on her face, as if she'd just discovered a major secret.

And she had, damn it. She'd discovered how easily she could turn him on, and how badly he wanted her. When she knelt down and began to move her small hands up his legs, her fingers making circles on his skin, he was done. That was it. The shower was over.

"We need to get out of here," he growled. "Right now."

"But I'm just getting the hang of it." She raised her eyes and gave him her beautiful smile.

"No kidding," he rasped.

He pulled her under the wide spray with him and rinsed them both, then turned off the water and slid the glass door open. Lifting her out to stand on the bath mat, he grabbed a large towel from the rack and dried her thoroughly before using the towel on himself.

"Sit," he said, urging her onto the little stool at the counter.

The hairdryer he'd used when getting dressed for the gig was still on the counter, plugged in. He dug out his brush and slowly and carefully dried her hair until it was a soft cloud falling around her shoulders. For him it was an exercise in self-restraint, teasing himself and knowing the prize was worth it.

"You make me feel so special," she said in a low voice, closing her eyes.

"You are special. And I plan to show you every chance I get."

He picked her up from the stool and carried her into the bedroom, pausing only long enough to draw back the covers before lowering her to the sheets. Lying beside her, he kissed her with a hunger threatening to consume her. He loved the silken feel of her lips, the wet warmth of her mouth, and the soft glide of her tongue against his. One hand molded to a breast, lightly pinching the nipple. He swallowed her gasp and pinched a little harder, her body arching up to his.

Dragging his lips away from hers with an effort, Marc took a long time worshiping her body, kissing every inch of her skin from the slender column of her neck to the slope of her breasts. He sucked and pulled on her nipples before moving his mouth down to the softness of her tummy, tracing the whorled flesh of her belly button with the tip of his tongue. He let one hand drift between her legs to find the heat of her pussy and gently rubbed the lips and the swollen button of her clit. Marc couldn't remember the last time a woman had reached deep inside him, making him feel so connected to her.

As he was tasting and exploring her and she squirmed in pleasure beside him, one of her hands slipped between them and found his throbbing erection. When she gripped his hard cock he jerked in reflex, the sensation almost too much to bear. His hand tightened convulsively on her, the heel pressing against her mound while his fingers dipped into her slick wetness. Jesus, she could make him come undone with just one touch.

Sucking in his breath, he nudged her to turn over and began to trail kisses the length of her spine, one hand caressing the sleek curve of her ass until he reached the dimple *there*, and traced it with his tongue. Music Lady was whimpering small sounds of pleasure and pushing herself back against his hand

and mouth. Suddenly, without warning, she rolled over and rose to her knees.

"I want to touch you, too," she told him.

Emma could hardly believe she was here again with this man. He was so magnificent. She could look at him forever. He lay beneath her hand, his body humming with sexual tension as she kissed him and licked his nipples, then she trailed her tongue over his abdomen down to his groin. He was like a new toy to her, willing to let her explore him in a way none of the men she'd been with up until now had been open to.

I guess when you pick bland men, you get bland sex.

Not that she wasn't aware of the other possibilities. She'd certainly read her share of erotic romances, and had suggested trying some of the things she'd read about, with a distinct lack of success. Andrew had just looked at her as if she'd lost her mind. With him, the whole process never took more than fifteen minutes from start to finish.

But Marc made her feel sexy. Desirable. Wanton, even, eliciting reactions from her that quickened her blood and made her pulse thrum. Showering with him had been the ultimate erotic experience—the two of them so close against each other, teasing, stroking. Rousing each other to a point of urgent need.

Although he made her feel anything was possible between them, she was always poised on the knife-edge of tension, waiting for rejection. Waiting for him to say it had all been a mistake. Waiting for abrupt dismissal. Wondering how many other women he'd brought home with him and how often he did it. Not that she, for one minute, thought he lived like a monk.

But tonight, everything just drizzled around in the back of her mind as she explored his very male body.

Wrapping her fingers around his thick, swollen cock, she bent her head and licked the bead of fluid on the slit with the tip of her tongue. A swipe across the velvety surface and she tasted the salty-sweet essence of him. His body jerked involuntarily but then she watched him every muscle in his body bunch in an effort to maintain control. She lapped at him again, loving the way his hot erection flexed in her grip.

Sliding a hand between his thighs, she cupped the heavy sac of his balls, stroking the soft skin covered with baby fine hair. When she moved her head lower to run her tongue over him, he groaned and tightened his grasp on her head, lifting it from his body.

"Enough," he growled, his voice rough and edgy. "If I'm not inside you in the next ten seconds, I might lose my mind."

His words ratcheted up her pulse, made the walls of her sex clench in anticipation.

He rolled her to her back, reached for a condom, and sheathed himself in a single smooth movement. Bending her legs and spreading them wide, he positioned himself at her opening. Thrusting smoothly with his hips, he drove inside her. Already wet and aroused, she took him easily, accepting him gladly into her body.

She felt complete in a way she never had before, as if all her life she'd been waiting for this moment.

"Look at me," he commanded in his husky baritone that sounded almost as if his guitar had transmuted itself into his body. When she locked her eyes with his, he said, "You are everything I've ever wanted."

An erotic charge swamped her. She so desperately wanted to believe him. To believe the connection she'd sensed from the beginning was as strong for him. Did he mean it, or was it just something he said in the heat of passion? Why would a man like Marc Malone feel that way about her? Impatiently, she brushed the stray thoughts away and tamped down her ever-present insecurities to give herself over to the moment. Fire for this man surged through her, and right at this moment, she didn't want to think at all. Just feel.

When he moved, a slow in and out thrust, the friction of his hot erection against the tight walls of her sex sent bolts of electricity everywhere in her body. She planted her feet on the bed, arching her hips up, trying to take him deeper inside her.

His laugh rumbled in his chest. "Don't rush me. I want to savor and enjoy every minute of this."

Nice and easy. That's what he said.

And it was exactly what he did, pulling back until just the head of his penis was filling her then plunging into her with a slow glide. In, out. In, out. His flesh dragged against hers in a hot, sensual dance. The lust that had coiled low in her belly and had begun unwinding in the shower now spiraled rapidly through her. Every nerve sparked. Every muscle trembled with unfulfilled hunger. She clamped her inner muscles around him, wanting to hold him in place. But the slow, steady movement of his cock only pushed her higher and higher until she was desperate for release.

Bracing himself on his hands, he bent his head and captured one taut pebbled tip in his mouth, pulling on it before he nipped it lightly with his teeth, then soothed it with his tongue. Need jolted her. When he gave the other swollen bud the same treatment, she tried to hold his head in place but again his low, husky erotic chuckle vibrated against her, and he bit down gently again.

In desperation, Emma wrapped her legs around his lean hips, locking her ankles at the small of his back and hugging him to her as tightly as she could.

"You ready to ride with me, Music Lady?" His voice was thick with passion and not quite steady. "'Cause I'm going to take you on the ride of your life."

"Yes," she gasped. "Please. Now."

His mouth took hers in a bruising, predatory kiss as he lifted his body and drove into her with a heavy surge. And then he moved with fast, hard strokes, pulling them both to the familiar precipice, taking her on the wild ride as promised. Everything ceased to exist except this man and the way he made her body explode with pleasure. Up, up...the orgasm hovered just out of reach.

She sensed his effort to hold on, waiting until she was there with him while she writhed in an agony of frustration. But then in seconds he stiffened and shouted her name, pumping his release into her as she shattered over and over. She was in a black velvet space where she whirled and spun and felt nothing but the clenching of her own body and the pulsing of his thick cock.

Limp, spent, legs falling to the bed, she continued to tremble with the tiny aftershocks. Although he was shaking with the aftereffects, Marc bent to kiss Emma again; this time a kiss so full of emotion, it nearly brought tears to her eyes. He slid carefully from the clasp of her body, disposed of the condom, and returned to enfold her in his arms, spooning them together.

She was thoroughly sated. Limp. Stretched in the lassitude of complete satisfaction. And the feel of Marc curled around her was so comforting. Despite her best intention, sleep dragged at her even as the need to leave hovered close. One tear slid down her cheek as she closed her eyes.

The movement of her body woke Marc, pulling him up from an erotic dream where he was buried deep inside Music Lady. Only this time she was on top, riding him, her breasts offered tantalizingly just beyond his touch. She smiled but when he stretched out his hand toward her, she suddenly began to dissolve in front of him. That was when he realized the woman he'd wrapped himself around had maneuvered herself out of his embrace and was sliding quietly out of the bed. He reached for her but she was already on her feet.

Pushing himself up to a sitting position, he raked his fingers through his hair and attempted to kick his brain into start.

"Hey." He cleared his throat to rid it of the gravelly sound of someone just awakened from sleep. "Hey, ML." When she didn't answer him he said louder, "Music Lady?"

She paused with her jeans in her hand and turned to him. "I have to go. You know why."

What the hell?

"No. No, I don't. Why can't you stay until it's light out? What's the big rush?" He was sleep-drugged, cobwebs impeding his ability to think and for a moment, despite his previous good intentions, anger sparked through him as she readied to leave.

"It's just better this way."

"Why?" He didn't understand the fear in her voice. The panic. He swung himself out of bed, stark naked, and put his hands on her shoulders. "I don't want you to go. Doesn't that matter?"

"I can't." She pulled away and reached for her clothes again.

Once again he wondered if she was hiding some terrible secret. Or just using him to take a wild plunge into an unfamiliar world.

You promised yourself to give her time to trust you. Don't screw it up now.

But swallowing the anger was like swallowing wood chips. Hard to get past the lump in his throat. "Wait. I have a present for you."

She froze in place, her eyes widening. "A present?"

"Uh huh. Hold on." He opened the top drawer of his dresser and then handed her a neatly folded T-shirt. "Take a look at it."

He watched as she shook the T-shirt with Lightnin's logo on it. She held it up to her body and laughed when she saw it came down to her knees.

She giggled. "It's a little large."

"I know." He took the shirt from her and slipped it over her head. "I was afraid you might not wear it outside your house—wherever that is—but I know women like T-shirts to sleep in." He gave her a tentative grin. "I wore it once because I wanted you to go to sleep with my scent all over you." His smile turned tentative, unsure of her reaction. "Okay?"

Please say yes. Please take this small part of me home with you. Please come back and see me again.

For a moment he thought she might pull it off and hand it back to him, but then she nodded.

"Thank you." She grabbed her clothes. "But now I really have to leave. I just wish you'd try to understand."

Marc rubbed his face, trying to think of some way to keep her there a little longer. Take her to breakfast. Really talk to her. But he couldn't seem to find any answers. He just knew this obsession with leaving was driving him nuts. He followed her as she headed out to the living room where she'd left her purse. Again he didn't bother trying to find anything to put on, simply followed her, nude.

"I don't know what I'm supposed to understand. We have something good going on here. Don't we? Something really special?"

It was true as far as *he* was concerned. His feelings for her had deepened and became more complex every time he was with her. He hoped desperately those feelings were returned, even a little.

She turned to him, her clothes and her purse in her arms. "I don't know what we have, Marc. And I'm really confused. About a lot of things. Maybe if you knew all about me, you wouldn't like who I really am. I...might not be your style."

He bit his inner cheek. She was more than special. He wanted to share other parts of his life besides the club and his bed. Wanted to talk about things they liked and disliked. Things they liked to do. How they saw their lives unfolding. What were her hopes and dreams? Was she interested in his? How could they get to that point? All questions he'd never worried about so much with other women in his life now ran rampage through his mind.

Jesus! Why did this all have to be so complicated?

"Impossible. No way could I feel less than I do about you. More, probably." He brushed his knuckles along her cheek. "I'll say it again. Don't you know how very special you are to me? Even in such a short time?"

She glanced away. "I'm not so special. We come from two different worlds, you and I. I wonder if I'm nothing more than a novelty to you."

Her words infuriated him, and he struggled to contain the anger threatening to rear its head. "Not so different if we learned about each other. And the person I am in the daylight might not be what you think at all. Stay and let me take you to breakfast. Just breakfast. You have to eat anyway, right?"

"I have to go to work." She headed toward the door.

"Then we can go to breakfast right now. Come on." He reached for her again.

She stopped and looked up at him. "I just have to go. Okay?"

In her eyes he saw a mixture of stubbornness and fear of...what?

If he pushed her he'd lose her. The knot in his stomach told him that. Swallowing the immediate retort that bubbled up, he nodded. "Okay. For now. But when can I see you again?"

"Soon?"

"When?" he persisted. He didn't know how long he could wait to be with her again. "Will you come back to the club?"

"Um, I think so." She edged toward the door.

"We're there for two more weeks, although I damn sure don't want to wait that long to see you again."

"Two weeks?" She wet her lip and twisted her hands together, anxiety flashing across her face.

"Uh huh."

"Then where do you go?" she asked.

He watched her carefully as he answered, trying to be as casual about it as he could but alert for her reaction.

"We have a week off then another really good club. One we've played before." *Yes, Music Lady. We'll be gone from Aftershock. Will you follow us—me—or will this be the end of us?* He had so much he wanted to share with her, like the excellent opportunity almost within the band's grasp. Usually he consulted with his family but for a long time now he'd been hoping to find the right woman to be part of his life. He harbored the hope when they really got to know each other, ML would be that person. He was almost afraid to open himself up to her any more in case she decided to just disappear. Again. "So will you?

Come back? I'd like it a lot if you did."

She hesitated so long he was afraid she'd say no. Then she nodded. "A-All right. I will."

"When?"

"I...soon." Impulsively she blew him a kiss. "Bye, Guitar Man."

She yanked the door open and raced to her car leaving him standing there once again, bare-assed naked, watching her drive away. Somehow he had to find out who she was and how to get in touch with her. Meanwhile, he hoped she meant what she said and she'd be back at Aftershock.

And next time, he'd make sure they stayed awake a while and talked. So he could learn more about her and tell her about himself. He wasn't about to give up on his Music Lady.

Chapter Eight

*E*mma straightened up the files on her desk and shut down her computer. The alarm she set on the machine had dinged to let her know it was noon. Time for lunch. She worked by herself in an interior office on the fifth floor of a building and without an alarm, she'd have no idea if it was day or night.

The morning had dragged on as if it had lead feet, and she had a world-class headache from the manuscript she was editing.

Of course, it could also be the fact that I got almost no sleep last night.

But she had to admit, it had definitely been worth it. Oh yeah, more than worth it. Marc Malone made her feel...oh, unlike any way she'd ever felt before. He woke her body and taught her what real sexual pleasure was. But it was more than that. There was emotion behind it, as if he was trying to tell her something with his actions.

She had been so tempted to crawl back into bed with him when he asked her to stay. To cuddle next to him again. Sleeping with Marc was so very different than just being in the same bed with Andrew. Which was what it had been. With Marc it was a sharing of bodies and souls. The emerging Emma was drawn to it like a junkie to a fix.

And the knowledge frightened her more than anything else.

She was really riding a dangerous edge here. She wanted to throw herself fully into this relationship, just as he kept asking her to, but she was finally discovering who she really was. Making a commitment of any kind so soon was scary. What if it turned out to be a hurricane that blew itself out? She'd be left with the wreckage and no idea how to put the pieces back together.

On the other hand, what if it didn't? What did they possibly have in common to build anything together?

You are such an idiot. You have a guy who treats you like gold when you let him. Who's accepted the situation on your terms, at least for now. Who obviously wants a solid life and isn't bringing you to death or just using you for blanket bingo.

So what was the damn problem?

Lifetime habits didn't just go away. She might be rebelling now but if her relationship with a rock musician came out of the closet, what would her family say? Her friends? Except, of course, for Annie, who'd be on the sidelines cheering her on.

She could hardly believe she'd driven home wearing nothing but the Lightnin' T-shirt. And she'd crawled into bed still wearing it for the three hours of sleep she managed before her alarm went off. She was just glad her boss gave her flexibility in her hours. But then, people who edited textbooks and did it well weren't exactly in plentiful supply so they took good care of her.

Right. No long lines to apply for boring jobs.

Her job was almost a metaphor for her life until that night at Andrew's–dull, rigid, manipulated into acceptability. She thought of all the notes she'd jotted down on story ideas, character outlines, little tidbits of ideas. She hadn't even found the courage yet to start her first story. She shuddered as she imagined the reaction of her parents and all their friends if she managed to write and sell an erotic romance.

Coward.

Oh, yes. Definitely.

She saved the document on her computer and pushed away

from her desk, massaging her aching temples. Marc wanted to know when she was coming back to the club. She hadn't given him an answer because she wasn't sure herself. She was still straddling the fence, one foot in each of her worlds, the old and the new, wanting to ask him how long he stuck with one woman yet knowing how childish that would sound. How insecure.

Okay, I am insecure. And I'm not asking the question because I don't want to know the answer.

No. She wanted to pretend it might go on forever. Of course, that meant she'd have to go back to Aftershock.

Ninny. If you're going to jump, just do it. You know you want to. Go back. See him. Tell him your name.

But she couldn't seem to make the leap. Her anonymity, her lack of commitment was her safety net. She still had a safe place to run back to.

Scaredy cat.

With a sigh, she told the receptionist she was going to lunch and took the elevator down to the lobby of the building. She started in the direction of the glass exit doors, searching in her purse for her sunglasses and paying no attention to anything around her. She'd almost reached the glass doors to the sidewalk when a hand closed over her elbow.

"I've been waiting for you," the male voice said.

Emma stopped, tensed, and turned around. And there was Andrew. "What for?"

"Because we need to talk." He prodded her toward the exit. "I'm not giving up on us, Emma. I won't let you chase me away."

Whoever would have thought plain, old oatmeal Andrew would be this persistent. She was over feeling bad for him, although her conscience did twinge once in a while. Now she was annoyed. She already had enough inner conflicts to deal with. She didn't need this.

Go away, Andrew.

But no, he was still attached to her like a barnacle.

"Andrew, we have nothing to talk about. It's over. *We're* over. Please. I want to get some lunch."

"Good," he said. "So do I. We can have lunch together." Outside he took a left, urging her with him. "There's a nice little restaurant a few doors down where we can get a quiet booth and hash this out. I spotted it when I parked the car."

Oh, great. Right where people I know might see me.

"There's nothing to hash out," she cried, trying to pull away from him, her anger ratcheting up even more. For God's sake. Why did he have to decide now to be assertive? This was a side of him she'd never seen in the two years they'd been together.

Oh, right, idiot. Because you always went along with everything. Never created a bump in the road. He doesn't know how to deal with this disruption of his life. And face it, Emma. That's mostly what this is about.

"I don't think you want to make a scene out here in public, do you?" he asked in a quiet voice.

Any residual friendly feelings she might have had for him were rapidly dissipating.

"Or you'll what? Turn me over your knee and spank me? Hardly your style. Especially where people can see you and your perfect image would be stained." She gritted her teeth. "I don't want to make a scene anywhere. I just want you to leave me alone. Or are you going to tattle to my parents again if I say no?"

"I thought you had lost your mind and they should know about it."

"How flattering," she spat.

"Listen, Emma. You owe me." He moved them along the sidewalk. "Let's just have lunch and talk. Okay?"

Emma sighed. He obviously wasn't going to go away no matter what she said. She hated the thought of making a spectacle of herself out in public this way. She'd just have lunch with him, be firmer than she was the other day, and make him go away.

"All right. Lunch. But then that's it."

They were already at the restaurant. Andrew opened the door and stepped back for her to precede him. For one hysterical moment, she thought about turning and racing down the street.

What if anyone she knew saw them together? Or worse yet, her parents? They'd definitely assume she and Andrew were getting back together. The thought made her shudder. But she knew, rationally, running wouldn't solve the problem, and she'd still have this situation to deal with. She'd just have to hold Andrew to his word they'd do this quietly.

She followed the hostess as she led them to a booth in a far corner. Of course. Trust Andrew to ask for something as private as possible.

"Thank you." He smiled at the hostess as he and Emma slid into the booth opposite each other.

"I'll send the waiter right over to take your drink orders," the woman said as she whisked herself away.

"How about a glass of wine?" Andrew asked.

Emma raised an eyebrow. "At noon? You never drink in the middle of the day."

"I know you enjoy a glass of white. You seem so...." He shrugged. "Uptight. Edgy. I thought perhaps it would relax you."

She forced a calm she didn't feel, reminding herself none of this was really Andrew's fault. He couldn't help who and what he was. And the plain truth, he was the man she'd chosen. Until last Saturday night.

"Thank you." She picked up the menu and made a show of studying it. Not that she had any appetite left.

The waiter returned with her wine and a soft drink for Andrew, and took their order. Luncheon steak for Andrew, quiche Lorraine for her.

Emma studied the man across from her. He was so different from Marc, but the very difference described the two parts of her life—the one disciplined and neatly arranged, the other wild and messy but exciting. Like discovering if you ate forbidden chocolate you wouldn't necessarily get fat.

If she wanted to maintain any semblance of control over this conversation, maybe even part on some sort of friendly basis, she'd have to start the conversation.

"Andrew." She set her wine goblet down very carefully. "I

want to admit, first of all, I probably—no, strike that—did in fact behave with disregard for you, both Saturday night and Sunday. For that I owe you an apology."

Okay, there it was. Would he be smug about it? Dismissive?

His reaction stunned her instead. He reached across the table and covered one of her hands with his. "We all have bad days, Emma. I'm going to assume we can put this behind us and move on from here."

She slid her hand out from beneath his as easily as she could, picked up her wine again, and sipped lightly. This was not going to be easy.

"Actually, Andrew, that's not really how it's going to happen." She looked at him with a direct gaze. "I didn't do this very well so I'm going to try and do it better now. You need to accept the fact we're not going to be seeing each other any more."

He took a slow, deliberate swallow of his water, leaned back in the booth, and fiddled with his sport jacket sleeves. "I can't believe you're still on the same kick, Emma. You know how good we are together. Everything was settled. In its proper place. The way it should be."

If she had any sense after that line she'd just get up and leave. Those few words summed it all up, the tenor of their relationship and of her life. And him. But she forced herself to see this through, hoping it would be for the last time.

"And that's part of the problem." Another sip of wine. She welcomed the warmth of the liquid, washing away the bitter taste of what she'd allowed her existence to become before the night she ran. She'd thought she wanted what he offered but in reality, it was only what everyone else wanted for her. "It's my fault, really. I'll take all the blame for it. But Andrew, I'd be doing us both a big injustice if I married you when I've realized this isn't what I want at all."

He frowned. "I don't understand. What's wrong with what we've got?"

She sighed. "I'm not sure I can even explain it, except to say

I've always done what others expected me to. Even dating you, Andrew. You're exactly the type of man my folks have always told me I should marry, and I thought they were right."

"They are," he insisted.

She shook her head. At that moment she was actually sorry for Andrew, so satisfied with his monotone life. Unwilling to see if there were colors waiting for him out there. She had the sad feeling he'd never have his own epiphany. "They're not. Everything we do is safe. Predictable. I might as well be sixty instead of almost thirty for as much excitement as there is in my life."

"Excitement is highly overrated," he grumbled.

Emma was silent while the waiter set their orders in front of them then leaned forward again. "Maybe for some people. And maybe for them—and you. What you have is as exciting as you want it to be. But not for me."

"It used to be," he said stubbornly.

"No," she answered in a measured tone. "I only thought it was." She paused and wet her lips. "I realized I don't love you, Andrew. Certainly not enough to marry you. I'd be hurting us both if I did."

With precise movements he cut a bite of his steak, forked it into his mouth and chewed. All the while Emma could almost see his brain working.

"So what *is* enough, Emma? Tell me how I can change?"

Oh God, this was harder than she thought.

"Changing isn't the answer. I repeat. I don't love you. I know I behaved badly Saturday night and I was rude on Sunday. I should have taken the time to explain properly what I'm feeling."

"Right." He nodded. "And then we could work on it together."

"No, we can't." She put her fork down and drained the rest of her wine. "How can I make you understand I want more than this? More excitement in my life. More fun."

"Fun?" He sounded puzzled. "We have fun."

"No. We don't. We've being doing exactly the same thing

every week since we started seeing each other." She waved a hand in exasperation. "We don't even have any variety in our sex life. No explosions. No fireworks."

Not like what I have with Marc, a man who pushes all my hot buttons and makes love to me as if I'm the most precious commodity in the world. Who taught me how great erotic is.

But that begged another question. Why was she still holding back with him? For the moment she tamped the thought down hard, stuffing it in a far corner of her mind to concentrate on the present.

Andrew's face reddened. "Our sex life is very normal, Emma. Or maybe that's what bothers you. Has someone been putting ideas in your head?"

"Oh, my God." She flopped against the back of the booth in frustration, thinking, *a stone is a stone is a stone.* "Maybe I just woke up one morning and...never mind. There's no way I'll ever make you understand I just want...more."

"More." His fingers clenched tightly on his fork.

"You'll never know how much I regret the way I handled this. You're a good man and don't deserve to be hurt this way. But it's over between us. We're not getting married. We're not even going to date. Can you at least accept what I'm saying? Then we can both move ahead with our lives."

Anger and pain shone in his eyes. "I'm not giving up. Unless you tell me there's someone else, I'm not letting you walk away."

She stabbed at a piece of lettuce on her plate.

Someone else? How can I possible tell him about Marc when I won't face the answers myself?

"The point I'm trying to make is I've finally realized I want different things out of life. I want a different *life.* I apologize again for handling this badly but there it is. The truth. You need to let go." She put down her napkin and slid from the booth. "I don't seem to have any appetite today."

He stared at her. "Emma, I—"

"I'm truly sorry, Andrew. I am. But you need to find someone else."

She practically ran from the restaurant, tearing down the street. Had he followed her? Was he even behind her? She turned the corner and slowed down, pressing a hand to her chest, her heart racing beneath her palm.

Well, this had been a wonderful waste of time. She wished Andrew hadn't caught her off guard the way he did. She knew she owed him a better explanation than what she'd thrown in his face Sunday but she'd wanted time to put the right words together.

Yeah, sure. Except now there weren't any right words.

She slowly walked along the sidewalk, people in a hurry pushing past her. Every few seconds, she checked to see if Andrew was following her but no, he wasn't there. At last she came to a hot dog vendor's cart and bought herself a large soft drink. It was all her stomach could handle at the moment. She sat on the wide ledge of concrete planted at the end of the sidewalk, hitched her purse strap over her shoulder, and took a large gulp of her drink. The chilled liquid cooled the raw feeling in her throat and helped settle her erratic pulse.

How had things gotten so messed up? Why couldn't she be happy with what Andrew offered?

But the answer was clear, so there was no sense going over the facts again. Even though she knew what she wanted, did she have the courage to grab it? And this wasn't just about Marc, although, he was fast becoming a big part of it. No, she needed the freedom to explore herself and her life, to not be afraid of new things. By now she was past the initial exhilaration of the joy ride and what the excitement held for her. The big question was what did she do next?

The intensity of her feelings for Marc, especially in such a short period of time, actually frightened her. She had so little experience with men that were the complete opposite of Andrew. And her tenuous self-confidence made her wonder if she could believe all the things Marc said to her. Did he really care for her, as he indicated, or was she just selling herself a bill of goods?

As she finished her drink, her cell rang and she fished it out of her purse.

Annie. Of course. With the third degree. Just what she needed right now. Still, she'd gotten her friend involved in this. Maybe she could cut this short and tell Annie she needed to get back to work. She wasn't up for dissecting her situation at the moment.

Sighing, she pressed the Talk button.

"Hi."

"I thought for sure I'd hear from you this morning." Annie chuckled. "Or did you have to call in sick at work and go to sleep?"

"No, nothing like that. I went to work." *And doing a half-assed job.*

"Wait. I thought you fixed things up with Marc, the sexiest bass player in the world."

At the mention of his name heat surged through her and her pulse stuttered. "I did. I just...I did."

"And?" Annie wasn't about to let go of it.

"And everything's okay." *Sort of.*

"Okay? Okay?' Annie's voice rose. "What the hell do you mean? I thought after the little grab and grope in the parking lot, you'd be going home with him again."

Emma gasped. "You *watched?*"

Annie laughed. "Well, of course. I was dying of curiosity. You didn't think I was just going to hang out twiddling my thumbs, did you?"

"I don't know. There were a lot of hot guys in Aftershock. You could have paid attention to *them.*"

"I'm surprised you even noticed, the way your eyes were fixed on your sex god. What a lip lock he had on you."

"I know," she whispered, remembering the electric feel of his mouth on hers.

"So give. What happened? Did you go home with him again?"

"Um, yes. Yes, I did." Heat crept up her cheeks, equal parts of embarrassment and sensual excitement. *No. I will not be ashamed of it. I am the new Emma, embracing life for the first time.*

"Did you get around to telling him your name? And are you going back to the club again?"

Another sigh. "No. And yes."

There was a heavy moment of silence. "You're planning to see him again, but you still didn't tell him your name? What is the matter with you?"

She didn't know if this was just a short-term thing for Marc, despite everything he said. If he didn't know who she was then he couldn't track her down if in the future he was bored or between girlfriends. Or whatever. Open wounds took a long time to heal, and despite her Guitar Man's assurances, she still had her own insecurities to deal with.

"Annie, try to understand. This is the most excitement I've ever had in my life, but I don't know if this...thing with Marc will last. Not giving him my name is my safety net."

"So if it doesn't work out, you can run back like a scared chicken to your old life, right?" Annie didn't wait for her to answer. "Emma, I thought you had more guts than that. You get up the nerve to reach for the brass ring but you're afraid to hold on to it? Afraid you won't know what to do *if* it all falls apart? Or you get your shit together and he shows up someday in the future and kicks it all apart again?"

Emma just sat there, silently holding the phone. Annie had just nailed it. Put into words exactly what she'd been thinking. Yet she couldn't make herself stay away from Marc. What a mess she was.

"Listen, don't mind me and my big mouth," Annie said at last. "You do whatever's comfortable for you."

"You're a good friend, Annie. I know a lot of times you've gotten frustrated with me. Maybe even wanted to shake me out of my neat life. But you always know when to push and when to hold back."

"Just...enjoy yourself, okay? And I'm here whenever you

need me."

"Thank you." Emotion made her throat tight and tears threatened at Annie's words. If only her parents gave her such unqualified understanding. Annie wanted her to enjoy life. Her parents wanted her to be acceptable to their friends, with little regard for her feelings. She sighed. It was what it was. "I'll...call you tomorrow."

How different would her life be if her parents and Andrew gave her support like that? Of course, she probably would never have met her guitar man.

Marc!

She didn't even want to think about the hoops she'd have to jump through if their relationship actually grew into something real,. Then she'd have to explain it to her parents.

Emma glanced at her watch and realized it was time to head back to the office. And her nagging headache had worked itself up to a full blown one. She couldn't wait for the day to be over.

"Good rehearsal, everyone," Rick said, unhooking his guitar strap. "We've got the new tunes down real good. Especially *On the Edge of the Woods*."

"So we're doing both the video and the audio tape this weekend?" Garrett asked. He wiped his drumsticks and put them away.

"Yeah. We'll shoot the video at Jado's on Saturday, and I've got studio time booked for Sunday with Scotty Redman."

"He's doing the mix himself, right?" Garrett asked.

Rick nodded. "He always does."

"Good. That's good. He really knows our sound."

Marc listened to the conversation, feeling especially good about the whole thing. Scotty was a longtime friend as well as a top sound engineer. They'd been with him since the first demo tape they'd done. Although Marc loved writing the scripts, he was pleased he could focus on the project despite the uncertainty of the situation with his Music Lady. All the band's hard work, all the discipline and long hours, and crummy jobs were about to bear fruit.

He had no idea what the future would hold for all of them if this gig worked, but they needed to grab the opportunity while it was there. Stuff like this didn't come along all that often. How would ML react to it? Would she want to be part of it all with him?

The missing piece of my life—the right woman to share this with.

But first I have to make her trust me enough to tell me her name.

Garrett, the one who always wanted to see the other side of the coin broke into his reverie. He frowned. "We're really rushing and cramming everything into two days, you know. Is this one of those cross-your-fingers-and-hope-it-all-works-out things?"

Marc leaned against a high stool at the back of the stage, idly plucking his guitar strings, watching everyone's reactions.

Rick shoved his hands into the pockets of his jeans. "Look. The opportunity came out of nowhere and it was either jump on it or lose it. We really don't have a choice here." He held up one finger. "One. This gig just opened up because another band had problems and had to back out." Another finger. "Two. We're getting better than our usual rate at both places because both Scotty and Jado had time available and are willing to cut us a big break." He glanced around. "You guys want to dump this? Is that what you're saying?"

"No, Rick. We're not. We're just asking question, okay?" Danny Chavez, the lead singer, slung a towel around his neck. "So what happens after we get this done?"

"Then I take the video and sit down with Butch Meredith, Deep Blue River's manager and see if we can strike a deal."

"He's already seen us at Aftershock," Garrett pointed out. "Why do we have to turn ourselves inside out to get this video done for him?"

Marc could tell Rick was losing patience. "He wants to hear the new song and see us perform it. And, I don't know, there are other things he'll be watching for. I'll load the video onto my laptop and we'll sit down and talk."

Danny shoved his hands in his pockets. "This is nothing on you, Rick, but don't you think we need someone whose business this is to do the sit-down? Maybe get us more than one shot with these guys?"

Marc saw a muscle jump in his friend's cheek but the guy kept his cool, just as he always did.

"I understand your concern." Rick rolled up a cord with deliberate movements. "But I think this is the right way to play this. Right now one shot is all we're being offered. And only because an opening act scheduled had to cancel. Otherwise we wouldn't even have this two weeks before the concert date. And there are plenty of other bands their manager could have contacted."

"Let's remember Rick's the one who met their manager and developed the relationship with him." This was something Marc thought he needed to remind everyone of.

"I know that. Can't a guy put his two cents worth in?" Danny asked.

Rick put the cord down and blew out a breath. "Of course. But if I can make this work, get us the chance to open for Deep Blue River at the Amphitheater and we do a kickass job, we'll get more dates with them. Plus, their record label guys will be there, and we can kill two birds with one stone." He studied each of them thoughtfully. "If we blow it then a different contract wouldn't matter, anyway, because we'd be toast."

"Rick's right." Marc hitched his hip onto a stool on the stage and cradled his guitar. "You all remember when we put this band together. We identified the strengths each of us has and assigned responsibilities. It's worked real well so far." He studied Garrett, the worrywort. "Rick got us the gigs here and at the other two clubs we wanted to play, and he got us good money. Right?"

"Right."

"Yeah."

"And he's been our point man on this whole deal." Marc went on, keeping his voice calm and steady so he could get this across without an argument breaking out. They'd blow the chance before they could do anything with it if they lost it now. "The connection is his, something worth a whole lot more than bringing in a stranger, even if deals like this are his only business."

Garrett threw up his hands. "Okay, okay. No big deal. It was just a suggestion. I thought it would help if Rick had one less thing to worry about."

"Rick's fine." Marc turned to the guitarist. "Right?"

"Yes." Rick's answer was short, clipped, but his face was unreadable.

"And right now we all need to relax and not get on each other's case. This could be the big break we've been waiting for."

"We've done opening act tours before and ended up going no place," Danny reminded them, "and Rick, that's not on you. Shit happens. But we're putting all our eggs in a real big basket here."

"And we'll be fine," Rick said. His words were carefully measured but every line of his body screamed tension. "As long as we're ready and hit our marks."

"We'll do it," Marc said. "Okay, guys?"

The other two nodded.

Everyone was silent for a long moment until Rick finally smiled. "Okay, then. I say rehearsal every afternoon this week except Saturday when we shoot the video. Sunday, we record and mix and Monday, I sit down with Butch Meredith. We all good?"

There was a chorus of yesses.

"Then go home, shower and eat and be back here for the first set."

Marc locked his bass in its velvet-lined case and headed for the back door when Rick stopped him with a hand on his arm.

"Thanks."

"No big deal. You and I have been doing this a lot longer than the other two, and they might get a little hinky once in a while. But it's all good now."

"Thanks to you."

"So do I get more money?" he asked with a hint of laughter.

Rick chuckled. "Right after I do. Listen. I saw your woman come back again last night."

"Yeah, she did." For a moment heat surged through him, combined with anxiety. He hated the uncertain nature of their relationship, the tenuous feeling still swirling around it. He thought of her nearly every moment except when he forced himself to focus on the band and wondered if she thought of him, too. What kind of job did she have? Did daydreams of them interrupt her work?

"Hey, buddy." Snapping fingers brought him back to the moment. "Where did you go?"

"Uh, right here." He gave himself a mental shake.

"So how's that going? Any better?"

Marc dragged his fingers through his hair, thinking of how once again she tried to leave without telling him until he woke up and caught her. And hating it. "I'd say...yes and no."

Rick quirked an eyebrow. "Well, nothing like telling it straight out."

"I know, I know. No, I really don't know." He looked at Rick. "Jesus, is that me talking?"

"'Fraid so. What's the problem now?"

"The sex is great. *She's* great. The best woman I've ever met." And just like that the thought became reality.

"And you can tell that after being with her only twice?" Rick sounded skeptical. "You've never said this about any other woman you've been with."

No, because they were all a product of the club environment and not what I really had in mind for myself. It wasn't what rang my chimes. I want normal, whatever normal is. Probably different for everyone. But how to convince Music Lady?

"I could tell it the first time. But the thing is, she still won't tell me her name. Or give me any way to get in touch with her."

Rick studied him. "Are you sure she isn't married?"

"I'd bet money on it. Unfortunately we've both seen women in that situation before and she doesn't act like they did. No, it's something different. Almost as if she's afraid to tell me. Like she's one person with me and another when she runs home to whatever world she lives in."

"Well, I'm certainly not one to give advice on women. But if you feel there's really something there between you, then hang in there. Read the clues she gives you. If it's supposed to happen it will. I've seen screwier things in my life."

"I guess."

But Rick's words still rattled around in his brain after he left the club. And instead of heading home, he turned in the opposite direction toward his parents' house. His mother would be home from work now, either taking a casserole she'd made out of the freezer or figuring out where she could nudge his father to take her for dinner.

He loved his incredible relationship with both of his parents who were as much friends as Mom and Dad. It was the reason he could discuss things with them that would shock his friends. When he'd tell his mom about Music Lady, she'd probably suggest he walk away. Still, she was a good sounding board for him, and exactly what he needed right now.

He rang the doorbell twice, his signal, and pulled on the front door at the same time. Open. Good.

"Marc?" His mother's voice called form the kitchen. "That you?"

"One and the same."

Frannie Malone was standing at the counter but she glanced over her shoulder when she heard him come in. He hugged her and planted a big kiss on her cheek. "How's my favorite girl?"

She laughed. "You must be between women if I'm your favorite." She ran her eyes over him and he knew what she saw— torn jeans and an old T-shirt he'd worn for rehearsal. The stubble on his jaw and the wildness of his hair. What she always called his derelict image. "Not that any woman would want you looking like this." Then she kissed his cheek. "Of course, I personally think she'd be lucky to get you."

"Mother's don't count. You're prejudiced." He opened the fridge and took out a cold can of soda, popped the top and took a healthy swallow.

The stove timer dinged, and his mother put the casserole on the counter into the oven, set the timer and turned to him.

"You know I'm always glad to see you, honey, but I know how busy you are right now. So what brings you here in the middle of the week?" She grinned at him. "Hungering for a home-cooked meal?"

Marc chuckled. It was a well-accepted fact in the family his mother's culinary skills were limited to casseroles and any kind of breakfast food. As a result, both the senior Malone and the three boys had become skilled cooks. Kitchen time had been a time to bond, to vent, to laugh and enjoy. And when all the boys were old enough, to be flavored with generous sips of an excellent wine.

"Thanks, anyway." He looked everywhere but at her, struck with a sudden case of nerves. This might be the most important thing he'd ever come to her with and for a moment, he wasn't sure he wanted to hear her reaction. *Shut up. This is why you're here.* "I think I just wanted some of your sage insight and advice."

"Uh oh." She took down a glass, filled it with ice water, and sat across from him. "Spill it, kid. What's up?"

Marc rubbed his hand over his face. He knew what he had to say would sound stupid even to himself, but he needed someone's opinion besides Rick's.

"Okay. Here's the deal. And try to listen not as my mother, okay?"

She laughed. "That's a pretty big order but I'll try."

He tilted the can and took a long swallow of his soda. "I met this girl. Woman. Female."

"I *hope* she's female." Frannie sipped her water calmly. "But what's going on here, honey? You haven't discussed a female with me since you were sixteen, so this one must be special."

He nodded. "She is. Very special." His whole body tightened. " I...have very strong feelings for her." *And growing stronger by the minute.*

"No kidding? Strong enough to bring her over for Sunday brunch? Or would you be rushing things too much?"

"I...don't think I could just yet." How the hell was he going to explain this to his mother? Not that ML wouldn't fit. Of all the women he'd dated, she was the most likely candidate. He had the feeling his family would love her, if he could ever make this work.

"Oh?" Frannie arched an eyebrow. "Is she gun-shy? I hope she's not someone I wouldn't want to meet. I thought you had better judgment, sweetie."

"Worse than that," he blurted out. "I don't know her name."

"What?" His mother stared at him. "Please tell me you're joking. Or, wait a minute. You've only seen her and not met her, right? Although...no, you wouldn't have feelings like this for someone you haven't met. I know you better."

"Nope. I have actually met her. I probably shouldn't be telling my mother this but she's spent the night with me. Twice. Sort of." He raked his fingers through his hair. "God. Mom, I could really use your take on this."

Frannie shook her head. "Maybe you'd better start at the beginning."

He swallowed more of his cold drink. "Don't smack me down at the details, okay?"

"I'll put away the paddle," she joked, and he knew she was trying to put him at ease.

"She came into the club a couple of weeks ago on a Saturday night. And Mom? I swear, it's like electricity zapped between us so strong you could see it. I'd never seen her there before and just by the way she acted, I had a feeling she'd never been in *any* rock club."

"Do you happen to know why she showed up when she did?"

He shook his head. "No. And I can't...." He stopped. "Let me finish first. Questions after."

"Okay. You're right."

"So, okay, the more I watched her the more I wanted to know her. I followed her out to the parking lot after closing and I...kissed her. Jesus. It was like stepping into a roaring fire. So I asked her to come home with me."

Frannie held up her hand. "I think we skip what came next."

"No kidding." Heat crawled up is face. "So then I see her in the grocery store the next day and she acts like she doesn't know me. And I'm telling you, I was pissed as hell." He got up to get another drink before he went on. "So then she comes back a week later, apologizes all over the place and, um...."

"She goes home with you again," his mother guessed. "Fade to black here. So what's the problem?"

"I feel things for her I've never felt for another woman. Not just sexual but real emotion. And I think she feels the same way."

"But?"

"She won't tell me her name. I call her Music Lady."

He expected a shocked cry but instead his mother was silent for a long time, drinking her water, staring over his shoulder as she absorbed his story. He was acutely aware of how absurd the whole thing sounded. She'd probably tell him to run like hell, and if he had a brain that was what he'd do. But Music Lady had become so much a part of him, he knew he'd never be able to do it.

Which was why he was here, in his mother's kitchen, spilling his guts.

"Well," she said at last. "This is definitely a new twist for you."

"Tell me about it."

More silence. Marc jiggled his leg, impatient for an answer. "So what do you think?" he asked, unable to contain himself any longer.

"Honey, I don't know what you want me to say."

His eyes widened. "Are you serious? Hopefully something

wise and insightful. Maybe that I'm not a dork or an ass or whatever might be holding her back."

She laughed. "You're neither, I can assure you. Your father and I did our best to make sure of it." Then her face sobered. "You know as a good mother I should tell you to forget about her. A woman who won't tell you her name has to be hiding something. Maybe something you don't even want to know about."

"You think that hasn't occurred to me?" He rubbed the stubble on his jaw. "I'm not stupid." His grin was rueful. "At least not much. But I really don't think she's married. She wouldn't be able to spend the time with me she does if she had a husband at home waiting for her."

"Unless her husband works nights," Frannie pointed out.

"I still don't think that's it. And you know I've seen married women in that situation before hanging at different clubs. Unfortunately." He stared down into his cold drink. "This is going to sound so dumb, but I don't believe she's that kind of person. Anyway, it feels like...something different. I'm telling you, Mom. Maybe it's just my gut talking but she's...how can I explain this? More like the girls I knew in high school."

Frannie chuckled. "That may not be the greatest comparison, Marc. I remember some of the girls you dated back then."

He had to smile. "I was in my immature wild stage. I got over it fast. Anyway, you know what I mean. She'd never even been in a rock club until last Saturday. Can you believe that?" He frowned. "Maybe it's against her religion or something. You think?"

"I think if that was the case, she wouldn't have gone home with you. Twice. No, she's got to be afraid of something."

He tried to replay every scene with ML in his mind, looking for a clue—anything that he may have missed. "But what?"

"Can't answer without knowing a lot more about the situation. I'm just guessing but speaking strictly as a woman, I'd say she has trust issues of some kind. Maybe she had a bad experience. If you really have feelings for this woman, even under these circumstances, you'll have to make her believe she can trust you enough to tell you about herself. You respect women, sweetie. And that should be obvious enough to her to help lower those barriers she's put up."

He sighed. "Easier said than done."

"Honey, if she's what you want and you think she's worth it, then you can make the effort." She laughed softly. "Your brothers will be home this weekend. Want me to send them to the club to scope her out if she shows up?"

"No!" Marc was horrified. He loved his brothers and was very proud of them, but they were the last people he wanted involved in this. "Don't you dare."

"Just teasing." She drained the rest of her water. "Sorry I can't give you any better advice here. Unless I can meet her for myself, I'm really shooting blind."

"Okay. About what I figured. But thanks for listening. I'm willing to bet there aren't too many other moms whose sons could go to them with something like this. You're one in a million, you know?"

"I'm flattered by such high praise but really, I just love you and want what's best for you." She paused. "This is the first time I've ever heard you this serious about anyone, Marc. As your mother, I'd really like to see you settle down with someone. But you'd need someone pretty special, someone who can roll with the pinches the music business delivers."

"This one *is* special," he insisted. "Despite everything. And I really could see her here for a Sunday brunch. I think you guys would like her a lot."

"Then hang in there. And speaking of music, how are the new tape and the video coming?"

"Good, good. Mom, I think this is going to be the big break for us."

"You've certainly worked hard enough for it. All of you. And I know how much you want it. So what happens next?"

"We're doing everything this weekend and on Monday,

Rick's going to sit down with Deep Blue River's manager. By Monday night, we'll know if he bites and the deal is on."

"You know we'll be crossing our fingers for you. I personally think the band has got what it takes."

"From your lips to Butch Meredith's ears," he told her, standing up and giving her a hug. "You don't now how much your support means to me. The whole family."

"We love you," she said in a fierce tone. "Don't ever forget it. I'll send you good thoughts that this thing with Music Lady works out."

"Thanks. I love you guys, too." He disposed of his empty soda can and dug into his pocket for his keys. "Okay. I'm gonna run along."

"You sure I can't talk you into dinner?"

"Not tonight, I want to work some more on the script for the video and iron out some glitches on my part of the new song. But soon. I promise."

His mother rose and walked him to the door, giving him another hug. "Take care, Marc. And be careful."

"I will. Thanks, Mom." He headed slowly to his truck, shoulders slumped.

Well, that didn't do anything except to underscore what I was already thinking. Why is it when I finally find a woman I'm pretty sure will complete my life, the whole thing has to be so squirrely?

He drove home, restless and edgy, trying to settle himself down for tonight's gig. Would she be there tonight? Would she come home with him again? She'd stepped into his world and in an instant, carved out a place for herself in his heart. What did he need to do to make her feel comfortable enough to let him into hers?

Chapter Nine

I'm not going back there tonight.

Emma repeated it over and over to herself until it echoed repetitively in her brain. She chanted it like a mantra as she drove home from her little shopping expedition. She changed into shorts and T-shirt and sat out on her back porch with a glass of wine. Repeating the words aloud as she managed to choke down a sandwich, she even thought of calling Andrew, still feeling guilty about the way she'd treated him, but blew off that idea before it was complete. So she hadn't been as nice to him as she might have been. But Andrew wasn't even listening to her, and there wasn't much she could do about that.

The Emma who'd been with Andrew would have been shocked at doing something so crazy, figured out how to do penance, maybe even groveled to Andrew. But the new Emma—after Andrew—wanted to kick her old existence to the curb and dig down for the courage to taste life. And courage was what it had taken to give her hair the new look—her blonde hair, now with more silver had an outrageous purple streak. Nothing she could wash out, either. Every time she looked in the mirror, she shocked herself all over again.

And the new clothes. God, Annie had been a pit bull, stashing her in a dressing room and bringing her items to try on—tight jeans, some with designs and tank tops and pretty tees to go with them. Vivid colors so unlike anything else in her closet. A new wrapping for a new person.

So by nine o'clock, deliberately blanking out her misgivings, she was in the shower, soaping herself, washing her hair, and mentally reviewing her wardrobe for something to wear.

I'll never be able to make it through work tomorrow if I don't get some sleep.

But at ten-thirty, she was dressed in new white jeans and a royal blue tank top with a blue and white print blouse thrown over it. She slipped on new white sandals she'd been saving for...something.

As she dressed she got the strangest feeling, almost as if with her new clothes, she was putting on a different personality. Emma was in the closet with her dull colors and sensible clothes. She looked in the mirror and saw Music Lady, a woman with silvery hair and a distinctive purple streak. A woman whose skin glowed and whose eyes shone with anticipation. Who had a confidence lacking in Emma. In her mind she could almost hear the familiar sound of Lightnin' and her hips swayed a little.

She was Music Lady!

Enough! Get moving.

In minutes, she was in her car heading toward Aftershock.

Something was missing when she walked in the door and she frowned when she saw the empty stage.

"Band's on a break," the bouncer told her, taking her money and stamping her hand.

Annie had told her that's what they were called. Bouncers. Not doormen. "It's not an upscale condo building, sweetie." Her friend had chuckled at her.

"W-When do they start again?" Emma asked.

"In a couple of minutes. Time enough to get a drink."

The crowd was a little thinner tonight, making her journey to the bar a little easier. She got her usual bottle of beer, a drink she was actually beginning to acquire a taste for, and glanced around to see if she could locate Marc. The first thing she saw was Lacey, the over-the-top redhead from the other night wearing jeans that looked painted on and a halter top that was barely decent. She had her hand on Marc's arm and was leaning toward him, a predatory smile on her lips. Emma might have been annoyed if she hadn't seen the flash of irritation on Marc's face and watched him jerk his arm away as he leaped up onto the stage. He obviously didn't like what she was saying because he shook his head and turned away to pick up his bass. He moved to the side to speak to the drummer and plucked a few low notes on the bass. The drummer nodded to him, and Marc stepped back to his usual place.

When the redhead tossed her hair and moved away, Emma worked her way to the front of the stage just as the band kicked into the opening number of the set. Something bluesy with hard rock overtones. *Gritty* was the word that came to mind. Marc was entirely focused on the music, not noticing her at all, but she just stayed in place, swaying to the melody.

Tonight she tried to listen to the words, to understand what the song was about. It seemed to be about a man searching for love but every woman gave him the same old, tired routine. She thought the title might be *She Did It To Me Again* since that was the chorus, repeated over and over again, with Marc and the drummer laying down the low, heavy sounds she was fast becoming addicted to. It vibrated through her body, just like the other nights, shimmering in waves from her breasts to her very wet sex.

For the first time, she managed to pay attention to the other band members, recalling their faces from the picture she'd found on their website. The drummer Garrett, almost frenetic in his movements. Rick, the lead guitarist, making his fingers dance at a dizzying pace over the strings. And Danny, the lead singer, with a voice as smooth as aged whiskey and a register that spanned three octaves. Even when he hit the high notes, the music was compelling rather than abrasive.

And when they all brought their voices together in four-part harmony, Emma thought angels couldn't have sung better. That was, if angels sang rock and roll.

Her hips bumped and wriggled, and she tossed her head back, but not so far she lost sight of Marc, wild on the stage as the power of the song built and built. When he joined in on the lyrics of the last repetition of the chorus, Emma felt as if she had been pulled on stage into the magic they were creating. When Marc screamed, *"She did it to me"* she had the eerie feeling he might have been singing to her.

He's singing to Music Lady. And that's who I am when I walked in here. A totally different person.

And then the song was over, the last notes lingering in the air like sparks of electricity. Still hugging his bass, Marc let his gaze roam over the room. The moment he spotted Emma, his eyes locked with hers and she was surprised there was a stream of fire sizzling between the two of them. After a moment, one corner of his mouth lifted in a slow grin and Emma was afraid she'd melt down right on the spot.

Then they were into the next song, and Marc was again immersed in the music.

She stood in the same spot through the entire set, taking occasional sips of her beer, but mostly watching Marc avidly. Hungrily. Caught up in the hypnotic sound of his bass. The attack of nerves that she'd battled on the drive over eased a little but she still saw herself as an outsider in an alien world. Part of it, she realized, was her own insecurities, her fear that she was a fraud. Someone playing a role that wasn't well rehearsed. She was feeling her way in this new environment.

When she looked at the other women in the crowd, all so much more comfortable with the scene and into it, it struck her that this was one of the main reasons she continued to keep her identity secret from Marc. Despite the spectacular sex and his reassuring words, she couldn't get past the fear he'd take a look at her and decide she was too dull and boring for him. Even Annie couldn't reassure her enough to shore up her confidence. She couldn't seem to get rid of her sense of inadequacy to the other women she saw.

But you're the one he chose.

She knew that. Still....

And of course there was always the question of how her family and friends would react to *him*. Talk about a stranger in a strange land.

You're a coward, Emma Blake.

But at that moment the set ended and Marc placed his guitar in a stand on the stage. He spoke to the lead singer then jumped off the stage to where she waited. Her pulse rate accelerated and her breath caught in her throat. She loved the wild look about him when he finished a set, the disarray of his hair from the movement of his head and the edge of excitement that was almost visible. She wanted to throw herself at him and kiss him, even here in front of all these people, a reaction so unlike her normal self.

But all that quickly dissipated like smoke blown away in a breeze.

"Let's take a walk outside." His fingers rested on her elbow with a reassuring touch but he sounded strange.

Her stomach clenched. Was he about to tell her to leave? Was it over this quickly? She felt slightly nauseous as he urged her through the door to the parking lot and guided her toward the back of the building.

It's okay. I knew this had to be over soon. I'm not his type. He's figured it out. I can't keep up. I can't—

They stopped just past the corner of the building. Marc pulled her around to face him, cupped her face in his hands and pressed his mouth to hers. Emma was so stunned for a moment she just stood there, unresponsive. But then she wrapped her arms around his neck. Boldly, she opened her mouth and welcomed his tongue inside, tangling her own with his. Holy God, he tasted so good. So distinctly...Marc, her Guitar Man. He kissed her until her head swam an onslaught of sensations threatening to drown her.

Magic. She didn't know what else to call it.

He lifted his head only when they were both in danger of

oxygen starvation.

"I watched for you all night." His voice was husky and rough with desire. His gaze raked over her, heat sizzling in them. "You look sharp, ML." He let the strands of the purple streak sift through his fingers. "Love the hair. And the clothes. Wow!" His eyes ate her up.

"It's...sort of the new me." She wet her lower lip. "I'm glad you like it." She hadn't realized how anxious she was about his opinion until she heard his words. Saw the look in his eyes. The knot of tension inside her lessened a fraction.

"I liked the old you," he insisted. "But now, just...wow," he repeated. He couldn't seem to stop touching her hair. "I was afraid maybe two nights in a row would be too much for you."

Their lips were still so close, she could feel his breath inside her mouth when he spoke.

"I almost didn't come," she whispered, tightening her arms around his neck.

"I'm glad you did."

"When you dragged me out here, I was sure you were going to tell me I was too much of a pain in the rear and not to bother you any more."

"What?" He licked her bottom lip. "Are you kidding? Never."

"Whew." She relaxed, the tautness easing more fully from her body. "Because I'd hate that. But...I'd understand."

He frowned. "You would? Why?"

She shrugged. "You know. I always run away. Won't go to breakfast with you. Won't even tell you my name." *Because I'm afraid that any minute you'll figure out Music Lady doesn't sparkle. I'm just plain old boring Emma Blake who hides behind a cloak of anonymity because I don't have all that much to offer. That I'm really a fraud, despite the hair and clothes....*

He tucked her hair behind her ears, his eyes searching hers. "I'll accept that you have a damn good reason for that. Or at least one you think is good. For the moment. It's better than not seeing you at all."

Everything inside her relaxed a little. He wanted her! He still wanted her! "I know you think I'm being stupid."

And she was. She was just damn lucky he was willing to put up with her quirky hang-up. He didn't seem to have a problem letting his world see them together—the band, the crowd, the club employees. Why couldn't she do the same?

Because she was a freakin' coward just taking chances for the first time in her life.

He brushed his mouth against hers. "I think you're being ML. And that's good enough for me right now."

Emma pressed herself against him, heat surging through her when she felt the hard thickness of his cock through both of their clothes.

"Thank you."

"I need to get back inside. We have one more set to do. Can you stay?"

She nodded.

"Good." He smiled. "I'll be playing especially for you."

Marc cradled ML in his arms and smoothed damp tendrils of hair back from her face. One of these nights he'd figure out how to slow down the first time and not take her like some horny teenager.

He wondered if they'd ever reach a point where the sex was less explosive, less dynamic. Less emotional. God, he hoped not.

Her head nestled on his shoulder, her eyes closed, and her lips slightly curved in a satisfied smile. Her satiny skin retained the rosy flush of sex, and her nipples were still taut peaks. Marc trailed his hand along the line of her body, following the dips and swells, the curve of hip and thigh. Jesus, she was a pure treasure. So much more than any other woman he'd known. A total assault on every one of his senses.

The connection between them from the beginning had been more powerful than anything he'd ever felt, and the intensity of it just continued to increase. He still didn't know how he'd gotten lucky enough for her to go home with him that first night. And to come back again. And if he had to play by her rules to keep her, so be it.

At least for now.

"Hey, Music Lady," he said in a soft voice.

She opened her eyes languidly. "Hey yourself."

"So. You said earlier you'd never been to a rock club before. Does that mean you don't know much about the business?"

She quirked an eyebrow at him. "To be truthful, I don't know *anything*. I felt so stupid because my friend knew all about your band, and I had to Google you to even realize who and what you are."

"So no rock clubs? No wild night life?"

She blushed. "No. 'Fraid not. Just didn't do that scene." Snuggling closer and burying her face against his chest, she asked, "Do you think I'm weird? Want to change me for a more up-to-date model?"

For the first time, he was beginning to understand what her hang-ups were. But maybe the kind of life she led, the overwhelming nature of the club scene and their unexpectedly explosive sex was the reason why telling him her name was such a big deal. It was like exposing who you really were to someone and not knowing if that person would be turned off. Or something. But rather than doing that, it only made him fall for her a little bit more.

He didn't think he'd ever met someone who'd never been to at least one rock club. He wondered exactly how sheltered her life was. Had been? Okay, so she was a little bit of a novice in bed. That only told him she hadn't had many lovers. And that was good. Very good. He wanted to teach her everything himself.

"Hell, no. Are you kidding? It's not a big deal but just where *did* you go?"

She lowered her eyelids but not before he saw embarrassment flash for a moment. "We went to...other kinds of place. And not too many concerts. I really led a much different kind of life than you have."

"Not really so different," he contradicted. "You don't know anything about me except what you see in the club and here. I think you'd be surprised at how my normal life really was. Is." Wouldn't she just be shocked if he introduced her to his mom and dad and his brothers? He cleared his throat. "But maybe we can play a little game. Exchange a little information."

She tensed. "Marc, I don't—"

He touched a finger to her lips. "Hush. Nothing big or important. Just little stuff. Any time you want to stop we'll call a halt to it. Okay?"

"Okay." But she said the word as if she didn't quite believe him.

"It's not a trick, babe. I promise." He moved his head just enough to feather a kiss over her lips. "I'd never do anything to make you uncomfortable or unhappy. I just thought it would be a fun way to get to know each other a little." He tightened his arm around her. "So. You can go first. One question."

"Hmm. Let's see." She chewed her lower lip, a habit he'd come to recognize as her nervous meter. "All right. How did you start playing the bass guitar?"

"Easy. My dad played bass in a band in high school. He hung on to that guitar until I got old enough for him to pass it along to me."

"So your *father* plays guitar?" She stared at him.

"Yes, but don't start thinking he was some long-haired freak rockin' around the country. He and the guys played clubs around the area while they were in college and for a while afterward until they all got too busy with work and families."

"That sounds...." She frowned. "Not like what I expected.

He laughed. "I figured. See? I told you I might not be what you thought. Okay. My turn. What's your favorite color?"

She answered immediately. "Blue."

"A good color. My favorite, too."

"Me, again," she said. "When did you start playing in a band?"

"In high school, just like my dad. Favorite food."

"Pizza. Are any of the people in this band ones you played with in high school?"

"No. Favorite season."

"Spring."

"I like winter." Now why had that just popped out? Because he liked the cooler weather so much or because it was an opposite season from the one she named? He'd never really given it much thought.

"Really?" She tilted her head back slightly to look at him. "You like the cold?"

"I like having a fire going. This house didn't have a fireplace so I put in a gas-fired one." He laughed. "If we ever get out of the bedroom, I'll show it to you."

"I love fireplaces." Her smile was unexpectedly shy. "They're great in winter, aren't they?"

"Uh huh." He studied her face, saw the hint of a smile curve her lips. "Maybe this winter we can cuddle in front of mine." *Because I want you to still be around when winter shows up. And not just this one.* "What else do you love?"

"Mmm, let me think." She wrinkled her forehead in a frown of concentration. "Warm chocolate chip cookies."

He grinned. "No kidding? Me, too. The world's best comfort food."

She looked a little surprised. "Really? You need comforting?"

Marc didn't think that was such a startling fact but again, he was starting to understand more about Music Lady and her perception of his life. He could tell by the expressions chasing across her face with each answer that she was seeing him in a different light. Much more three-dimensional. Maybe even more acceptable in the world she grew up in.

"We all need comforting now and then, Music Lady." He stroked her cheek. "It's part of who we are. Who *I* am, anyway." He teased the strands of purple hair. "But then why the hair? The new duds? New wrappings?"

"Because I—" She tensed against him.

He could feel her withdrawing and wanted to kick himself

for being so stupid. Getting her to reveal pieces of herself was like a complex treasure hunt and he had to tread very carefully. pulled her a little closer. "Never mind. It's not a big deal. I told you, I like the look. It's sharp. And if you're comfortable with it, that's all that counts."

And so it went, until he'd told her all about the battle with his parents to skip college and stick with his music. Their acceptance finally and their support. Meeting Rick at a party and putting Lightnin' together. The struggle for recognition. In return he'd learned enough tidbits about her to begin piecing together a picture of the woman she really was. Smart. Funny. Sometimes shy.

"Okay, enough Twenty Questions for tonight."

Emma didn't know whether to be relieved or not. On the one hand, she wanted to know so much more about Marc. Each question and answer had been a revelation, shaping him differently in her mind. On the other hand, the more she exposed her inner self to him, the greater the danger was out of her depth. She needed to just be Music Lady with him, someone with spark and a newly found adventurous spirit. Someone who could be sexually uninhibited with him, fulfilling fantasies she didn't even know she'd had.

She still lived with the fear that Marc would take a look at her one day and think she wasn't enough to satisfy him. And the specter of her parents always hovered just out of range in her thoughts.

He lowered his head to hers, his kiss this time hungry, almost needy. But Emma had an answering need, the thing that kept driving her back into his arms. One small taste of him would never be enough. His flavor was more intoxicating than any alcoholic drinks she'd ever had and had seeped into her system.

He licked the inner surface of her lips before thrusting inside and touching every inner surface. She answered him just as greedily, sliding her tongue over his and pushing it into his mouth.

She shivered at the touch of his fingers along the line of her neck and over the hollow of her throat where her pulse was beating fast again. She remembered the first night they were together, how unsure of herself she was, how hesitant as he coaxed responses from her. But each time they were together she became a little bolder, a little less reticent. Willing to be a more active participant.

Pulling his mouth from hers, he slid moist kisses over her cheek and along the sweep of her jaw, nipping the soft skin and soothing it with tiny licks. Heat exploded inside her. He cupped her breast and his thumb rasped the nipple already sensitive from their earlier lovemaking. She gasped slightly when he pinched it and arched her body up to his touch, wanting more.

"Making love with you is like making music," he murmured, his lips against her breast. "Your body is like my guitar, responding to every touch and caress. Jesus, ML, you are so incredible."

"You, too." And he was. His words were as arousing as his touch, scrambling her thoughts.

What could she do? She didn't think she could give him up.

When he lifted one leg and caressed it lightly from ankle to hip, she stopped thinking. Every place he nipped lightly on her thigh then soothed with kisses felt as if a match had struck her there. When he finished with the first leg, he rolled her toward him again so he could work on the other one. He stroked and licked and tasted until she was a writhing, panting mass.

"You get to have all the fun," she gasped, needing to torment him the same way.

With the edge of daring being Music Lady gave her, she slid her hand between their bodies and down his stomach to the thickness of his cock. When her fingers closed around him, she heard an answering gasp, the sound sending a bolt of fire rocketing through her. She squeezed gently as his fingers tightened on her nipple again, and he grazed it gently with his teeth.

ML's hand inched its ways slowly up and down his throbbing length, his cock flexing each time her thumb brushed over the head.

"Jesus, babe," he murmured against her skin. "When you do that my balls tighten up like a fist. You'll make me lose control."

"I like it when you do." She was growing so much bolder with him each time, both in actions and words, but she couldn't seem to help herself.

"But not too quickly." His voice trembled with the effort to hold it together.

Reassured, Emma rose gracefully to her knees, and with a movement she was still becoming comfortable with, bent to touch her tongue to the head of his cock. He jerked beneath her and when she took him fully into her mouth, his hands gripped her head, angling it this way and that. A groan rumbled up from his chest, and her lips against him curved in a smile.

Not bad for a novice, Emma.

An unfamiliar feeling of power surged through her, knowing that she could provide this man with a degree of pleasure close to what he gave her. She managed to find a rhythm, moving her mouth up and down, his cock pulsing in her mouth. Then, without warning, he pulled her head up and urged her onto her side again.

"You just do it to me, ML," he rasped. "That mouth, God."

Heat flamed inside her, a surge of pleasure as great as anything he brought her physically.

Just go with the moment, Emma. Worry about the rest later.

His hand skated over her damp pubic curls to find the slickness of her heat. Her clit, already sensitive, was still swollen and she jumped slightly when he touched it.

"Your body's still ready for me," he crooned.

Oh, yes, she was so very wet, more so when his touch slipped along the length of her slit and found her opening.

While he was busy stroking and caressing her, his fingers

inside of her, she pushed her hand between them to touch his cock again, rubbing the hard length and insinuating itself between his thighs to cup his balls. Squeezing them. Loving his sounds of pleasure and the tensing of his body.

Growling with need he rolled her to her back, stretched out between her legs, and lapped the wet length of her pussy.

"Ohhhhhh." Was that her making those erotic noises?

As he moved his mouth and tongue over every exposed area of pink flesh, Emma writhed in pleasure, hitching her hips toward his mouth, her fingers clutching at his hair. He licked and tasted, swallowing her essence as if he could absorb her entirely into his system.

"Oh, oh, oh."

The little rippling sounds of pleasure seemed to stoke the fire in him hotter and higher. He lapped faster, pulled the nub of her clit into his mouth, and sucked on it deeply. When he eased two fingers inside the wet walls, her pussy clamped down on him like a vise. Each time he touched her it seemed, the need inside her grew.

Suddenly all his finesse disappeared.

"I want inside you. Right now." His voice was so hoarse with passion she almost didn't recognize it. He rose to his knees and lifted her legs over his shoulders. Spreading her wide, he positioned himself at her opening and drove into her with one full, hard stroke.

"Marc!" She moaned his name as her body clenched around him, her muscles of her pussy gripping him hard as sensation after sensation rushed through her.

"That sound drives me wild," he growled, pulling back then plunging into her again.

"More," she cried, wanting nothing more than this man filling her and driving her to the brink of erotic insanity. "God, Marc. Now, now."

He slammed into her, harder, faster, pumping, pumping, pumping.

One more thrust and they exploded together, consumed by

flames, a cataclysmic eruption that sent her spinning into space. She shook and shuddered, unable to breathe from the sheer force of it.

At last he collapsed against her, bracing himself on his forearms. Beneath him, Emma shivered with the aftershocks that rippled through her, a fine layer of perspiration covering her skin.

Emma had no idea how long they lay there, his arms wrapped around her keeping her tight against his body. She didn't know whose heart thundered louder, his or hers.

At length he slid from the clasp of her body. Rolling to the side, he tugged her against him, feathering kisses over her face. She could feel her eyes wanting to close. Maybe tonight....

Then she sighed and pushed away.

"I have to go." He had no idea how much she didn't want to.

"Why?" He was almost pleading with her. "Why can't you stay?"

"I-I just can't." She wet her lips. "I have to go to work." She jumped from the bed, grabbed her clothes from the chair, and began to frantically pull them on.

"Please. I want to take you to breakfast. Talk some more."

Wordlessly she shook her head, stuffing her feet into her shoes and grabbing her purse. As she raced toward the front door, Marc leaped out of bed—naked, as usual—and hurried after her. He caught her as she was unlocking the front door, his hand on her shoulder.

"Please," he repeated. "Just breakfast, okay? No more questions or anything."

"I-I can't, Marc." If he didn't let her go now, she was afraid she wouldn't be able to. It got harder and harder to leave each time. Only the fear of unknown repercussions kept her moving.

"You'll come back to the club again, right?"

She looked at him, seeing the uncertainty on his face. That one thing made her heart turn over and convinced her to keep seeing him. If there were consequences, she'd figure out how to deal with them. She hoped. But right now she had to get away.

"Yes. Yes, of course."

Then she was out of the house, flying toward her car. When she glanced back, she saw that once again he was standing on his porch. Naked. She hoped his neighbors weren't up early and peering out their windows.

As she drove away, the inescapable fact smacked her in the face: he was in her blood. In every part of her. The more she saw him, the less likely she could ever let him go.

She prayed he felt the same way. That he meant everything he said.

Why is it that everyone wants to have a meal with me?

If it wasn't so irritating, Emma might have found it funny. Andrew had all but hijacked her for a lunch she didn't eat. Marc seemed obsessed about taking her to breakfast. Now her parents had insisted she come for dinner.

So here she was, sitting at the familiar breakfast room table, trying to make intelligent conversation with her parents and not succeeding too well. And while the meal was excellent, as usual, the tension in the air stole her appetite.

"You haven't even called all week," Angela Blake protested.

"Mom, I've just been busy," Emma told her, gritting her teeth.

Busy trying to straighten out my brain.

Two intensive nights listening to the high energy music of Lightnin' and spending demanding hours in bed with Marc had nearly worn her out. So for the last two nights, she'd stayed home trying to separate her feelings from her rational self. A daunting task, no matter how she looked at it. Besides, she needed the sleep. She couldn't keep dragging herself into work like a limp noodle and catching cat-naps when no one was looking; her saving grace was the fact she had her own office and could close her door. But sooner or later, her boss would catch on and then she'd be toast.

But the band had only one more week at Aftershock, and she had no idea where they were going next. She had such a strong sense of being in over her head with Marc, of falling into a world that was entirely foreign to her. On the other hand, the thought of not seeing him again was too depressing to contemplate.

I am a freaking mess.

"Emma? Are you there?" Her mother's voice broke into her thoughts. "Are you with us here?"

"Yes, Mom. Sorry." She glanced over at her mother who was staring at her.

"What on earth have you done with your hair?" She sounded so horrified she might have been asking, *why did you paint your face green?* It was the old now-you've-done-it voice.

"I just...livened it up a little." Emma tried to keep from squirming.

"With purple? And the rest of the color's different."

"Just a little change," Emma said with a touch of defiance. "I was in the mood for something different."

Angela smoothed her napkin in her lap. "I thought about inviting Andrew tonight. I guess it's a good thing I didn't. He'd probably take a look at what you've done to yourself and walk back out the door."

Emma was barely holding on to her temper by now. All her life she'd been her parents' "good girl" and been rewarded with approval and pats on the head. Now that she was unexpectedly moving into a new phase of her life, changing things about herself, their disapproval was both hurtful and irritating. She wanted to scream that she wasn't twelve years old any more.

"Well." She calmed herself with a sip of iced tea. "It's a good thing you didn't invite him because we aren't seeing each other any more. You know that, right?"

"I don't know what's wrong between the two of you but your father has convinced me not to stick my nose into your business."

Emma glanced at her father and mouthed, *I owe you, Daddy.*

Her father made no acknowledgment, just forked another bite of food into his mouth.

"We haven't seen you in a while," her mother went on, "and we just wanted to spend a little time with you."

"So, kitten." Her father leaned back in his chair and wiped his mouth. "Your mother tells me you and Andrew had a little spat or something."

Okay. Here it comes. So you're not on my side after all. Well, what did I expect?

Through her entire life, whenever she'd done something that violated the boundaries the parents set for her even the least little bit, it was always her father who was supposed to be the voice of reason. He was an attorney and a very good one, but she always felt as if he was prepping her for the witness stand. It had never been quite as obvious to her as it was until now.

"It wasn't a little spat." She took a swallow of her cold drink. "It was a lot more than that. But it's nothing you need to be concerned about."

They both looked at her with identical bewildered expressions.

"I don't understand," Angela said. "Everyone, all my friends, have been expecting a big announcement from the two of you. Andrew's mother and I—"

"Wait." Emma held up her hand. "You've talked to his *mother* about this?" Why was that so surprising? In her mother's circle that was the established pattern.

"Well, of course, dear. It's proper to consult with the mother of the groom when planning a wedding." She touched her immaculate hairdo.

"You know how well Andrew has fit in with us," her father added. "Your mother and I saw such a wonderful future for the two of you. We can't imagine what went wrong."

Emma had the feeling she had suddenly stepped into someone else's life. Or that she'd been sleeping for thirty years and woke up to find herself in someone else's body.

She carefully put down her knife and fork, refilled her iced tea glass from the pitcher on the table and slowly stirred in two packets of sweetener, giving herself time to collect her thoughts and biting back the angry words threatening to spill out of her mouth. She had to remind herself that her parents truly thought they knew what was best for her, but what defined "best" had changed drastically and they didn't know it. Taking a small sip before setting the glass down, she looked from one to the other.

"*If* there was a wedding, it would be *my* wedding. So don't you think I should have been the one you talked to first? Not to mention the fact that Andrew and I never officially became engaged."

"But everyone thought…" her mother began. "That is, the children of our friends followed this pattern and—"

"And you expected me just to fall into place. Right?"

Neither of them said a word, watching her as if she'd just told them she had an incurable disease. And maybe in their world, breaking out of the accepted social pattern was just as devastating.

"I know you and Mom are worried, Daddy, but there's really nothing to be concerned about here. Andrew and I have just decided our…relationship was a mistake, and it would be better to go our own ways."

"Not according to Andrew," her mother said.

"What?" Emma was startled. "What do you mean? Has he been talking to you again?"

Her father nodded. "He came to see me at the office this week to plead his case."

"Oh, my God." She threw up her hands. "What is wrong with him? Are we teenagers here or something?"

"Now, kitten." Her father's voice had taken on that overly tolerant tone, as if reasonable words would bring about the reasonable conclusion that was always his goal.

But Emma was tired of this conversation.

"Don't 'kitten' me, Daddy." She hated that childhood nickname. "I'm an adult. Almost thirty years old. I make my own decisions about my personal life. I find it insulting that Andrew runs to you like I'm some idiot casting aside the prize of the century and expects you to, what, talk sense into me?"

Her father shifted uncomfortably in his chair.

"Oh, my God," she said again. "He can't accept the fact that it's over so he figures you'll take up for him. So we can fall into the 'accepted and proper' pattern again, right? Holy crap."

"There's no need to use vulgar language," Angela told her.

Vulgar language? Holy crap is vulgar language?

Listening to them, Emma was struck by just how sterile her life had been up until now. She shuddered to think how she'd been so accepting of it. Content enough that Annie had believed dull, boring Andrew to be the perfect person for her. And almost two weeks ago, she'd believed it herself.

She took a deep breath and let it out slowly.

"Look. I know Andrew is a really nice man, and it's my fault for letting everyone—including him—believe we were headed down the bridal path. But I don't love Andrew. I'm not sure now I ever did. It's like...like...." She chuffed in frustration. "Like I woke up one day and discovered my world had been gray and now I realized there were colors. Can you even try to understand that?"

"Your mother tells me your old roommate Jacie was in town a week or so ago and you had lunch with her." Her father shook his head. "I always did think she was a wild one. Now she's filled your head full of ridiculous ideas."

"Oh, my God," she repeated yet again. "Jacie is *not* wild. She's a happily married woman completely in love with a husband she raves about. I don't even feel one-tenth for Andrew of what she feels for Michael. She has a wonderful family and a career she thrives on. What do I have? A job editing textbooks and reruns of old movies every Saturday night. What is so bad about wanting something different?" She looked from one to the other. "What if I'd married Andrew and *then* realized I'd made a mistake?"

"A lot of women would love to have a dependable man like Andrew for a husband," her mother pointed out.

"And so I'm sure they'll be lining up for him once he lets them know he's available. He's just not for me."

Her father studied her carefully. "I don't suppose visiting a rock and roll bar had anything to do with it, either."

Emma froze in shock. How in God's name did they know that?

"You didn't think we'd know? Andrew told me when he came to my office."

"What? He *followed* me?"

Thad Blake nodded.

"And then what did he do?" Oh God, what if he'd followed her to Marc's? How did she explain that?

"He said he waited in the parking lot for a little while but you never came out. He wasn't about to go into that...*place*, and after a while some man came and told him he couldn't keep sitting there, and he'd have to leave."

"He sat there like some stalker?" A bubble of hysterical laughter wiggled its way up her throat.

Her father nudged his plate away. "He was very concerned, Emma."

Emma pushed her chair back and stood up. "I'll just bet he was. Concerned." She almost spat the word. "Enough to follow me but not to wait around to see if I was in trouble? Listen to me. Andrew was *concerned* he was going to lose a cook and housekeeper and someone who wouldn't rattle his chain. Holy crap!"

"Emma!" Angela admonished.

"Crap, crap, crap." Emma repeated, feeling as if she were ten years old, throwing a tantrum and about to get her mouth washed out with soap. "Do you both realize that in a couple of weeks I'll be *thirty years old?* I can go wherever I want. With whoever I want. I don't need permission anymore."

"Honey, please." Angela looked at her, distress stamped on her face. "We raised you to be a good girl, a decent woman. Not go places where they have things like...drugs."

"Drugs?" Emma tried to get a handle on the anger

threatening to burst forth. "There are no drugs in the places I go to. And the people are very nice. Don't pass judgment on things you know nothing about. Have you ever even been to that kind of club?" She threw her hands up in the air. "Of course not. And they weren't even in my universe growing up. Not in my carefully selected group of friends."

"There's no crime in not going certain places," Angela fretted. "Or liking certain things."

"No. But there is in prejudging them." Emma swallowed the urge to scream. How did she let them dictate her life all these years? "Why couldn't you have given me the freedom to make my own choices? Didn't you trust me?"

"We gave you a good life, honey."

"Yes, and I'm very grateful for it. But now you have to let me figure things out for myself. I'm going to be thirty years old. Give me a break here. Please."

"Emma," her father began.

"No. This was a mistake." She took a couple of deep, hopefully calming breaths. "Look. I love you both. I really do. And I appreciate that you want certain things for me. But I'm not a child. I need to make my own decisions. And if what I want isn't what you had in mind, I hope *you* love *me* enough to accept that." She kissed each of her parents in turn. "I'll call you tomorrow. Please don't worry. I'm really fine. Just battling with a case of arrested development."

Her anger boiled over again as she pulled away from the house, grabbing her like a living thing. It grew and expanded as she drove through the streets until she reached her destination. Rocking to a stop in the driveway, she turned the engine off, then ran up the porch steps and banged on the front door.

"Open up," she yelled when nothing happened at once, and pounded away again.

"What's the matter?" Andrew pulled open his door and stared at her. "Emma. Have you lost your mind?"

"I'm wondering if *you* lost yours. You *followed* me?"

"Try to understand," he said, attempting to placate her.

"Understand what? Damn, Andrew. Are you turning into a stalker? I'd never have believed it of you."

"Listen." He looked over her head at the street. "Why don't you come inside and we can discuss this rationally?"

"Two reasons. I'm never coming inside again and I'm not rational." She fisted her hands and dug her nails into her palms, reaching for some measure of inner restraint and wanting to smack Andrew for being so dense. "We're finished, Andrew. Try to get that through your head. I don't love you. Maybe I only thought I did. But I saved us from making a big mistake."

"Your friend Annie put you up to this." He delivered the words in a hard, flat tone.

"Annie?" She heard her voice rising and swallowed hard. "Annie has nothing to do with this. Don't you think I have a mind of my own?"

"If you did, we wouldn't be standing here now having this argument."

"What? Are you saying I'm stupid? Or dumb? Easily influenced? "

Was that how he saw her? What her parents expected of her? Another Stepford wife to take her place in their social circle?

How did I never see this side of him before? He's not bland, he's controlling. He was only bland as long as I didn't object to anything.

Ohmigod!

"Listen to what I'm going to say, Andrew." She made herself speak slowly and patiently because she didn't intend to go through this again. "I will say this one last time. Don't ever presume to follow me again or go behind my back to my parents. It's pointless because I make my own decisions. And marrying you isn't one of them."

She spun on her heel and hurried back to her car. The tires squealed as she backed out into the street and pulled away.

Well, that went well.

But she had to admit, while she'd insisted to everyone what a grownup she was, she didn't act like one where Marc was concerned. Not telling him her name. Afraid to let him into her world. Hiding behind secrecy like a kid sneaking out of the house.

Yet she still held back. Maybe because she didn't understand enough of his world. Didn't trust that what the two of them had was real and important. Or was she still afraid of what would happen if she gave him a glimpse into hers?

The one thing she couldn't ignore was the relationship growing between them. More than just sex. More than thrills. She needed to quit riding the fence.

But it's all so new to me. I'm not ready yet. And I'm not sure I ever will be.

Chapter Ten

$\mathcal{M}$arc was trying to pull himself together as he drove to the site where the band was shooting the video. His Music Lady hadn't come back for the last two nights. Why not? Had he pushed too hard? Had his little game of Twenty Questions scared her off? Or all the information he'd given her about the business he was in?

Maybe he was just imagining she was into him. Wishful thinking. She was obviously stepping into a world she knew nothing about. What was she really looking for? Did she think he wasn't exciting enough for her? Or too exciting? Was the sex suddenly too over the top?

Shit. I'll drive myself crazy doing this.

Any sleep he managed had been fitful, his dreams invaded by erotic images of her naked in his bed. Under him. Over him. The feel of her when he was inside her. The scent she wore clung to his sheets, tantalizing him. And at night, at Aftershock, his eyes kept straying to the spot where she usually stood, her sweet little body swaying to the music.

He'd been encouraged by the information he'd pried out of her in such a slick manner. Maybe she didn't think she was giving him clues to herself, but all those little things were indicators of the real person she was. A person who was becoming even more special to him.

What would she say if he told her just how "everyday" his background really was? Parents with real world jobs. Two brothers at the university. A family who bonded over cooking. All the things making up the real fabric of his life. Would they make him more or less interesting to her?

Better get yourself together, buddy boy, or the band will eat your ass for lunch. Can't screw up this video.

Everyone was already at the studio when he got there. Rick's cousin, Jado, had built a stellar reputation shooting videos for bands and was doing this on a Saturday as a favor to Lightnin'.

"Family always comes through," Rick had told them.

They would pay Jado, of course, but a pittance compared to what he usually charged. And he had a top-notch facility and the equipment to go with it.

The song they'd chosen was called *On the Edge of the Woods*, about the lure of the darkness of the trees and the sunlight that washes it away. Jado's studio was in a rural area with a thick forest-like expanse bordering it, so they'd decided to shoot the video outside. Something to enrich the flavor of the song.

The band members had agreed all four of them didn't need to hang over the shoulders of the two professionals. Since this was Rick's project, they were leaving it in his hands. Even Garrett had agreed that was the best. Then he'd go home for sack time before his meeting with Butch Meredith.

"Hey, guy." Rick walked over and clapped him on the shoulder. "All set?"

Marc nodded. "Did you think I wouldn't be?"

"Nope. I asked the same thing of Garrett and Danny." He shoved his hands in his pockets, took them out again, the air around him jittery with his nervous energy. "We're cramming a lot into forty-eight hours to get this done so there's no margin for error here. You're not letting...stuff screw with your head, right? What we talked about after rehearsal the other day?"

Marc bit back a retort. He hoped he hadn't made a mistake talking to Rick about Music Lady. "This video has been my focus,

Rick. I know writing the script is a huge responsibility and it makes me feel great you guys trust me to do this."

"That's because you're very good at it. You really have the length and timing down pat, and you get creative with the stage directions. That's what makes our videos so good."

For just a moment tension shimmered between them. Was that a real compliment or was Rick patronizing him? Suddenly losing confidence in him?

Quit imagining things. Rick is just doing his leader of the band thing.

"People have no idea how complicated it can get to produce a three-to-five minute video. I know we're a little on edge with this particular one because of what it can mean."

"Which is why we've walked through it so many times this week," Rick reminded him.

"So then have faith in us. In me. I'm good to go, Rick. I'm a professional. You should know that by now. Besides, I know Jado's giving us a dirt-cheap rate so I want him to know I appreciate it.

"Just making sure."

He might have said more but Jado was suddenly next to Marc, hooking him up with a tiny mic that would be invisible to the cameras.

"As usual," he reminded Marc, "don't worry about the quality of this soundtrack. This is just to sync with the real tracks you'll lay down tomorrow. "

Marc grinned. "Thanks, Jado. Cause this is my first time doing this, right?"

Jado clapped him on the shoulder. "Just covering all my bases, guy. This one's pretty important, and we want to make sure every detail is covered. No sweat."

"He knows it," Rick said. "He's just being his smartass self. We're set to begin at Scotty's studio tomorrow at ten in the morning. You worked out the details of the final product with him?"

Jado laughed. "Yes, Mr. Obsessive. When he's finished the

mix of the sound tracks, he'll bring it here and the two of us will finish up. Don't worry. You'll get a quality finished piece out of this, my man." Jado winked at Rick and walked back to his equipment.

Marc looked at his friend. "We'll be fine, Rick. We rehearsed our asses off this week on this. And everyone's psyched about it."

He lifted his guitar case out of the Jeep, and they headed over to where the other band members waited. Marc knew they could do this. No doubt about it. There was a magic to the way the four of them blended that made them top sellers in the city's rock clubs. Now it was important to make sure it would translate to a big concert stage. And the best part was there wouldn't be a lot of time to think about Music Lady.

He hoped.

"Okay, everyone," Rick called. "Get tuned up." He inclined his head toward a place at the edge of the trees. "Jado's marked the spots where he wants us to start. So, let's do it."

"I'm telling you, you're a fool if you don't go back there tonight," Annie said, popping a potato chip in her mouth.

She and Emma were lying on loungers in Emma's backyard and indulging themselves in junk food and sweet tea. Emma had rehashed the conversation with her folks and her confrontation with Andrew until she was sick of the sound of her own voice. But she was stuck on two things: why had it taken her thirty years to wake up and smell the roses, and how could she put her anger at Andrew to rest?

Annie, of course, was more interested in coaxing her back to Aftershock.

"I don't think I can explain it to you," Emma said. "I can hardly explain it to myself. But Marc is...is...larger than life. There's so much raw masculinity, so much energy surrounding him that everyone and everything else fades into the background. Annie, when he's up on stage, really into his music, he's in another world. I see the crowd so mesmerized by him, the excitement he generates, and I wonder what in hell I'm doing there."

"Correct me if I'm wrong, but I'd say having a good time." Annie crunched on another chip.

Emma chewed her bottom lip, frustrated. These days, she didn't seem to be doing a good job of explaining her emotions about anything to anyone.

"Sometimes it's like I've walked into the set of a movie," she said slowly. "By mistake. And while Marc has made me welcome, I worry any minute he's going to discover it's—this, *us*—is all a big mistake and the whole thing will disappear." She swatted at a fly buzzing around her head. "I'm nothing like the women he's used to being with."

"How do you know what kind of women he hangs with? Please don't tell me he's low class enough to talk about them."

"No. Are you kidding?" She blew at a stray hair on her forehead. "But I see the women who come to the club. How they are. How they dress. There's one especially that looks at Marc like she wants to eat him alive."

"And does he look at her the same way?"

Emma rubbed her forehead. "Well, no, but I feel, I don't know, *dowdy* compared to her. Them."

"First of all, chickadee, no one would ever call you dowdy. Besides, you've spiced up your hair. Got some new duds. But maybe the difference is what attracts him to you." Annie crunched another chip and swallowed. "He doesn't seem too anxious to kick you to the curb." She paused. "And what would be so terrible if you gave him your name?"

"No. No, no, no."

Their differences continued to plague her despite his cute little Twenty Questions game and the other tidbits he'd managed to pry out of her. And what little she'd learned about him. His family. His father played guitar. He had two brothers in college. But what did his father do? His mother? She sensed a normalcy she hadn't quite expected but there were still so many unanswered questions. And over and above it all, she was still scared. If this...thing...between them fell apart, which she kept expecting it to do, she needed to be able to hide behind the old Emma.

Annie raised her eyebrows. "Why so definite about it? What's the problem?"

"It's like being Music Lady is a new identity for me. Emma's dull and boring but Music Lady is appealing and exciting. And maybe a little but mysterious."

"So you think you can hook him by wrapping yourself in a cloak of secrecy?"

"Uh huh. That's part of it. As Music Lady, I can be everything Emma's not."

Annie quirked an eyebrow. "Like what?"

Emma shrugged. "You know. Into the music." She brushed a hand over her head. "Purple streaks in my hair." She bit her lower lip. "Good...together with him."

Her friend laughed. "You mean wild monkey sex, right? Ohmigod, you're blushing! I'm right." Then she sobered. "But even then I'll bet he sees the essence of Emma. Did you ever stop to think what you offer might be what he really wants? Not the girls from the club scene?"

"I don't know." Emma pressed the icy cold glass to her forehead. "I just don't know."

"Well, I do." Annie sat up and swung her legs over the side of the chair. "You're going back to Aftershock tonight if I have to take you and dump you there myself. Holy crap, Emma. I'm so glad you broke out of your shell. Don't crawl back in because you're afraid of something that might not even happen."

"I know, I know." Emma worried a fingernail. The sad truth was she really didn't need Annie to give her a push. She'd already decided to go back to the club. She just couldn't make herself stay away from her Guitar Man. He'd awakened emotional and sexual feelings in her she hadn't even known she was capable of.

"Then it's settled. At least keep seeing him until you know

what's going to happen one way or the other."

Her mind kept tripping over a disturbing thought, one that popped up whenever her confidence drooped. "But...what if all he wants from me is sex? What if this is just a different kind of game for him?"

"From what you've told me about him and the way he is with you, I don't think that's it. If he was just looking for a little different flavor, he'd be over it by now. But if it somehow turns out you're right, then enjoy every minute of it while it lasts. Now come on. We need to quit lazing around and do some shopping."

Emma frowned. "Shopping? For what?"

"Some snazzy duds so you can knock Marc's socks off tonight."

Hours later, she parked at the edge of the jammed lot at Aftershock, turned off the engine, and took a deep breath. She'd let Annie call the shots during their whirlwind shopping tour, and now she was geared up in a pair of tight white jeans and a hot pink tank top designed to show off every one of her assets. Her silvery blonde hair hung in shining waves to her shoulder and large gold hoops sparkled at her ears. Newly polished toenails glistened through the straps of hot pink sandals Annie had insisted on.

The old Emma was fading as the new Music Lady surged to the forefront, even though she was battling a bad case of nerves.

The moment she opened the door to the club, it was like the first night all over again. Sound blasted at her in waves, the yelling of the crowd a counterpoint to the loud volume of the music. She had to wait while the bouncer processed the people in front of her then gave him her ten dollars and held her hand out for the stamp.

"Glad to see you again." He grinned and winked at her.

He recognized her. Emma relaxed fractionally. At least this wasn't like walking into strange territory anymore. She'd take every advantage she could get.

The press of bodies was even tighter tonight than the first time she'd been there. She had to shove her way to the bar this time. Mostly everyone ignored her, caught up in the thrall of the music. By the time she reached the bar, she was sweaty and panting and she hadn't been there for fifteen minutes.

"Lone Star," she shouted at the bartender who was busy pouring three drinks at a time. She'd been drinking beer since the first night and surprisingly it wasn't too bad. He nodded, grabbed a bottle out of the well beneath the bar, handed it to her, and took her money all without even raising his eyes. *How did he even do that?*

Then she was back to shoving and elbowing, ignoring glares and a few curses as she bulldozed her way to her usual spot in front of the stage. People were moving frenetically in place, and Emma couldn't tell if they were dancing alone or with someone else.

The band was bathed in a red glow, the music heavy and wild and building to a crescendo. Marc was pulling the now familiar very erotic low sound from his guitar and leaning forward slightly to sing into the microphone in front of him. His hair, as usual, was wild around his face, the light bathing him. The sight was so sensual, Emma felt the pulsing beat all the way from her breasts to her sex and on to her toes. Her entire body seemed to be in tune with the sensual bass guitar.

And the guitarist.

The last notes of the song pierced the air and hung in the shimmery darkness for a long moment. Then the crowd began clapping and stamping and screaming for more. Emma managed to move herself an inch or two to the left so she'd be in Marc's line of vision and did her best to wait patiently. He threw his head back, shaking his hair out of his eyes and took a step back. The lighting changed from red to a soft yellow. His gaze tracked over the front of the crowd...and then landed on her.

The grin he gave her pumped up her heart rate, and she smiled back at him.

"Later," he mouthed. "Don't leave."

And then they were into the next song, and Emma was caught up in it just like everyone else.

She could hardly believe when the set was over. Marc leaped over the edge of the stage but before he could reach her, he was stopped by a couple who obviously knew him. Then it was a group of guys. Then the same stupid redhead—what was her name? Oh, yeah. Lacey. Queen of the groupies—who acted as if she wanted to drag *her* Guitar Man off to a corner. This time Marc's anger with her was obvious. Emma was seized by an insane desire to grab the woman and yank her away by her hair.

Ohmigod. Is that me?

She swallowed a giggle.

She watched Marc edge tactfully but steadily away from the two females until he was beside her, touching her arm.

"Let's go outside or we won't have a minute to ourselves."

Emma was aware that the redhead gave them the death stare of hate as they moved toward the door.

"You have a lot of fans," she commented when they were out in the parking lot. "They seem very enthusiastic."

"Yeah." One corner of his mouth turned up into a lopsided grin. "Sometimes *too* enthusiastic."

"Especially one of them." *Great, Emma. Sound like a jealous bitch much?*

Marc twisted his lips in a grimace. "That's Lacey. Nobody I'm at all interested in. Or ever have been," he added quickly.

"I've seen her the last few times trying to corral you."

Marc cupped her cheeks with his warm palms. "Forget Lacey. She's nothing to me. And never has been. You're who I want to be with. Believe me."

As if to prove his point, he pulled her into his arms, his eyes searching every inch of her face before his mouth brushed against hers. The light contact ignited sparks in her bloodstream and sent her pulse points throbbing. He ran his tongue gently over the closed seam of her mouth, sending shivers skating along her spine. His warm hands slid up the length of her arms to her shoulder, then along the column of her throat until he at last cradled her head between his palms.

"I'll never get enough of your taste," he murmured just

before licking every inch of the surface of her lips and plunging his tongue inside her mouth.

Emma clung to him as everything faded away—the jammed parking lot, the people standing outside smoking, other couples doing their own thing—until she and Marc were just an island in the sea of darkness. The kiss was endless. He turned her head this way and that seeking a better angle, all the while his tongue stroked hers and tasted every inner surface.

Her nipples hardened painfully, and the pulse beating at her core echoed throughout her body until she was sure he could sense it. Feel it. She pressed him, rubbing herself against the obvious bulge of his erection and moaning softly.

"Jesus, ML," he gasped when he broke the kiss. "I hope we don't go up in flames just standing here."

She gave an unsteady laugh. "Me, too. Although I was afraid we might."

He tucked a strand of hair behind one ear. "I missed you, Music Lady. Wondered what you'd been up to. I think about you a lot, you know."

"I-I think about you, too."

Was this the moment to ask him, why her? Why not any of the other women throwing themselves at him? But she wasn't sure she'd like the answer so she just nodded.

He took a step back, and his gaze traveled the length of her body and up again. "You look damn fine tonight, Music Lady. Sharp outfit. I hope you picked it out just for me."

She knew she was blushing. She'd have to remember to thank Annie for another great shopping trip. "Thank you. I-I did."

"Listen. I've got a lot of stuff to tell you but you know we have one last set to do. Will you stay?"

She gently bit her bottom lip before answering him. "Okay."

"Will you come home with me again tonight? Please?"

Another hesitation on her part. She was glad he didn't take it as a given. That the choice was always hers.

"Yes. I will."

"Good." He kissed her again, brief but not less incendiary, and took her hand. "Let's go back inside, and I'll get you another beer. The band has a tab. You shouldn't have to pay."

"But—"

"No buts. Come on."

She wanted to ask him how many other women he bought drinks for, but squelched the nasty worm of jealousy trying to burrow its way into her system.

Enjoy it. Just enjoy it.

Again, as they worked their way to the bar, people stopped Marc. Talked to him. Joked with him. All the while he held tightly to her hand. They glanced at her questioningly, but she stayed quiet. Marc was warm and friendly to everyone, taking care of the people who paid to see him perform. It was obvious he was sending two signals to her at once—*I respect your anonymity so I won't introduce you or put you in a position where you'd have to give your name, but I'm going to keep you close and let everyone know you're mine. Yes, mine.*

The idea was at once both thrilling and frightening to Emma. Another step forward into this new world. But Marc's touch was reassuring.

It seemed to take forever until he managed to get the beer for her and lead her back to her usual spot.

"I'll be playing just for you," he whispered in her ear before leaping back onto the stage.

A voice rose just enough to be heard over the crowd. "He'll get tired of you soon, you know."

Emma turned and found the redhead's face inches from hers. She blinked. "What?"

"You're not his style. I am. So why don't you just take your little self out of here and leave the big boys to us."

She looked away, doing her best to ignore the woman. Not to get riled.

Lacey poked her arm with a sharp-nailed finger. "Did you hear me? You're out of your league here."

Her words were so close to what Emma had been thinking.

She didn't need someone like this redheaded bitch reinforcing it. She breathed a sigh of relief when the first notes of a song split the air and the sound filled the room, killing any further ability for Lacey to be heard.

Emma made herself focus on the music, on Marc, shutting everything else out of her mind.

The final set was electrifying, jam-packed with an energy that pulsed through the club and wrapped itself around the people there. By the last song, the crowd bumped, swayed, and gyrated as one person, as if an extension of the music poured over them. Emma was almost regretful when the band said goodnight.

Almost.

People crowded the stage clamoring for Marc's attention, along with the other band members, while they packed away their instruments. Emma tried to make herself invisible, leaning against the wall by the back door. She breathed a little easier when he was able to break free. With his guitar case in one hand and the other firmly clamped around her arm, he hustled her out the door.

"Before someone else wants to hang out with me," he muttered. "Where's your car?"

She pointed to the spot she'd managed to squeeze into.

"Okay. I'll come around from where I am on the other side. You can follow me like always. Okay?"

She nodded.

"Then let's do it."

Emma was a bundle of nerves as she followed him to his house, and she couldn't have said which of the many things caused it. Maybe it was taking a stand with her folks after all this time, something she was many years past due for. Or venting her anger at Andrew. Or dumping her uncertainty on Annie and hearing her friend tell her life was for taking chances. She smiled in the darkness of the car. Maybe it was even the purple streak in her hair or the slightly sexy new clothes. And the confrontation with that bitch, Lacey, certainly hadn't helped.

She definitely wasn't used to women like her—hard, edgy, balls-to-the-wall. Could you say that about a woman? Whatever it was, she had the feeling she was about to cross some line tonight, and she wasn't quite sure she was ready for it.

But I'm going to do it because my heart—yes, my heart—tells me I should. And whatever happens, happens.

When Marc unlocked his front door, she was prepared for him to grab her and kiss her senseless the way he usually did. But instead as he walked in, he flipped a switch to light a small table lamp and placed his guitar next to an armchair. He then turned to her with that crooked grin in place.

"I thought maybe tonight you might actually want to see what my place looks like." He winked. "I mean, before I hustle you into the bedroom and rip off your clothes."

She giggled. "That might be nice." And yes, she really wanted to see all of where he lived. See another side of the man who made hot music and even hotter love.

When she'd placed her purse on the lamp table, he took her hand and pulled her into the middle of the room. "I even cleaned up for you just in case. Although, I had to kind of rush through it."

"Oh? How come?"

"I'll tell you later. Well, what do you think?"

She moved in a slow circle, taking everything in. The floor was a polished hardwood with a colorful rug in the conversation area. Part of the room was filled with comfortable, overstuffed furniture; most of it arranged to face a big flat screen television mounted on one wall. On another wall was a framed modern painting in vivid colors.

"You like modern art?" she asked.

He shrugged. "I like this one. My cousin painted it. She gave it to me for a housewarming gift."

Hmmm. So he had a family and they did things like people she was used to. The more he revealed of himself, the more she came to believe him when he gave her bits and pieces of his so-called normal background—more normal than she thought in the beginning, for sure. It widened her comfort zone, helped her feel a little less insecure about this whole thing with her Guitar Man. Was it really possible that their background weren't as different as she imagined? Could they find more and more common ground, something beyond the hot and sweaty sex? Did his background mean that she could really believe the things he said to her in the heat of passion?

Geez, overthink much?

Emma circled the room, once more. Next to a big armchair was a stack of magazines, the top one with a guitar player on the cover. On the coffee table in front of the sofa, a pile of notebooks had been neatly stacked, precisely aligned. Oh yes, he'd gone to some trouble here no matter what he said.

"Did you do all this yourself?" she asked, knowing what a humungous job it must have been, especially the floor.

"A lot of it. My dad and my brothers helped."

More normal stuff. First about his dad. Now the family picture was fleshing out more, changing more her perspective of him. She wondered what his mother was like. Controlling, like hers? Or supportive of her children? Warm and friendly or cool and distant? Was there a preconceived image he had to live up to or was he lucky enough to have a family that encouraged him to be himself? *Unlike my own.*

Enough! Turn off the brain.

"Don't sound so startled. Did you think rock musicians were hatched like chickens?" He laughed.

She lowered her gaze, embarrassed. "No, I...I mean...I didn't think at all, I guess."

"Well, now you know."

In front of a wide window, she saw a dining table and chairs and in the middle of the table, a piece of statuary representing a band.

She grinned. "Is that supposed to be Lightnin'?"

"Yeah. I have a friend who does this kind of work."

Emma didn't want to ask if the friend was male or female. She didn't want to know. So she just smiled and said, "It's a beautiful piece."

He dragged her into the kitchen, cleaner than anyone's she'd ever been in, including obsessive/compulsive Andrew. The countertops were gleaming granite, the stove and refrigerator brushed aluminum, and an array of appliances stood precisely on one counter.

"Wow! This is beautiful. Do you actually use it?"

He nodded. "My family's big on cooking. Everyone one of us gets into it." One corner of his mouth kicked up in a smile. "Except my mother. I think she's missing the cooking gene. But she makes killer casseroles."

"This isn't some kind of a joke?" She could hardly believe what she was hearing. But then she remembered running into him at the grocery store. If she'd thought about it at all, she figured he was there to buy a week's supply of frozen dinners. But he *cooked?*

He shrugged. "What, you don't think rock musicians can prepare food from scratch?" He touched the tip of a finger to her lips. "Shh. It's a big secret. Don't tell anyone. You'll ruin my image."

"Too late," she said, only half joking. "Your image is already changing."

And it was. Family, a cousin who painted, and now cooking? What else didn't she know about him? What else had she deliberately chosen not to find out because it was the safest way?

His face became dead serious. "Good. That's what I want." He took one of her hands and rubbed his thumb over her knuckle. "I'm not just the guy you see on stage, ML. That's who I am in public, but in private I'm a lot more."

Was he really? She wanted to desperately to believe it. A kaleidoscope of images collided in her mind—her cooking in his magnificent kitchen, curled up on the couch with Marc watching television (anything but war movies), rocking a baby...A baby? *Reel it in, Emma. Don't get ahead of yourself here.*

She sucked in a deep breath to steady herself and let it out slowly. "Okay."

He cocked his head. "Does that damage my sex appeal?"

"No. Not at all." It actually made him seem more real to her. And somehow even more dangerous. Because she couldn't pigeonhole him, couldn't keep him in a little slot marked "not real". It was easier to let herself go with a living figment of her imagination. Seeing him as a real person whipped up the emotional whirlpool to a dangerous level. Especially when his thumb was caressing her with a slow sensual movement.

She eased her hand out of his and glanced around again, trying to distract herself.

"I can't believe how neat this kitchen is," she commented.

"My mom taught me always to clean as you go," he explained. "That way you never have a mess when you're done. Meanwhile, we haven't finished the tour. Come on."

He took her hand again and led her down the hallway toward his bedroom. Opening a door opposite his, he turned on a light. "Guest room." He waved his hand at the space. "But as you can see, I haven't exactly been planning for any guests."

A quick look told her the room was filled with workout equipment, various pieces of electronic equipment, and some unopened boxes.

"I work out as often as I can. Helps me keep in shape. The rest of this is junk I haven't figured out where to put yet." He indicated a door to the right. "That's a second bathroom, one of the things that sold me on the place. So if I ever put this room to use as a bedroom, it has its own bathroom."

"It's...nice. More than I expected."

Far more. That first night she saw him as a free spirit, immersed in his music and hotter than a furnace in bed. But this man was putting down roots. Creating a solid life for himself. Not at all what she expected. She didn't think Marc would want these kinds of things.

So maybe you misjudged him, you idiot.

He turned her toward him and brushed his fingers against her cheek. "Good. I wanted you to like it."

She sensed the pride of ownership that he was trying to be so casual about.

"Okay, tour's over." His voice was husky, edge with hunger and need. "My self-control's about at an end. If I don't get a taste of you in the next sixty second I might expire."

Her pulse raced and her blood heated. Shivers of excitement skated along her spine. Deep in her sex, hunger and need throbbed for this man who made her body sing like his music.

Yes. Hurry, hurry, hurry.

He tugged her into his bedroom where the only light came from the bedside lamp and the moonlight shining in through the wide window. Emma could feel the tension of restraint radiating from Marc's body as he pulled her tank top over her head then ran his fingers deliberately through the fall of her hair. He studied every feature on her face before his gaze lowered to the swell of her breasts above the lace of her bra.

Oh, yes, her lingerie was new, too, also courtesy of Annie.

Not that she'd been addicted to dull cotton before, but these undies had real pizzazz. She couldn't wait for him to get a load of the thong.

Resting his hands on her shoulder, he bent his head to trail a line of kisses across the upper slope of her breasts then licked the fullness with the tip of his tongue. Almost lazily, he drew each nipple into his mouth, silky fabric and all, and sucked on them until they were rigid and taut.

Emma trembled and leaned her head back, closing her eyes, giving herself over to sensation. Marc's lips were hot and soft at the same time, cruising over her skin with delicate care, igniting her every place they touched. When he reached behind her to release the catch on her bra and slip it off, she almost breathed a sigh of relief. She then cupped her breasts with her palms and held them out to him. An offering. A bold move for her but with Marc, bold was becoming almost a motto.

Fire sparked in his eyes. "Oh, yeah. Hold them just like that so I can look at them and kiss them and lick them. Tonight, Music Lady, I'm going to take it slow if it kills me. And it just might."

Chapter Eleven

*H*e worshipped her breasts. That was the only word Emma could use to describe what Marc was doing. Standing there, the two of them, him still fully clothed, her naked from the waist up, he concentrated on those mounds as if his life depended on it. He sucked her taut buds, nipped them, soothed them and drew circles around them with the tip of his tongue. Grazed his teeth over the flesh around them. Licked some more. She trembled with the effort to hold the firm mounds out to him, and her legs were so weak she wasn't sure how long she could continue to stand upright.

At last he raised his head, moved her hands to his shoulders, and kissed her like a starving man, tasting everywhere inside her mouth. She couldn't stop the flame scorching her with its intensity. She felt it clear down to her core, clear in the wet heat of her body. Her own small tongue slid over his, stroking it, coaxing him deeper inside that hot, delicious cavern.

When he lifted his lips from hers, they were both shaking. He touched her shoulders, her arms, her breasts. His eyes were like hot coals searing her every place he looked. In slow motion, he unsnapped her jeans and lowered the zipper, the rasp of the teeth unnaturally loud in the room. His hands slid inside the jeans and cupped her ass, his breath hissing between her teeth when he touched bare flesh.

"No panties, babe?" His voice had a strangled sound to it.

"Take off the jeans and you'll find out." Her new temptress attitude was definitely more Music Lady than Emma. Or maybe the two were merging.

Emma clung to his arms as she toed off her brand new sandals and kicked them to the side. She stood shaking with anticipation while Marc deliberately slid the white denim down her legs. She leaned on him while he knelt and lifted each foot, one at a time, from the jeans before tossing the garment onto the pile with her tank and bra.

"Lordy, lordy." He sighed when he took in the miniscule white thong, made of all lace.

She was well aware her dark golden curls were visible in the tiny openings of the material. She wet her lips, trying to calm the sudden surge of nervousness. The old Emma still hovered in the background. For now. Marc's fingers tightened on her hips as he took his time licking the triangle of lace, lapping it and tugging on the soft curls with his teeth. His tongue pushed the lace into her slit and traced the length of her from top to bottom and back again.

The walls of her pussy quivered, and the thong became soaked with her juices. When he took the fabric between his teeth and tugged it down, she had to dig her fingers into his shoulders to keep from sinking to the floor. By the time he rose to his feet, they were both trembling with need.

His eyes never left hers as he shucked his clothes, dropping them on top of hers. She stared at his cock as it sprang free, thick and swollen, rising like a spear from his groin. She wanted to swallow but her throat was suddenly dry, and she remembered the taste of him the last time she took him in her mouth.

As if she'd been doing it forever, she dropped to her knees and cradled Marc's shaft in her palms. For a woman of her age, she was sexually unsophisticated as far as oral sex was concerned. None of her partners, including Andrew, had been much interested in it. But Marc had used his mouth on her and brought her untold pleasure. He'd liked it when she did it the other night so maybe she could do it again now.

With only a hint of shyness she licked the broad head, capturing the bead of fluid sitting precipitously on the slit. Salty, she thought, but also with an earthy flavor. Just as before. She licked again. And again. Tension radiated from Marc's body; his hands curled into fists at his sides. Oh, yes, she was pleasing him.

"You're killing me here, babe," he growled.

She hummed her satisfaction, opened her lips wider and slid them over the head and onto the fat, wide stalk. The sensation of his thick erection stretching her mouth was so erotic, she persisted, working her mouth down a little at a time. When she'd taken half of it, she slipped one hand between his thighs and cupped his balls, gently squeezing them.

His taste excited her as much as the sudden sense of power the act gave her and pleasure surged through her. After years of placid, uneventful sex, wondering what all the fuss was about, she realized this—*this!*—was what her friends had giggled about. And avoided discussion about for the most part when they figured out she was outside the circle.

Tentatively, she moved her mouth lower but she'd reach a point where she couldn't take any more of him.

"Stop." Marc's fingers pressed into her jawline.

Emma froze. Was she doing something wrong?

Marc's laugh was laced with frustration. "I'm not saying you're doing a bad job. The problem is you're doing a damn good one. But I need you to stop before I lose control."

He urged her head back and his cock slid from her lips. Gently, he helped her to stand.

"You don't know how good you make me feel. Jesus. It was incredible." He threaded his fingers through her hair, pushing it back from her face.

"Then why—?"

He touched a finger to her lips. "First of all—and this is not a slam in any way—I'm guessing you haven't done this a lot. You have to work up to it, babe. To learn how to angle your head and let me slide down the back of your throat." He feathered a kiss over her lips. "And I'm going to teach you, because no way are we crossing this off the list. But right now I want you on your back on the bed and me between your legs."

He lifted her, bent enough to pull back the covers, and placed her carefully on the sheet. He stood looking at her for a long moment, hunger flashing in his eyes, before climbing onto the mattress and kneeling between her thighs.

Emma had never been so aroused in her entire life.

Marc made himself stop and take a deep breath. What was it about this woman that the moment he touched her, his control always frayed? He'd never wanted a woman the way he wanted her. And it wasn't just sex. If that were the case after the first couple of nights, the edge would be off. He'd have settled down into a pattern with her, and it wouldn't be every time he saw her. He wanted this to go forward, but hell! She wouldn't even tell him her name. Yet deep inside, he knew they had something pretty special. He just didn't know what to do about it.

He took a long time with her body, trailing slow wet kisses starting at the sensitive spot behind her ear, over the slope of her breasts, down her tummy, pausing to swirl the tip of his tongue in the indentation of her navel. He licked the seam where each thigh and hip joined, a light touch that skimmed her flesh before moving down the length of each leg. He paid special attention to her knees and ankles, even the arches of her feminine, graceful feet. He couldn't seem to get enough of tasting her. He wondered if he ever would.

At last, when she was trembling beneath his hands, he spread the lips of her pussy with his thumbs and allowed himself a long, slow lap of pleasure. Her taste was intoxicating, sweet and tart at the same time, the flavor of it surging through his system. He flicked the nub of her clit back and forth, the bundle of nerves swelling beneath his touch. Her sensual little whimpers made his cock throb and his entire body tighten.

Stiffening his tongue, he thrust it inside her, tiny spasms in the walls of her cunt flexing against the intrusion. It was one of the most erotic things he'd ever experienced. Each time he sensed her closing in on an orgasm he backed off, soothing her then arousing her again.

He was so close to his own release now, the memory of her soft mouth on him an incredible aphrodisiac. He needed her to catch up because he sensed his control fast unraveling. Fucking her with his tongue, he stroked her clit again and again. *Rub, rub, rub*. He drove her up to a precipice, pushing her there, and when he could tell she was hanging by a thread, he sheathed himself with a shaky hand and drove into her with one fluid movement.

He tensed for a long moment, steadying himself, enjoying the feel of her around him like a tight, wet fist. Then he let himself go, pumping into her as she shattered around him, shouting "Music Lady" as he poured himself into her. At last he collapsed forward, exhausted, physically drained but filled with an emotion he dared not give a name to.

Emma couldn't ever remember being so thoroughly exhausted yet so filled with pleasure at the same time. She hadn't thought it possible for sex to be mystical, but with Marc that's exactly what it had become. Every part of her body sang as if touched by some enchanted fog drifting over it and surrounding her. For a fleeting moment, she wished the rest of the world would disappear, and there would be nothing and no one except for her and Marc.

Too bad such a thing wasn't possible.

Dragging more air into his lungs, he shifted position to pull her into his arms and gave her a gentle kiss. She could taste herself on his lips, an exotic awareness that flooded her senses. Lifting her hands, she smoothed her fingers through his hair, moist with the perspiration of exertion and inhaled his scent, a combination of musk and something earthy. She was sure the outdoors would forever be sexy and intoxicating.

He molded her to his body, her head cradled against his shoulder, one of her hands resting against the damp matte of his chest hair. His hands idly stroked her down the length of her back and the slope of her buttocks.

"You okay?" he asked when his breathing had evened out.

"More than okay. Much, much more."

"Good. That's good. So. Favorite television show."

She frowned. "What?"

"You know. Twenty Questions. I ask, you give me an answer, then it's your turn."

"I answered a bunch the other night. Why do you want to know this stuff, anyway?" A tiny knot formed in the pit of her stomach. She couldn't give away too much information to him. Sure, it was great they were learning more about each other, but what if she slipped and gave him clues she didn't want him to follow? She was torn between sharing intimacy that went beyond sex and opening the door to the real Emma too wide.

"Like I said earlier. We've got something special going here. I don't want to lose it. I'm hoping I can get you to the point where you trust this enough—trust *me* enough—so we can move forward with this."

Trust? Was that possible? She was growing more and more comfortable with him, but she trusting someone meant giving up a part of yourself to them and that little clutch of fear made her hold back a little. What would it take for her to cross that boundary completely? On the one hand she was so ready to do this. On another, fear of rejection held her in its grip.

"ML?" He nudged her. "Where did you go?"

She shook off the mental tap dance. "Huh? Oh, sorry." *Make an excuse.* "I just get lost listening to your voice, I guess."

"Not a bad thing. But as I was saying, I want to know anything about you I can." He winked. "Besides, I've got good stuff to tell you tonight, so come on. Play along. Favorite television show."

"Hmm. The Good Wife."

"Really?" He grinned. "Not American Idol?"

"I don't watch...." She swatted at him. "You're teasing me. No fair."

"Okay, okay. Anyway, it's your turn now."

They tossed questions back and forth for a few minutes. Emma caught glimpses of Marc she didn't see on stage or in bed. Things that made up the real person. Was that what he was doing with her?

Her confidence grew each time they were together, and she was feeling better about herself when she was with him. But what if she took that final leap? The specter of her parents loomed over her along with their friends and the people at her office. The purple streak in the hair had already been a cause for comment. What would they think of Marc?

Grow up, Emma. You aren't sixteen any more.

"ML?"

"Yeah?"

"Where did you go?" He stroked his thumb down the line of her jaw. "You drifted away for a minute."

"I'm here."

"Ask me if I have any big news."

She looked at him, startled. "Do you?"

"Ask the question," he prompted.

"Okay, okay." She flopped back on the pillows. "Marc, do you have any big news for me?"

He grinned. "Maybe."

"No fair," she cried. "That's not an answer."

"Hmm. I think you're right. Well. You know we're only at Aftershock for one more week."

Emma tensed. Was he leading into a goodbye? Giving her time to adjust to the fact in seven days this would all be over? Was this his big news? Surely he wouldn't do it so casually. Would he?

Why not, you idiot? All you show up for is sex. Has he had enough? Didn't you worry that was the way he saw you? Now the shoe's probably on the other foot.

"So what's next for you?" She hoped she sounded more casual than she felt.

"Two things." He kissed her forehead and wound his fingers through her hair. "The biggest thing is a possible huge concert date at the Amphitheatre."

She leaned her head back so she could see his face. "The Amphitheatre? The big concert facility? I see ads for it all the time. That really *is* huge. A big deal for Lightnin'."

"It is. You have no idea."

She sensed the excitement rippling through him, like music in a finely tuned instrument.

"So give," she said. "I want all the details."

She listened carefully while he explained about Rick Trajean's connection with the manager of Deep Blue River. About the band forced to cancel as the opening act at the Amphitheatre. And about the invitation for Rick to meet with Butch Meredith with a good video of the band he could critique and decide if Lightnin' would be a good fit for Deep Blue River. If they were professional enough. Exciting enough.

"We're really humping this weekend to get the video finished and fine-tuned. There's so much that goes into it, and we've only got two days."

"Is that what you did today?" She pushed herself up on one elbow so she could really look at him. "You must be exhausted."

His grin was so seductive she thought it should be illegal. "I can always find energy for you, ML."

She brushed her lips across the stubble on his jaw. "So tell me about it. How you do it? You know."

"Well." He cupped a breast, lightly rubbing his thumb over the nipple. "We did the video portion today. Shot the visual as well as us singing and playing the song. But we won't use that sound."

"Why not?"

"It's scratchy. Not blended. It's just so we'll have the lip movements to blend the soundtrack with. Tomorrow we'll lay down the real tracks—"

"Lay down the tracks?" she interrupted. "What are tracks?"

"Recording of the actual song," he answered. "Each vocal and each instrument is captured in a separate track. Then the sound engineer will do the mix and sync it to our singing on the video. And if it all comes together, we'll have a polished video like the ones you see on The Music Channel. Or YouTube."

"I don't watch The Music Channel." She was embarrassed to admit it, wondering if he'd think she was a dork.

"YouTube, then." His thumb continued to idly rub her nipple. "You know what YouTube is, right?"

"Uh huh. Of course I do. *But I don't go there to watch rock bands*. Of course she didn't need to tell him that.

"There you go. And if we're really, really, really lucky, the gods will smile on us and the whole thing will come together in a perfect package."

"And you can do that all in two days?" She had so little knowledge of how anything like this worked.

"We have to. It's all the time we have and anyway, we fell into an empty slot in everyone's schedule so we got bottom rates for it."

She kissed him lightly. "Marc, that's so exciting. When will you know?"

"Monday after Rick meets with Butch Meredith."

She hated herself for asking the next question. "But the week in between you'll be gone someplace else, right?"

"Actually, it's an off week for us. We planned it that way. Now we'll have time to rehearse our set. If we get the gig. Deep Blue River's record guys will be there and if they like us...."

His voiced trailed off even though the exhilaration radiating from him was electric. Even Emma knew this could be a very big break for the band. She wanted to be thrilled for him—and she was, but also far from ready to let him go. She was just so afraid if all this happened, the fragile relationship growing between them would somehow disappear.

And there was the old Emma, still uncertain and unsure.

"Hey." He moved his hand away from her breast and pulled her down into his arms. "If we get the date, would you like to come and see it?"

Her heart thudded. "The concert? Really? You could get me a ticket?"

He laughed. "I could do even better. I'll get you a pass. Tell you what door to come in and what to do. What do you think?"

"When is it?"

"Next Sunday night. Can you make it?"

Emma nearly shook with suppressed delight. Make it? How could she not? And it was her birthday! What a great present.

"I'd love it. Are you sure it's okay?"

"Absolutely." He hugged her tightly. "We'll get a limited number of passes, and I really would like you to be there."

Ohmigod! He wanted her to be there with his friends. Out in a place much bigger than Aftershock. So she was important enough for him to include her. She wondered if the redhead she'd seen at the club would be there and if so, who was bringing her? And would she be all over Marc?

But then a thought struck at her, diminishing her enthusiasm. "You'd have to know...."

"Your name?" he finished, as if knowing what she was about to say. "Would it really be so bad for you to tell me?"

Would it? Why did she continue to cling to such concealment, like some kind of security blanket? She'd been intimate with him in ways she'd only imagined before. But they were so different. From separate worlds. Now it was more than the inability to get past the fear that the bubble would burst, and she'd need a place to hide and heal her broken heart. She was equally nervous about bringing him into her world, worried people would only see the rocker with the tattoo sleeve and long hair and not the intelligent, caring, solid individual she was coming to see him as. The normal things she'd learned about him.

No. She wasn't ready to chance it yet.

Scaredy-cat.

"I know you think it's stupid," she told him. "I'm sorry. If you want to change your mind about the concert...."

"No." His arms tightened around herm and he feathered a kiss over her forehead. "I'll work it out. I respect you enough, ML, to wait until you trust me enough to tell me yourself. To really let me into your life. "

"Thank you." She pressed herself against him. "You're just so...thank you." Her heart squeezed at his words and tears clogged her throat. Maybe they did have something real here if she could just take that last step. She could see happiness with him shimmering just beyond that final barrier if she just had the courage to reach out and grab it.

"I definitely want you there at the concert. With me." Another light kiss. "You'll really get to see first hand what this business is all about."

"Are you sure?"

"Of course I'm sure. It's a very special night for me and I want to share it with you. How can I make music without my Music Lady?"

"This is like a dream come true for you, isn't it?"

"It's what every musician works for. Pushes himself for. Dreams of." He kissed her forehead. "Don't you have dreams, Music Lady?"

Of course she did. Could she tell him?

"Well?" he persisted. "Come on, everyone has dreams."

"Yes," she answered in a small voice. She'd never let anyone in on this secret. "I want to write."

"Yeah?" His eyes lit up. "Sounds great. Write what?"

"Um, well, romance novels." Her heart of heart's desire. She had notebooks filled with scribbled ideas, still shoved in a box in her closet where no one would find them. Her hidden dreams that she'd never had the guts to go after. Kind of like the way she was afraid to take that final step with Marc.

"So why don't you?"

She shrugged. "I don't know." But she did. Not enough

courage. Not enough faith in herself. Fear of criticism by her parents. By the few men in her life. Especially Andrew.

"ML, listen. Music was *my* dream and when I was a lot younger, I was afraid to reach for it. All of us in the band were. Except maybe for Rick. But we took one step and then another and look where we are now."

"There's a lot of rejection in the publishing business," she pointed out.

"Just like in the music business. But if you settle for nothing, then nothing's all you'll ever have.

Just like she'd been willing to settle for Andrew.

"If it's truly your dream," he went on, "you should give yourself a chance. Worst case, you won't be any worse off than you are now. Right?"

"I guess so." If she could accept what Marc was offering and give herself completely to him, trust and all, then she could also reach for her dreams. Somehow believing in him and believing in herself all became wrapped up together.

She glanced at the red numbers on the clock beside the bed and sighed. It was that time again.

Each time it got harder and harder for her to do this: pull away from him and leave before dawn. Her heart was seriously involved now, and she had to admit to herself how much she'd enjoy waking up in his arms. Having breakfast with him. Maybe cooking for him in his magnificent kitchen, although if cooking was his thing, she'd let him wait on her. Reading the Sunday paper together. All the things making up a relationship. She was so conflicted, as if her heart was taking flight while her feet were locked to the ground in cement shoes.

But she was fighting thirty years of ingrained behavior that refused to let go. Breaking the final tie was damn hard.

He tensed beside her. "Can't you stay? Just a little longer? I still want to take you to breakfast."

"No. I'm sorry. I...I really have to go."

Reluctantly, she eased herself from his arms, slid from the bed and dressed quickly. He had no idea how bad she wanted to stay, but sticking to her routine was another part of her self-protection. At least it was the weekend, and she could sleep in. Thank God.

"You'll be back next week?"

"Of course. But...maybe not every night. Okay?" She needed some breathing room. Time to get her head straightened out again. She hadn't let him know that next Sunday, the night of the concert, was her birthday. Truthfully she wasn't sure yet if she was going to. She couldn't figure out why he kept choosing to spend so much time with her instead of someone like the redhead from the club. Someone flashier, more outgoing, more into "the scene".

"I'll take what I can get." His voice was strained but his smile was warm.

"Thank you."

As usual Marc climbed out of bed naked and followed her through the house to the front door. "Music Lady?"

She turned, her hand on the doorknob. "Yes?"

"Just...this."

He cradled her face in his warm palms and pressed his mouth to hers. His tongue slipped inside as if it belonged there, tasting her inner surfaces, drinking from her. He kissed her until she couldn't breathe.

"Keep that in mind until I see you again." He stroked a finger along her cheek.

This time he didn't come out on the porch to watch her leave, simply stood in the doorway. The image of him burned itself into her brain. Along with a thought she wanted desperately to dismiss.

She was falling in love with Marc Malone.

"A concert?" Annie's eyes widened. "He's getting you a backstage pass to a concert?"

"Uh huh." Emma took a bite from the slice of pizza she was

holding.

The two women sat cross-legged on Annie's living room floor, the pizza box between them, a half-empty bottle of wine on the coffee table along with two glasses. She'd slept late, exhausted in a well-sated way from the hours with Marc. Then Annie called late in afternoon demanding the latest details and offering wine and pizza as a bribe.

"And they're opening for Deep Blue River?"

"Maybe." Emma chewed, swallowed, and took a sip of her wine. "They're making the tracks today and blending everything for the video."

"*Recording* the tracks," Annie corrected. "And mixing the sound."

Emma lifted an eyebrow. "Since when are you so familiar with the lingo?"

"Since I was sixteen and hung up on rock music and soaking in everything I could like every other teenager. Except you." She laughed, but her face sobered instantly. "Honey, I did not mean anything by it. Okay? Please?"

Emma tucked her hair behind her ears. "I know you didn't. I'm just now beginning to realize all the things I missed out on." She took another sip of wine, wishing that her parents could be half as understanding. That they could see beyond the Emma they'd created. The thought of explaining Marc to them very nearly gave her a case of the hives. "Still, I can't keep blaming my parents. They raised me the way they'd always lived, my friends were the same and I guess I was oblivious to everything else."

"Too bad I wasn't around." She swallowed a bite of pizza. "I'd have turned you into the original wild child."

"I'll bet. And gotten me grounded for life."

They were both silent for a long moment.

"So when will they know for sure about next Sunday night?" Annie wiped pizza sauce from her lips.

"Tomorrow. Whenever the band leader meets with Deep Blue River's manager." Emma popped the last of the crust in her mouth.

"Deep Blue River." A long sigh drifted on the air. "I have every one of their CDs."

"You do?" Emma caught her breath. "So they really are famous?"

"Yes, honey. They really are. I know you have a CD player, in your car as well as your house. What do you listen to?"

Emma shrugged. "Glee. The Beatles. Michael Bublé."

"Okay, okay, okay." Annie drained her glass and refilled it from the wine bottle. "Education time. Deep Blue River is one of the hottest rock bands around. Especially here because they're home grown. Their last single debuted at the number three spot on the charts and in a week it was at the top."

Emma was curious. "So what do they sound like?"

Annie chuckled. "I'll put in a CD and you can hear them for yourself. Have some more wine, lean back, and prepare to be wowed."

She turned on her stereo, popped a CD in the player and hit the play button. Immediately the sharp sound of an electric guitar crashed into the room, a shower of notes that instantly filled the air. Then the heavy cadence of the bass guitar, building the foundation of the song. The drummer, and then all of it came together in music so powerful Emma was mesmerized. She simply sat, leaning back against the couch, letting the sound grab her until the final notes of the song had faded.

In seconds, the intro began to the next cut but Annie turned the volume way down.

"We can listen to them in the background now you've gotten the full impact,"

"I don't think Deep Blue River could ever be just background music. Holy crap, Annie. They're incredible. And I don't even know anything about rock music."

"See what you've been missing?" Annie winked. Then she sobered. "This is a huge deal, Emma. It could mean big things for Lightnin'."

"That's what Marc said. He mentioned Deep Blue River's record people will be there, too."

Annie sat back down across from her and tilted her head, studying her friend's face. "This could mean a lot of changes. If they're offered more dates, Marc could be gone for long periods of time. You think you could handle that?"

"Listen. I don't even know if he'll still want anything to do with me if this all happens for him. He'll be very busy and I'm...I'm...."

"You're what?"

"I keep having this feeling I'm just a novelty to him. A little different from all the other women he...hangs out with. But if the band gets this break, I'm sure I'll be history. I'm not glamorous or exciting enough to be part of that atmosphere."

"Emma Blake, that is just bullshit and you know it. You're making excuses again."

"Maybe. But maybe not. I look at all the other women in that club and realize how different I am. And can't help wondering what the hell he's doing with me." She couldn't stop comparing herself to Lacey, even though Marc had reassured her he wasn't into the redhead.

Annie snorted. "Yeah, right. You idiot. Men don't take 'novelties' home with them night after night. Or invite them to be their guest at a major concert event. Guess again, girlfriend. I keep telling you not to borrow trouble, don't I?" She rubbed her forehead. "Damn. Your parents and that dipshit Andrew really did a number on you."

"Whatever. It's just hard to get past all these years of thinking and living a certain way."

"Have some confidence in yourself, for God's sake. Show the guy some trust." Annie snapped her fingers. "Wait a minute. Next Sunday's your birthday, right? I don't suppose you bothered to tell him."

Emma ran a fingertip around the rim of her wine glass. "I know it's stupid but I don't know if I should. If the band gets this deal that's cooking, I keep thinking he'll want to be with women bolder than me. Women who know the ropes, who are better suited to his new lifestyle. To his fame. Then it's back to dull reality for me. The very thing I've been afraid of all this time What if when he sees me with all his friends and the women they have, he decides he I'm all wrong for him?"

"What if he doesn't?" Annie sipped slowly from her goblet. "Emma, I've seen you go through some wonderful changes in a very short time. Blossoming into a new, more confident, more vibrant person. That's the person you should take to that concert. Flaunt it, kiddo. You've got it. Let those other women know you've got what he wants."

"I hear you." Emma sighed. "I'm still catching up with myself and trying to figure out if I'm making a huge mistake or not. If I can tell him who I am. And if I don't, will he finally just wash his hands of me and tell me to get lost?"

"The choice is yours. But it sure would be a nice present for him on his big night."

"I know." She looked at Annie with a steady gaze. "And you're right. This is the right time to take that final step. If I want him I have to give him all of me."

"Good for you. But I'm here if you need me. To fall apart or to celebrate."

"I'm counting on that."

Chapter Twelve

"*And love comes easy*
On the edge of the woods."

Danny stopped turning and leaned against the thick trunk of an oak tree, let his arms fall to his sides and his head drop. The rest of the band had eased their way into the trees. Marc knew Jado would electronically fade each of them out of the pictures and bring in the image of the woman they'd been singing about, a fantasy woman who kept disappearing into the woods until they found the magic to make her stay.

The song made him think about Music Lady and the way she disappeared after each of their nights together. Why couldn't *he* find the magic to make *her* stay?

"Okay," Jado called. "That's it. I think we've got everything we need."

Knowing how important this was to Lightnin', Jado had brought another cameraman as well as various lights and people to set them. And taken great pains to get shot after shot so he'd have all the footage he needed.

It's a good thing he's not charging us his going rate. We'd be broke for the next ten years.

They'd plotted out what the video should look like ahead of

time. Some shots with instruments. A lot of them without. Now the band would get ready to go to work, and Jado would go into his studio to turn raw footage into incredible video. Then tomorrow they'd do it all over again with the soundtrack. And tomorrow night, the two electronic results would be blended into a video they all hoped would seal the deal with Butch Meredith and boost Lightnin' up a big notch.

Marc wiped his bass down and placed it carefully in its case. Garrett was breaking down his drums, and Danny was giving him a hand. Rick had walked over to chat with his cousin. Marc moved up to join them.

"Hey, thanks for everything." He bumped knuckles with Jado. "We really appreciate this."

Jado nodded. "I think we got a good piece of video out of this." He looked at Rick. "You're up for a late night tomorrow, right?"

"As long as it takes."

"All right, then. See you tomorrow night."

Marc was in the parking lot, stowing his guitar, when Rick walked over to him.

"Good job today."

"Were you expecting me to do otherwise?" Marc closed the rear door to the Jeep and glanced at his friend.

"You've been a little distracted lately, you know."

"I'm fine," he insisted. "And I'll *be* fine. For whatever we need."

Rick held up his hands. "Whatever. Just checking. And letting you know I'm here if you need to talk."

"I said I'm fine." Marc slammed the door to the Jeep then sucked in a breath and let it out slowly. "Sorry. I didn't mean to bite your head off. I know how important this thing is. You don't need to worry about me."

"We've been working toward this for three years," Rick reminded him.

"And I'm just as aware of it as you are. No worries here. Okay?"

"Okay."

They bumped fists and Marc climbed into his Jeep.

He'd meant what he said to Rick. He was, after all, a professional. But what if they got the gig with Deep Blue River? What if they ended up shuffling club dates around for the more desirable major concert venues, and he lost contact with the woman carving a place for herself in his heart?

Get your head straight, buddy boy. Time enough to worry about Music Lady after tomorrow. When you know what's really going to happen.

Monday, the band hung at Marc's house while they waited for Rick. Each of them did their best to look casual but they were all wound tight as a coil of steel. Garrett had a set of drumsticks with him and persisted in beating a tempo on the ottoman until Marc was ready to kick him in the ass. Danny had made himself scarce in the spare room, working off the nervous energy with the free weights until he was covered with sweat. When they were about ready to jump out of their collective skins, the doorbell rang and Rick walked in.

Marc tried to get a read on the situation but the guitar player was wearing his best poker face. For a moment his stomach pitched, and he had a sour taste in his mouth.

We didn't get it.

Then Rick's face split into a huge smile and he shouted, "We're in." He pumped his fist in the air and laughed like an idiot. "We. Are. In."

"He liked it?" Marc was trying to absorb the reality of the news.

"He didn't jump up and down, if that's what you're asking. But he watched the video several times, making notes while he did, then sat back and said we were a good fit for his guys, and we had the sound and energy he was looking for. And the appearance."

They pounded each other on the back, laughing, shouting. This was it. The chance they'd been working so hard for. A concert appearance with a band at the top of the charts and exposure to a major record label. If everything went well next Sunday night, they'd be leaping to the next level.

"Okay, settle down." Rick dropped down to the couch and let his gaze travel over each of them. "We have a lot of work to do between now and then. This week we can rehearse at the club while we finish out our contract there. Then I've got a place lined up for us to use every day next week. We pick the best of our material, including *On the Edge of the Woods*, and go to work."

Marc watched the others leave then closed the door and leaned against it. This was it. He could hardly believe it. A garage band the people said initially wouldn't go anywhere, and here they were. He wanted to call ML and share the good news with her, tell her it was really going to happen, but damn! He didn't have her name so obviously no number.

He couldn't ever remember being this frustrated. Why couldn't she trust him enough to open the last door? He'd done his best to show her his feelings, to get to know her, to ease her along, sensing how skittish she was. But now he wanted her here with him, wanted to enjoy this moment with her.

Wanted to work her into the fabric of his life as it moved into a new arena.

The next time you see her, you better be at the top of your game with her.

Emma picked at her food, wondering how she'd let herself get talked into this meal. She'd felt guilty she wouldn't be spending her birthday with them, but now they were at her about it again.

"I have other plans that day." Emma looked from one parent to the next. "I already told you that."

I love my family but I know what their agenda is. I'm so

tired of having this conversation over and over and over. And how is it a woman my age can still feel like such a child with her parents? I'm an adult.

I'm an adult.

I'm an adult.

Maybe if she repeated it enough she'd even believe it. But her mother and father had the ability to put her on the defensive, reducing her to the five-year-old child who'd broken an expensive toy belonging to someone else.

Suck it up, Emma.

Her mother's smile was just the slightest bit forced. "I know, dear, but you've been acting so strange lately, we thought a celebration dinner would be a good time to get things back to normal."

"Normal." Emma lifted an eyebrow. "What's that supposed to mean? I'm as normal as I ever was."

"Well, if your mother won't say it, I will." Her father set down his knife and fork precisely on the edge of his plate. "We don't understand what's come over you. Breaking up with Andrew. Going to strange places at night you've never been to before. Doing something to your hair color and putting in that god-awful purple streak. Avoiding us. Yes, avoiding," he emphasized when she opened her mouth to contradict him. "You think I don't know what you're doing? Letting your answering machine pick up and not calling back unless you're sure we aren't home?"

She couldn't really deny it. She had been dodging them, unwilling to answer their questions or explain something to them she wasn't even sure she understood herself. She took a sip of water, giving herself time to collect her thoughts.

"I wish you could understand. I'm not doing anything bad"— *much*—"and I'm going to be *thirty years old*. Don't you think I'm a little past having to make excuses to my parents or ask permission for what I'm doing?"

Angela Blake sighed heavily. "It's just we like Andrew so much. He's such a nice, steady young man. So dependable."

"So dependable," she echoed. *So boring.*

"What's wrong with dependable?" Her father demanded. "A lot of women would give anything to have a dependable man."

"But the choice of a man is mine, not yours," she said, biting back her frustration.

Yet how could she be so exasperated with them when the blame for this situation was equally on her shoulders? Until a few weeks ago, she'd gone placidly along in the life they'd raised her to lead, never dreaming she was missing anything. Until Jacie breezed through town and opened doors she hadn't even known existed.

Now her parents were having trouble understanding this new version of her and with good reason. The adventurous person who'd been hiding inside her very precise, very controlled self had burst forth without warning, and she continued the struggle and understand it. To figure out after all these years who she really was.

"Oh, honey, you're absolutely right." Angela reached out a hand to her daughter's arm. "We're just concerned is all. You seem so...different lately. Drifting away from us. We just thought it would be nice to spend your birthday together."

"Why don't you tell us what you've got planned?" her father asked. "Maybe we can join you."

Emma swallowed a hysterical laugh. "I don't think you'd be very comfortable. I'm going to a concert."

"We've been to concerts before," her mother said. "What wouldn't we enjoy?"

"This is a rock concert. You don't even like the music. And that's okay," she added hastily as she saw her mother's lips thin. "We each have different tastes. I just want you to acknowledge there's nothing wrong with it."

"I suppose it's dumb to ask if Andrew's going with you," her father said drily.

"Andrew? Why would it even occur to you? How many times do I have to tell you Andrew and I are no longer together?" Emma's eyes widened. "Let me guess. He's been bugging you again, hasn't he? I'm sure he's bending your ear, despite the fact

I asked him to back off." She pounded her fist on the table. "Damn him. He needs to get a life. A *new* life."

"Emma." Her father sighed. "He really would like the two of you to get back together again. All he's done is ask for our help."

"Not happening." She looked from one parent to the other. "It's over. I told him and I'm telling you again. He needs to move on. And what kind of man keeps bugging a woman's parents like this? It's not as if we're teenagers. No, you'll just have to understand that it's over with Andrew and me, and so will he. There's no fixing. No going back. It's done. Period. The end."

Angela smiled at her. "I guess it's just so hard for us to realize you're an adult. Almost thirty. And to accept that you've had some kind of epiphany or metamorphosis or whatever and are making big changes in your life."

No kidding. Hard for me, too.

"Mom. I'm definitely old enough. You can trust me to make good decisions."

Oh, yeah, right.

"All right." Angela rose and began to clear the plates. "Then let's just have dessert."

"How about if we have dinner the night before?" she suggested. "But without Andrew." She looked from one to the other, mentally crossing her fingers. She didn't want to shut them out completely. "Will that work?"

Her parents exchanged a look but in a moment they both nodded.

"And I'll do my best to tell Andrew he needs to start looking elsewhere," her father added.

"Thank you," Emma breathed. "I'd appreciate it."

"You definitely need a new outfit," Annie said.

Emma wrinkled her forehead. "Another one?"

"Absolutely."

It was Thursday night and they were at Annie's having their

own happy hour with margaritas from Annie's blender. She just hadn't been in the mood for Hot Salsa and besides, at Annie's she was much more comfortable. It occurred to Emma that she was soaking up a lot more alcohol lately than she was used to. But right now she needed liquid courage. Her brunch with her parents had been far less confrontational than she'd expected. But Andrew had been waiting in front of her house when she came home and that confrontation hadn't gone nearly as well. Only when she'd threatened to report him as a stalker did he get the message and leave. Hopefully for the last time.

Why hadn't she ever seen this stubborn streak in him before? Or was it the need for control? Either way, she was done with him. After Marc's invitation to the concert and the resurgence of all her fears, she'd stayed away from the club this week and had done a lot of soul searching. Trying to find the answers to who she was before and who she was now. When she saw Marc again, she wanted to be a lot less conflicted. When she was with him she tended to lose sight of everything else.

"Hey. Earth to Emma."

Her head snapped up. "Did you say something?"

"Apparently nothing you heard. Where was your brain? Not at here, that's for sure."

Emma sighed and sipped some of her drink through the straw. "Sorry. Just...thinking."

"About Mr. Hottie?" Annie laughed. "I pulled up the picture of the band again. My, my, my. He is one sweet, luscious man."

Heat crawled up her cheeks. "Actually I was mentally cursing Andrew again. And myself for acting like I was a docile child for so many years."

"Listen, girlfriend." Annie touched her arm. "There's absolutely nothing wrong with parents wanting their kids to have a nice, safe life. And for a lot of people that's definitely more than enough. But everyone's tastes are different, Emma. It just took you a lot of years to find out what yours really are."

"I know, I know. I'm just so conflicted."

"Okay. Do you really, really like this guy?"

"More than like, I think." She licked some of the salt from the rim of her glass. "Can you fall in love with someone so quickly, Annie?"

Her friend shrugged. "Sometimes all it takes is twenty-four hours. But Emma. If that's the way you feel about him, don't you think you at least should tell him your name? Playing that game is getting a little old."

Emma nibbled her thumbnail. "I just wish I could be sure how he felt about me. I have this panicky feeling that if the concert goes well and things go well for him, that's the last I'll see of him."

"Why? He might be on the road but today we have such things as cell phones and video chats." Annie grinned. "You've heard of those, right?"

"Of course. But he has to *want* to use them. Annie, I can't keep up with him. Who am I? An almost-thirty-year-old woman with a boring job and a boring life."

"Honey, if you were so boring he might take you home with him once. Maybe even twice. But that would be the end of it. Have a little confidence in yourself."

Emma chuffed a short laugh. "I can just imagine what my folks would say if I showed up at their house with him."

"Your folks need to accept the fact you're a grown woman making your own choices." She paused. "Are you ashamed of him, Emma?"

"Hell, no. I just wouldn't want them to make him uncomfortable."

"I think it's all in how you present the situation."

That was so true. The sharp edges of her relationship with her parents were easing. Maybe they'd be more receptive. Especially since his background apparently wasn't all that different from hers. If she wanted something permanent with him, she had to be the one to set the stage with her family. If she cared enough for him, then this was what she needed to do. Be proud of him. Show her feelings. Let everyone–*everyone*–know they were together.

"Meanwhile," Annie continued, "you won't be taking him anywhere if you don't tell him who you are."

"I know, I know."

Annie scooped some salsa with a chip and popped it into her mouth. "Maybe the night of the concert would be a good time. Especially if things go really well. He'll want to celebrate with you. You can tell him your name and about your birthday at the same time."

"Fine. Fine, fine, fine." She drew in a deep breath and blew it out. "I'll do it then." *And hope Miss Redhead isn't there or attempts to get in my face.*

"Then Saturday we need to go shopping and get you a new outfit. Which is how I started this conversation."

"Another new one?"

Annie nodded. "Something really special." She winked. "Just put yourself in my hands, girlfriend. I've got ideas."

Emma laughed. "That's what I'm afraid of."

"Just remember." Her friend was giving her the no nonsense look. "It's you he wants or this would have been over long ago. "He likes what you bring to his life. And he's proud enough of you that he wants to show you off."

"I can't help being nervous. You know that."

"This is going to work. I feel it, Emma. Now let's get you tricked out so you can knock the socks off everyone."

"I only care about one person, Annie."

"I know, but this is kind of your coming out party, sweetie. No more hiding in the shadows or keeping your name a secret. Showing Marc that you're definitely the prize he wants." She winked. "Not to mention his friends and all those groupies that hang around the band."

"Yeah?"

Annie smiled at her. "Yeah. This is it, Emma, The brass ring. Just grab for it."

In that moment Emma actually felt she might be able to do it.

This is stupid. Idiotic. I must be braindead.

It was early Thursday evening and for the second day in a row, Marc was prowling the grocery store where he'd first run into Music Lady. How long could he hang out with an empty basket before the manager got suspicious and called the police? But he figured since if he'd bumped into her there once before, she must live in the neighborhood and it would be logical for her to appear again.

Maybe she'd need something on her way home from work. Wherever she worked. He hadn't gotten around to asking her that yet. He was saving the more personal questions for when her skittishness wore off.

In the meantime, he had this insane need to see her. Make sure she was coming back to the club again. Two nights running, he'd even checked out Hot Salsa during Happy Hour to see if she and her friend were there having a drink. *Nada.* He missed her almost more than he wanted to admit, trying not to watch the door. Hoping each time it opened, she'd be walking through it. He just had to keep telling himself that she had a good reason for staying away, but for the life of him he couldn't figure out what it could be. He just hoped to hell she hadn't changed her mind about the concert. If this all came together, she was the one he wanted to share it with.

A flash of blue caught the corner of his eye and a thrill of anticipation ran through him. He turned, expecting to see her pushing her cart into the produce area and started in that direction. But when he looked again, he realized it was a total stranger. Disappointment was a bitter taste in his mouth.

Concentrate on what's coming up, buddy boy. On the things you can do something about.

Rick had met again with Butch Meredith that morning and brought back the contract for them all to look at as well. He also had the layout of the Amphitheatre and the list of what they could request, including one guest pass per musician. Marc wanted to be sure he'd see ML at least by the weekend to make sure she had hers.

Rich had given him some shit about requesting a pass for a woman who wouldn't even give him her name, but he'd put a cork in it fast enough. This could end up being a really big deal, and he wanted ML there to share it with him.

I must be nuts, fixated on a woman who won't let me know who she really is.

But he'd already figured out that this was a little more than a fixation. Although he'd changed the sheets on his bed, he'd left the pillowcases, hugging her scent to him at night when he fell asleep. How dumb was that? He was also plagued by erotic dreams of her that woke him with a boner beyond painful.

It wasn't just the sex, though. Not by a long shot. It was *her*. Everything about her. He wanted her not just in his bed, but in his life. The problem was how to convince her. Whatever had her wound up so tight internally, the battle was far from over. One thing was clear: trust played a big part in this. He was deliberately going slowly with her because of it. She was as skittish as a creature out of its element.

He just wished he knew what exactly that element was. The little Twenty Questions games he'd coaxed her into playing gave him more information than she realized. A picture blossomed in his mind of a woman with a sharp mind, an inquisitive nature, but one who for some reason had hidden behind barriers most of her life. If he could just find the key to knocking them down, he could tell her what she really meant to him.

And how do you feel, smartass? Are you in love with her? Can you be in love with a woman you know so little about?

The answer, plain and simple, was...yes.

But he wasn't going to find a solution to his problem wandering around among the tomatoes and apples. Sighing, he purchased potato chips out of a sense of guilt and headed home to get ready for work. If he was lucky, the woman of his dreams would show up.

Chapter Thirteen

Marc checked his watch again, wondering if the night would ever end. Keeping his shit together was becoming more and more difficult, and he didn't want to blow this chance. Rick had called a quick meeting between sets in the club's tiny dressing room.

"Okay, guys," he began. "We're packed tonight, probably because it's Friday night and our last week. Everyone seemed a little on edge the first two sets so let's have it. What's going on?"

"I don't know about anyone else," Garrett said, tapping his sticks against his thigh, "but this week has felt a month long."

"It's always like that when something you're waiting for is just around the corner," Marc answered. "But I've been edgy, too.

For a different reason.

"Okay, guys." Rick shoved his hands in his pockets. "Heads up here. We've rehearsed every day and performed at night so your time should have been well taken up. Next week's going to be even more intense. What we need to focus on is the fact we have forty minutes to impress everyone—the audience, the record people, promoters, even Deep Blue River. They're looking for an opening act for their next tour and we want to be *it*."

"You said Butch Meredith asked for a better cut of the video." Danny fiddled nervously with his sticks. "Did he say why?"

"No, but I'd say it's a positive indicator of his future plans and they include Lightnin'. This would be first class all the way so let's not do anything to blow it. Like letting a case of nerves distract us. Okay?"

"Yeah."

"Sure."

"You're right, big man."

Marc started toward the door when Rick touched his shoulder.

"You doing okay?"

"Fine. Peachy." Marc rotated his head, trying to work out an annoying kink.

"You just seem a little more tense than usual is all."

"I'm doing my job, right?" he snapped.

"Even better than usual." Rick chuckled. "Maybe sexual deprivation works for you."

"Yeah, right."

He was definitely feeling deprived and it wasn't all sexual. He'd had plenty of chances this week to heat the sheets with women who'd come on to him, especially that damn Lacey. But instead he watched the door every night, hoping to see ML walk through it.

He was in bad, bad shape.

"I'm good, Rick. You don't need to worry about me. I think I'll get some air before we go on again."

He started toward the side door, edging around the crowd. Aftershock was even more packed than usual, everyone determined to see the band's final performances. Even people he hadn't seen since week one crowded into every available inch of space—and some not so available—for a last look at Lightnin'. The deafening screams and applause at the end of each number they'd played created a field of energy crackling in the air.

Like Lightnin'.

"You might want to put it off a little while." Rick spoke directly into his ear to be heard over the noise.

"Oh, yeah? Why's that?"

"Turn around and you'll see."

When he did he nearly stopped breathing. Music Lady was standing right at the edge of the stage, fighting to hold onto her tiny bit of space among the crush of bodies. She'd obviously just arrived because she hadn't even taken time to fight her way to the bar and get a drink.

For some reason she appeared tentative, as if expecting him to blow her off. Then he saw Lacey standing right next to her, jawing in her ear. Well shit. He took the fastest route to her, up on the stage, across the platform, and then jumping off onto the floor. Right between her and Lacey.

"I was just giving your friend the lowdown on the band," Lacey smirked.

"I'll bet." Marc ground his teeth. Lacey had been the biggest pain in the ass for as long as he could remember. He didn't much like used goods and she definitely fell in that category. The Queen of the Groupies didn't take no for an answer. He grabbed ML's arm before Lacey could cause trouble. "Go have fun someplace else, Lacey. I told you. I'm not interested." He tugged ML into the little hallway behind the stage, elbowing his way through the packed crowd. "Don't believe a thing she says, ML."

She lifted her hands in a helpless gesture. "She told me you and she...."

Marc bit back the anger flaring inside him. "She wishes. Lacey's used goods. I'm not interested." He cupped her chin and tilted her face up to his. "In anyone but you."

The moment his gaze locked with hers, heat flamed between them and the uncertainty on her face was replaced with a hunger he was sure matched the one clawing its way through his body. Glancing at his watch, he saw he still had a few minutes before the next set. He took her hand and led her out of the club to their usual spot at the corner of the parking lot. Before she could say a word, he cradled her head and captured her lips in a predatory kiss.

Jesus, she tasted like a hundred kinds of wonderful.

She opened to him at once, surprising him with a need as strong as his own. Her small tongue danced with his, coaxing him to explore every inner surface of her mouth. Her hand slid up his arms to his neck; her fingers threaded into his hair as if she'd never let him go. He closed his eyes and let the intensity of their passion consume him. Everything around them faded away until there was nothing and no one except for him and his Music Lady.

When he finally broke the kiss, his heart was racing, and he was breathing like a long distance runner. Her body was pressed so tightly to his he could feel her heart pounding wildly, and the erratic touch of her breath on his face.

He studied her face, taking in the slumberous look of her eyes and her swollen lips. "I missed you all week. I was afraid you wouldn't come back."

"I said I would," she reminded him.

"I know. But...I mean, I don't even know how to get a hold of you if you just disappear."

"I'm not going to disappear," she assured him.

"But you're also not going to tell me your name, either."

"Not...yet."

He wanted to find the right words to say. He had a bad feeling that whatever poison Lacey had been spewing only underscored the self-doubts she constantly battled. "You know you're special to me, right?"

"I...I hope so."

"Well, you are. You can take it to the bank."

Did she believe him? Believe in *them*? Despite the new hairstyle, the hot new clothes, the slow releasing of inhibitions, she was still like a little bird poised to take flight at the first sign of danger. And he worried each time something would frighten her away. He wanted to tell her just how he felt about her. Was it too soon to say "love"? Was that what it was? Could he at least tell her she'd carved a place for herself in his heart, that he saw things in the future for them if they could get past the last of her reservations? He didn't know if she was ready to hear the words yet, not when she still guarded her identity the way she did. Besides, he wanted a silent but unqualified commitment from her first. He wasn't about to expose himself to a woman who could disappear like smoke and never return.

And how am I going to get around that?

He touched his lips to hers again before sliding his hands down from her face and wrapping his arms around her.

"I have something for you."

She wet her lips. "You do? A present?"

"Sort of. It's your pass for Sunday night."

A grin lit up her face. "Really? You actually got me a pass?"

He frowned. "Did you think I wouldn't? I gave you my word." There was the old trust issue again. He wondered if it had more to do with past experiences or her hesitation in a new environment. No question, he was miles away from any other men she'd been with.

"Do you have it here?" Her eagerness was hard to miss.

An encouraging sign.

"No. It's at home. You'll come home with me tonight, right?"

"Of course." She hugged him. "Did you doubt it?"

Yes.

"Just making sure. Come on. I'll get you a drink before we start the next set."

As he walked her into the bar, all he could think of was his impatience for the last set to be finished so he could be alone. With his Music Lady.

Emma couldn't believe how eager she was for both of them to get naked. She remembered how nervous she'd been that very first night, but each time she was with Marc the panicky feeling faded more and more. She'd tested herself by staying away from the club all week, examining her feelings, trying to make sure it wasn't just the novelty of spectacular sex and the attention of someone in a glamorous industry. A babe magnet who had somehow, someway chosen to be with her.

Part of the old Emma still lingered, feeding her insecurities. In the back of her mind she feared this would all blow up in her face any minute. But she had learned one very important fact during her week of denial—there was no way she could stay away from Marc Malone. Her Guitar Man.

This time the moment the door closed she was the aggressor, the one who grabbed him and kissed him until her senses reeled. Kissed him until neither of them could breathe. She plunged her tongue into his mouth and drank him in.

"Whew! Wow!" Marc pulled away and tilted his head. "Holy shit, ML. Maybe I should insist you stay away more often if this is what happens."

"No, no, no." She shook her head, hardly able to believe she was actually behaving this way. But her entire body hummed with need for this man, and she wanted him *now*. Her fingers trembled as she went to work on his shirt, pushing the buttons through the buttonholes.

"Let's at least get to the bedroom," he insisted, lifting her in his arms.

He carried her down the dark hallway. In the bedroom, he flipped the wall switch, turning on the bedside lamp before setting her on the floor. It was almost a race to see who could undress the other one first. Clothing flew everywhere and then she was flat on her back with Marc hovering over her, the passion in his eyes so strong it was almost singed her with its heat.

"Hurry," she urged.

"Not too fast," he murmured. "I want to touch every part of you. See all of you. I dreamed of you every night this week." He chuffed a laugh. "The boner I wake up with every morning gets bigger and harder every day."

"Me, too." She swallowed a nervous giggle. "Not the boner. I mean about the dreaming."

"Good. I'm glad."

He kissed her again, his hands sliding through her hair, the act one of possession as much as passion, then he moved his lips to the hollow of her throat. "Did you dream of me doing this?" He pinched first one nipple then the other. "And this?" He bit lightly on one pebbled tip.

The pulse in her womb ratcheted up, and she knew her sex was wet and ready for him. "Yes." Her breath came out in a rush. "Yes, I could almost feel your mouth on me."

"Like this?" he asked again, his lips cruising over her breasts, his tongue teasing the pebbled tips. The touch of his mouth sent sparks clear to her toes.

"Yes, like that." She arched into him.

"How about this?" One hand skimmed over her tummy, then his fingers threaded through the curls covering her mound to find her clit. The moment he touched it, fire speared through her.

"More," she begged. "Touch me more."

"Is this what you want?" He rasped his thumb over her sensitive nub again and again.

Every pulse in her body throbbed with delicious need. She widened her legs and lifted her hips to him, trying to tell him silently what she wanted next.

"Oh, yes. Yes, yes."

He kissed her tummy then lower, his tongue twisting through her soft curls until he found her clit again. She trembled beneath his touch as he tugged the swollen bud between his teeth and licked the hot tip. He pulled her into his mouth, sucking gently. She shook under the assault of multiple sensations. Her nipples ached and every part of her sex pulsed with hunger and need.

His skin was hot against hers, the fiery length of his cock burning against her thigh as he moved his fingers in and out of her.

"Feel how hard I am for you?" His words were edged with the roughness of lust. "I've missed you so damn much, Music

Lady. Missed this."

"Me, too," she whispered. "Touch inside me."

"With pleasure," he growled, sliding two fingers into her vagina.

She clamped down on them, hitching her hips to create friction. "Mmmh," she whimpered.

"Good, baby? I like to make it good for you."

He worked a third finger in with the other two, taking her clit into his mouth again until she didn't think she could stand it one more minute.

"Inside me." She could barely form words by now. "All of you. Please. Right now."

He slipped his hand from her wet grasp and rubbed her hot button as he reached for a condom and rolled it onto his pulsing erection.

Emma ran her hands over the hard muscles of his arms and back, relearning his touch, inhaling his familiar scent as she opened her thighs wider for him. She bent her knees to give him better access, digging her heels into the bed and arching up to him. With one hard thrust, he was inside her.

She was complete now. Totally connected to him. Emotions whirled through her like a hurricane, plucking at her heart as the feel of him invaded her body.

His mouth was on hers again, and she sighed into it as he filled every inch of her, the walls of her sex gripping him, clenching him, How had she lasted these past days without this? Without *him?* Her heart squeezed with the intensity of her feelings.

Then he lifted his head and fixed her with his hot gaze, and her thoughts disappeared like smoke.

"I don't know how long I can hold on to this, babe. I think we're both hanging on the edge."

"Yes," she urged. "Hurry. Now."

Balancing his weight on his hands, he pumped into her with a ferocity—a joining that shook her entire body, but she didn't care. It was exactly what she needed. Wrapping her legs around his waist, she hitched herself even closer, riding the wave with him as the orgasm uncoiled inside her like a length of rope caught in the wind. As if they'd received some silent signal, they exploded at the same time, bodies shaking and shuddering with the spasms, breathing raw in the otherwise silent room.

"Good God!"

Marc collapsed forward, catching himself on his forearms before rolling to the side and taking her with him. He was still deep inside her and, at the moment, it was a linking she desperately didn't want to lose.

His soft breath dusted her cheek, the dampness of his body fused with her. She wasn't sure whose heartbeat was banging at her ribs, hers or his, amazed at how in sync they were. She kissed his forehead and brushed the damp hair from his skin. Touching him always sent a surge of warmth through her. How would she survive if he walked away from her? Somehow she had to dig deep enough to conquer this unreasoning fear of hers. Or else face it head on and deal with whatever happened.

He smiled at her with lips swollen from their kisses, the look he gave her melting her like chocolate. "That was some way to start the weekend, ML. If we do it too often I might not survive."

She grinned at him. "Wimp."

"I'll show you wimp," he growled, pushing her onto her back again. Then he moaned, a rueful sound. "But maybe not right this minute. I need one to revive here."

Emma laughed. "I'll give you five."

"We'll see." He kissed her cheeks, her eyelids, her forehead. "You know tomorrow's our last night at Aftershock. Then Sunday, it's the big concert."

"Excited?" she asked. Would she see him next week? See him at all after the big concert?

Will Lacey be there? The little bitch. I should turn Annie loose on her.

"Yes and no." He eased himself slowly from her body, disposed of the condom, and pulled her against him. "This could be a really big break for us. And in this business, they're very hard to come by. You have no idea the intensity of the competition. Everyone who's ever played a high school dance is knocking on the doors."

"But Lightnin' is going to get that chance, right?"

"Yeah, thanks to Rick knowing Butch Meredith. It's a long story, one of those one-in-a-million things you hear about. Usually for other people. I'll tell you about it sometime. Anyway, when the opening act for this show had to cancel, Butch called Rick and here we are."

"And if this goes well?" she persisted. She was so conflicted, on the one hand hearing his excitement and wanting success for him. On the other, she was afraid it would be the thing drawing him away from her.

Be unselfish for a minute, Emma.

But there was the fear, filling her again as she waited for his answer.

"Hopefully more concert dates with them. Maybe interest from the record label. And more money."

"A lot more women, too, I'll bet."

Emma, why can't you keep your mouth shut?

Marc went absolutely still. "Are you worried?"

She tried her best to sound nonchalant. "I have no claim on you."

He cupped her chin and tilted her face toward his. "You know, you could if you wanted to."

She shifted her gaze away from his. All of her emotions warred inside her. She wanted Marc, her Guitar Man. Wanted a life with him. Wanted a joy ride that never ended but carried them into the future. Could she actually fit into his life? It'd be harder to fit him into hers, right? If only she could make a decision and stick to it. But vestiges of the old Emma clung to her like ancient cobwebs, tangling her mind.

"You don't understand. " *I've still got one foot in my other life and can't seem to pull it out.*

"Why not? What are you afraid of?"

That I won't be enough for you. That in the end, despite

what you say, you'll want a woman like Lacey who fits more into the scene. Someone who knows the ins and outs. Who won't accidentally say something stupid. Who won't embarrass you.

Emma worried about that almost as much as anything else. She saw herself as not cool and untrendy. Someone who could easily put her foot in her mouth and say the wrong thing at the wrong time.

"Nothing. Nothing at all." She wriggled from his grasp and pushed herself to a sitting position. As long as he held her like this way, she couldn't think straight. And she wanted desperately to believe nothing he said would change. "Hey, didn't you say you had my concert pass here?"

"Okay, okay, I get the hint." A muscle jumped in his cheek. "But this conversation is far from over."

"My pass, big guy?" Emma hated the uncertainty lingering in her brain. Just when she thought she had things under control, she'd had that sort-of confrontation with Lacey and she couldn't get the redhead's words out of her mind. Despite the fact that Marc kept insisting there was nothing between them, it brought all of her insecurities to the surface again.

Please, please understand, Marc. My Guitar Man.

He tensed for a moment then pulled her back into his arm. "Sure do. I'll give it to you before you leave." He licked her jaw lightly. "You know where the Amphitheatre is, right?"

"Of course."

"Okay, go to the back gate. It's where the roadies and performers enter. There'll be a guard there. Show him your pass and he'll direct you to the door you'll use. The guard there will tell you where our dressing room is, but I'll try to keep an eye out for you."

"What time should I get there?"

"We go on at eight, so if you get there at seven I can hang around the door looking for you."

"Then that's what I'll do. And I'll be on time. Definitely." She snuggled against him, pushing back her own misgivings to assure him. She shared his anticipation and knew what all this could mean for him, and she did want him to have this success. "I'm really excited about this, Marc."

"Excited enough to tell me your name?"

Her stomach tightened at the thought but she'd made a bargain with herself. "Maybe. Depends how good your performance is."

"How about my performance tonight?" He grinned. "The one right here? Doesn't that earn me points?"

"Hmm. I don't know. "She trailed her fingers over his stubbled cheeks and the line of his jaw, pressing her reawakening body against his. Sliding one leg over his, she rubbed her sex against his cock, feeling it pulse in response. *Yes!* "Maybe I should ask for a repeat just to make sure."

"How about a shower first?" His mouth curved in a predatory smile. "We do real good in the shower."

Hunger, so recently satisfied, surged through her again. "Yes, we do."

They took a long shower, leisurely soaping each other and teasing each other to a fever pitch of desire. Then they made long, slow, lazy love. Touching each other everywhere. Tasting each other. Emma had never spent such a sinfully satisfying night in her life.

"One of these nights," Marc told her in his deep, slow voice, "I'm going to show you a few things we haven't even tried yet. Think you'll be ready for me?"

She tried to read the look in his eyes. But all she saw was intense heat. She tried to imagine what things he could be referring to. Maybe something from the erotic romances she read and wrote? Acts she'd conjured up in her imagination? A shiver of anticipation glided over her. "I don't know. Will I like it?"

Red-hot scenes from the erotic romances she read flashed through her mind, things she'd never done but sometimes fantasized about. Would he do some of those things to her? Would they do them together? Anticipation shimmied through her, accelerating her pulses and making her nipples and clit ache with pleasure. Whatever they did, she was glad it would be with Marc, the man who made her body sing in three-part harmony. She wet her lower lip, breath hitching in eager anticipation.

"Oh, babe." He chuckled softly. "I promise you, you'll love it. We'll work up to it, okay?"

How much higher could they go? Emma skimmed her hand over his chest, rubbing the soft fur of the hair curled there and brushing against his nipples. Liquid flooded her sex as her movement drew a gasp from him.

Sleep wasn't even on the menu in the hours that followed. Marc was over her, under her, thrusting up into her as he showed her the best way to ride him. He used his mouth on her and groaned with pleasure when she did the same to him. They explored every inch of each other's bodies until they were almost too exhausted to move.

It was nearly five in the morning by the time they'd had enough of each other. For Emma, with so many of her fears still unresolved, there was a sense of urgency, as if she needed to cram days into hours but again she pushed the uncertainty away.

Don't borrow trouble.

"How about breakfast?" he asked as she pulled her clothes on.

She actually laughed. "You're really hung up on this breakfast thing."

His face was sober when he answered her. "The breakfast thing, as you call it, makes the difference between meaningless sex and something more. And while I have the feeling you might not believe this, right from the beginning I could tell we had something special going here and I want to see where we could take it."

Emma paused in the act of stepping into her shoes. She wanted to tell him she thought he was special, too, but she couldn't manage to push herself that last step. To give everything to him, nothing held back.

I'm being such a child. God, it's a wonder he hasn't just

gotten sick and tired of me and pitched me out. Doesn't that alone say something?

So tell him, you idiot.

She just couldn't make herself say the words. Was she going to lose him, not because he lost interest in her, but his patience wore thin?

Fear was the worst obstacle of all. And now, with the concert and all approaching, she was afraid that she wouldn't be able to keep up. Marc would see it and that would be the end of things. So how could she tell him now what her feelings were?

Finally she asked, "But how could you even know? I mean, the first night you were already asking me to breakfast. Looking for something more."

Marc climbed off the bed and stood before her in his glorious nakedness. "Because I knew then this was something different. Something more. I know you caught it. Sensed it. I don't know what's holding you back but sooner or later I'll find out and then I'll be able to tell you how I really feel about you."

"How can you be so sure this is more than what it seems?" *That you, the man who lives in a world of excitement, could be satisfied with me?* Annie was right. She'd been raised to fit a pattern, not to be herself. Before Music Lady began to emerge she was grateful for men like Andrew. Now she had trouble believing anyone like Marc would care for, never mind love the person she was becoming. Bot oh, god, she wanted it so badly.

"I know. Believe me." The look on his face was equal parts of earnestness and determination. "And like I said, if you'd just be honest with yourself, so do you."

"Kiss me, Marc." She wanted the reassuring touch of his mouth on hers before she had to leave again.

"With pleasure."

This was no kiss of passion, but one filled with emotion. It made her heart turn over and hope blossomed deep inside her. Hope she could believe his words and have faith in herself as well as him.

Sunday night. I'll tell him my name and how I feel Sunday

night and then we can go on from there.

He broke the kiss. "Let me get your pass for you."

Still naked, as usual, he walked her into the kitchen and took an envelope off the counter, then handed it to her. "Your pass for Sunday night. Put it on before you try to get into the facility and keep it on all time. It's your entry to the backstage area and the dressing rooms."

She opened it and took out a rectangle of plastic stamped Backstage Pass. The name of the concert facility was front and center along with the promoter and below that Aftershock. It hung on the end of a woven fabric lanyard.

"Thank you. I won't lose it."

"Will you be at Aftershock tomorrow night?"

"No. I'm...having dinner with my folks." It was the birthday compromise. "But I'll see you Sunday night right on the dot of seven."

"Be careful." He kissed her again as he walked her to the door.

She paused at the threshold and wrapped her arms around him, squeezing him tightly.

"What's that for?" he asked suspiciously.

"For good luck. For Sunday."

Then she hurried out to her car before she could say anything more.

Chapter Fourteen

*E*mma spent the day arguing with herself while Annie fixed her hair and makeup, and helped her get her outfit ready. It was her birthday. She was thirty. Time to finish growing up and act like an adult. Her determination from the other night still stuck with her, although at times it wavered slightly. Tonight, she would tell Marc her name. All about herself. And how she really felt about him.

Right?

Yes. She'd take the final step into her new future, the world she created in her mind for her and Marc, her Guitar Man. So much of it yet unknown. If she still had the courage when she saw him.

"Don't even think of chickening out." Annie snapped the case of eye shadow closed and studied Emma's face. "Time to put your big girl pants on, girlfriend."

"And if I'm misreading the whole situation?"

"Then you'll have had the ride of your life and be prepared for the next one."

Still, a hundred butterflies were beating their wings in her stomach as she was waved into the Amphitheatre parking lot. It took her a few minutes to find a parking space. Then she had to weave her way past two delivery-type trucks, one larger than the other, and a huge bus with Deep Blue River painted on the side.

If Lightnin' gets this job and it works out for them, will Marc be touring the country some day in one of these? And where will I be?

Stop that! Right now!

Hauling in a breath to calm herself, she showed her pass to the guard at the back door, who smiled and stood back for her to climb the few steps to stage level.

Emma had been backstage at community theater plays before, but that was nothing at all like this. The ceiling seemed miles above her head, and the entire place was a frenzy of activity. People moved everywhere, guys in jeans and T-shirts hauling strange looking items from one place to another. Someone with a set of headphones and a clipboard was talking into a lip mic and making notes. Others were walking around with no apparent purpose. In one distant corner, three men, one in a suit, were huddled as if discussing the fate of the nation. For Emma it was almost like falling asleep and awakening in a foreign country.

But an incredible buzz of excitement hummed in the air, like an electrical charge sizzling along the surface of her skin.

"Hey, Music Lady."

The low timbre of his voice made her body react instantly. Her every pulse point throbbed. Relief he was actually there waiting for her, along with heat, warmed her blood.

"Hey." She gave him a shy smile.

"Wow." His eyes travelled over her from head to toe and back again. "You look damn hot, Music Lady."

Her heart stuttered at the compliment. "Thank you."

Emma sent a silent thanks to Annie for dragging her to a boutique and outfitting her in embroidered jeans and layered tees. And also for convincing her to have her toenails painted a hot, sensuous pink.

He took her hand. "Come on. I want to introduce you to the rest of the band."

Emma stopped, suddenly frozen in place. "M-Meet the

band?"

Of course he intended to introduce her. She hadn't even thought of that, although she didn't think Marc was going to hide her away in some corner. Anxiety threaded through her as she wondered how they'd react to her. Would they like her? Accept her? Or would they take one look and try to convince Marc he was making a huge mistake? That she was just the old Emma hiding under a new veneer that could crack at any moment. She wiped her damp palms on her new jeans, her pulse racing. So much to worry about.

"No worries. I promise." Marc turned back to her, oblivious of all the activity around them, and wrapped his arms around her. "To them you're just ML. The woman I'm crazy about."

"C-Crazy about?" Her body suddenly felt liquid, as if she had no power to stand, and her heart was thumping. Had she heard him right? And why did she have to sound so much like an idiot?

He traced the line of her cheekbone and her jaw. "Surely you've figured it out by this time. And no, I haven't discussed you with them. Well, maybe with Rick, but he's my closest friend and a really good guy. They do know I'm...seeing someone, and I want to show you off." He touched his mouth to hers. "Just for a few minutes, okay?"

Butterflies began an overcharged tango in Emma's stomach, and her throat was suddenly dry. She hoped this didn't turn out to be a huge mistake, but she nodded and let him lead her through the maze of containers and cables covering the landscape of the backstage area. They circle around to the other side of the facility, past two doors to a third. Marc stopped, gave her a quick hug, whispered, "Just follow my lead," and opened the door.

The laughing and chatter in the room stopped the moment they stepped in. Emma tightened her grip on Marc's hand as she took in the other band members and what looked like half the women she'd seen at Aftershock. Although "women" might be too loose a term since they all appeared younger than she did. She didn't know if they were in relationships with the band members or were the groupies even she in her uninformed state had heard about. They were all staring at her with open curiosity.

Every muscle drew taut when she spotted Lacey in full makeup and revealing outfit, lounging on one end of the couch. Damn! What was she doing here? Which band member had brought her? She wanted to ask Marc, but everyone's attention was too focused on her.

Come on, Emma. You can hold your own. Don't let the bitch get to you.

But, of course, Lacey was the first one to speak.

"I see you have your 'friend' with you tonight, Marc, honey." Her smile was more feral than friendly, and she still eyed Marc as if he were her main course for the evening. "How about introducing her to everyone here? Make her feel part of the crowd?" She wet her lips, a slow glide of her tongue. "You know, like you always did with me."

Emma took in the too-tight jeans and tank top showing more cleavage than Annie's tiny bathing suit. Jealousy mixed with anxiety made every muscle in her body tense.

"She's just trying to stir up trouble," Marc whispered in Emma's ear. "I told you, Lacey was never anything to me." He put his arm around her and cradled her closer. "Everyone, this is ML. Don't scare her away, okay?"

"You think she's afraid of me?" The redhead ran hungry eyes over Marc, a sly look on her face. "Geez, sweetie. You know how dangerous I can be, right?" Her laugh carried the sound of envy and a hint of anger.

"I'll be sure to warn her, Lacey." Marc chuckled then murmured, "Ignore her. Pay no attention to her. I'll tell you again, she's not important to me, no matter what she says."

But Emma wondered uneasily if Lacey really did have history with her Guitar Man. Had she been important to him at one time, despite what Marc said? Was she just waiting to finesse Emma out of the picture? She had to beat back her clawing insecurities. The other women in the room were watching her, obviously waiting to see what would happen next. It was apparent they all knew each other well. Emma sensed a gauntlet had been thrown down and, for a fleeting moment, she regretted coming here tonight.

There were also a couple of men, laughing and joking with the women. Emma wondered if she had a sign on her forehead that read "Alien". Talk about being a fish out of water. She leaned a little closer to Marc.

A tall man standing at a table, covered with food and drink, put down the bottle of water he was holding, walked over to them, and extended his hand, a cordial look on his face.

"Hi. I'm Rick. Thanks for coming tonight and keeping Marc together." His smile was warm and Emma relaxed fractionally.

"Rick's the leader of our group. The one who got us this gig."

Emma shook his hand. "Nice to meet you."

Rick pointed at two of the men, one sitting on the couch, the other standing by a chair chugging form a bottle of water. "Garrett, our drummer. Danny, the lead singer." He indicated the other two men. "Jado, standing there with Danny did our video and Scotty, hanging out by the food, cut our tape. I'm guessing Marc told you about that. We figured they deserved to be here tonight, too."

The men acknowledged the introduction with a chorus of greetings.

She gave them a tiny grin but still clung to Marc.

"They don't bite." He led her over to the table. "Let's get you something to drink."

"Just water is fine." She didn't even want that but it would give her something to do with her hands.

Then, as if someone released a pause button all conversation suddenly resumed, filling the room with noise. The same buzz of excitement Emma sensed the moment she walked into the facility saturated the air in this room. Marc and the other members of Lightnin' looked calm on the surface but there was an unmistakable jitteriness to them.

"We go on at eight." Marc walked her over to an unoccupied

corner. "So in a little bit we have to head for the stage. Make sure the instruments are still in tune and do a last minute check to make sure the roadies set everything up the way they're supposed to."

"Roadies?" She lifted an eyebrow.

"You're cute, babe. I like being the one to teach you all this stuff." His eyes were hot. "All kinds of stuff." Then he brushed a kiss over her forehead. "I keep forgetting you're still learning the lingo. Road crew. The guys who haul the equipment, especially the sound system, and set everything up for the band."

Embarrassment rushed through her. Had he explained about this before? He must really think she was a dunce. "I'm sorry, but if you mentioned them before I don't remember."

"Don't worry, and I didn't. Playing at clubs, we usually do it ourselves. Save the bucks. But tonight we'll be using Deep Blue River's sound equipment, and their crew helped us with our instruments and stuff. They're pros. These guys have been doing it for a long time so they know what they're doing."

"And you made sure it was okay when you did your sound check, right?" She remembered him telling her about that.

"Yes, but we'll do one final look-see."

"Where will I be when you're on stage?" she asked.

"I'll show you." Looking at the other members of the band, he said, "See you guys on stage."

He took Emma's hand and led her out of the room and back the way they'd come. There was still activity everywhere, people moving in all direction, the hum of conversation like the counterpoint of a melody.

"Where's the other band?" she asked as they navigated the snake bed of cables stretching everywhere.

"Did you see the big fancy bus in the parking lot?" Marc asked.

"How could I not? It's huge."

"It belongs to them. They'll hang out in it until it's time to come inside to get ready."

"Oh." Something else for her to learn. *They should provide guidebooks for people who don't know anything about this business.*

"Here. This will be a good place for you." He lifted her up onto a large black box that held sound equipment during travel. "Sit here and you can see the whole thing."

He pointed toward the stage and Emma realized she had a full view of everything, albeit from the side. And she'd be out of everyone's way. Excitement sizzled over her at the thought of seeing Marc in action on a big stage like this. She hoped none of the women from the dressing room would come to stand near her. Especially Lacey. It was bad enough she knew plenty of women in the audience would be licking their lips over the sight of Marc on stage.

"I'll just wait here for you until you're finished, right?"

"I'll have to take care of my guitar and amp, but it won't take long." He stroked a finger down her cheek in a familiar gesture that always gave her hot shivers. "You go on ahead to the dressing room, because it will be chaos here during the equipment change."

"No. I'll just stay here." *Away from the predatory redhead.*

"Just go on ahead to the dressing room. Please? So I'll know where to find you if I get held up." He cupped her head and kissed her, thrusting his tongue deep into her mouth, his thumbs stroking her cheeks. When he lifted his head, they were both breathless. "That's to bring me good luck. See you when I'm done." He headed onto the stage, where the heavy black curtain blocked everything from the audience.

Emma watched the final preparation with fascination. It amazed her all these people knew exactly what to do and did it without getting in each other's way. She was startled when a tall, older, good-looking man in slacks and a collared shirt, sleeves rolled to his elbows, came to stand beside her.

"Friend of the band?" he asked.

"Uh, yes." Who was he?

He held out his hand. "Butch Meredith."

She recognized the name. Deep Blue River's manager. "ML,"

she said.

His touch was firm and strong, and she got a sense of solidity from him. His eyes were bright with intelligence and knowledge, and he was obviously completely at home in these surroundings. He exuded confidence, the kind earned with a successful track record. If Lightnin' signed with him, she believed he'd take good care of them.

He narrowed his eyes at her. "You're here with one of the musicians in Lightnin'?"

"Yes. Marc Malone." She bit her bottom lip. "He said I could sit here but if I need to move...."

"No, no, not at all. Just trying to identify all the players back here. Marc's a good guy. But then all of the members of Lightnin' are." He grinned, apparently trying to ease her nervousness. "Don't worry. Everything's gonna be great. I believe those boys are going to kick things up a notch for themselves tonight."

"Thank you." She folded her hands tightly in her lap and looked back onto the stage.

The rest of the band was in place and the hum of conversation had faded almost to a whisper as instruments were tuned yet again. Marc and Rick stood together, facing each other, bits of music floating back to her.

Butch Meredith had moved away from her to stand to her right at the edge of the stage, and she realized the women from the dressing room had gathered in a cluster just to her left. Lacey, the redhead, sauntered over to her.

Oh, God, not her. Anyone but her.

"So. You and Marc know each other a long time?" The same nasty tone she'd used in the club.

"Yes," Emma lied, somehow knowing she shouldn't tell this woman the truth.

"Funny I've only seen you at the club a few times." That sly look crept over her face again. "Marc and me have known each other forever."

"How nice." Emma turned her head deliberately away, hoping the woman would get the signal. She clung to Marc's assurances he and Lacey had never been together, that he didn't even like her. But she could tell the woman would scratch her eyes out given the slightest chance. She was doing her best to make Emma feel out of place.

Lacey walked back to her friends and from the corner of her eye, Emma saw her whispering and pointing. Fine. She could whisper all she wanted. But Emma was Music Lady. She was special. Marc certainly told her often enough.

Suddenly everything got so quiet Emma could even hear the muted conversation from the audience filtering through the curtain. The intensity of the excitement in the air changed, ramped up. Anticipation was like a living thing. Emma could almost feel it sizzle in her blood. The lights on the stage darkened, and a voice from somewhere boomed through the sound system.

"Okay, everyone. Let's party."

Lightnin' hit the opening chord of their first tune, the black curtain rolled smoothly open, the spotlights hit the band and music blasted into the Amphitheatre to the cheers of the audience. Just like that Emma was snared by the magic of it, the elation, the thrill, so intense she almost forgot to breathe. The atmosphere was so heady she could see how people were caught up in it, addicted as if to a drug. She zeroed in on Marc totally engrossed in his music, head thrown back, hair wild around his face as she'd first seen him, the pure energy of the tune reaching out to grab her.

All through the first number, Emma sat with her fingers wound tightly together, so nervous for the band she was afraid to breathe. But then she began to relax and soon, she was bouncing on her seat and tapping her fingers on her thigh as the rhythm vibrated through her. When she heard the intro to the song they usually closed with at night, she could hardly believe their set was over. It seemed as if they'd just begun.

They hit the final notes, Danny in his usual pose with one arm extended, hand reaching up, Rick, lifting his guitar over his head in what she'd learned was his signature move, and Marc in the wild pose she loved so much. For a moment, there was dead silence. Then the audience erupted, screaming, cheering, chanting, the noise level deafening until the curtain closed.

Butch Meredith was back to Emma's side. "Told you they'd get it done." He grinned at her then headed over to talk to the three men who'd been standing off to her right.

Emma could hardly catch her breath she was so excited. Everything the band hoped for was about to come true. Deliberately she pushed away the unease, the worry. If they moved on, she'd be left behind. Everything she had with Marc would be gone, not much more than a memory she could haul out at night.

No. I won't let that happen.

She had no idea how long they'd have to stay at the Amphitheatre or when they could head to his house, but when they did she planned on making this a birthday she'd always remember.

Sliding off the huge black crate she'd been sitting on, she watched for Marc to walk off the stage. The roadies were already out there, setting up for the main act, but Lightnin' was huddled in a tight little circle, talking. Then she saw Butch join them, shake all their hands, and guided them off the stage in the opposite direction. Finding a out of the way space by the exit door, she attempted to make herself invisible for what seemed like a long time, trying to decide what to do. Everyone else with the band had disappeared by now.

Maybe she should go to Marc's house and wait for him. Or just go home.

But he'd told her to go on ahead to the dressing room. He'd left from the other side of the stage so he was probably already there.

I'm a grown woman who can certainly find the way to the dressing room by myself.

Making her way down the hall, she found the place she was looking for and heard the sound of voices even before she opened the door. It sounded to her as if everyone was talking at once.

Good news. Of course everyone's excited.

She walked in, looked around...and stopped. Her heart stopped, too.

Marc stood against the wall with his shirt open, and Lacey was plastered against him like white on rice, her mouth attached to his in a lip-lock unlike any Emma had ever seen. One leg was wrapped around his hips and a hand planted firmly on his butt. Marc was gripping her shoulders. Someone—maybe more than one person—was encouraging them with piercing wolf whistles and loud clapping.

"You get him, Lacey," one of the women yelled. "That's the way."

"You always get so damn lucky, Marco Polo." Emma thought it was someone from the band but she couldn't be sure.

Pain lanced through her; maybe the worst she'd ever felt. Everything inside her seemed to shrivel up and die. If she could have evaporated into the air she would have. Instead she seemed frozen to the floor, sick with a sense of betrayal, her heart cracking into pieces.

He lied. That was all she could think. Not have anything going with Lacey? Not interested? All lies. But why? What was the point? Her heart felt as if an axe had pierced it, the pain radiating through her body. A sense of total betrayal consumed her. From start to finish everything had been a fraud.

It was all a fake. Pretend. A line he fed me. Why? It's not as if he can't have his pick of women. But damn it, he seemed so sincere and I almost bought it.

Maybe he was intrigued by the "good girl" Emma. And when all was said and done, that was who she really was. The purple streak? The new clothes? Dancing to the rock music? That belonged to Music Lady, a role she apparently didn't play very well.

So why this charade? Why bring me tonight? To humiliate me?

Oh God, it hurts. It hurts so much.

The pain nearly doubled her over and for a moment, she couldn't even catch her breath.

The instant everyone spotted her, the conversation and noise died as though an off switch had been flipped. Marc's gaze landed on her, and he shoved Lacey away from him.

"ML." He started toward her.

"Don't come near me. Don't come anywhere close to me."

She ran from the dressing room, barely avoiding all the obstacles on the floor, tears clogging her throat and blinding her eyes. She should have known the exhilarating joy ride would come to a crashing halt. Didn't they always? How long could you safely ride the edge of danger, anyway?

This one?

She'd hoped it would be forever. What a stupid fool she was.

"ML!"

She heard him shout her name, but she just kept on until she got to the back door and slammed out into the parking lot. Her hands were shaking so badly she could hardly fish her car keys out of her jeans pocket. She was fumbling with the lock on the door when he caught up with her, grabbing her and pulling her around to face him.

"Stop," he said, breathing hard. "Listen to me."

But when she looked at him, she saw the bright red imprint of Lacey's lipstick on his face and she felt sick to her stomach. She jerked her arm free, stumbling against the car.

"Get away from me. Just...get away from me."

She finally got the door unlocked and herself inside. Marc was still trying to hang on to the door when she backed out of the parking space, but she floored the accelerator and knocked him to the ground. By the time she was out of the lot and onto the street, the tears had broken free in earnest, flooding her eyes to the point she couldn't see. She turned into a gas station, stopping at the far side of the building, and sat there while the sobs ripped out of her as if yanked by a giant fist.

After a long time the waterworks eased and she mopped her face with tissues from the glove box. Her throat was raw and her body ached all over.

I was so afraid of this. Afraid he'd realize we weren't meant for each other and want Lacey instead. Or someone like her. I was fooling myself all the time.

Lacey hinted to her they had a history and the clinch made it obvious. Anyway, the redhead was far more savvy, far more experienced than Emma. She'd just swooped in and picked up wherever it was she and Marc had left off.

The image flashed across her mind again, and tears well up once more. Lord, hadn't she cried enough already?

Maybe I should have waited for him to explain.

Yeah? Explain what? Everyone in the room knew what was going on. They're probably all laughing at me. Damn rock musicians, anyway.

She had no idea how long she sat beside the darkened building, wondering if she would be able to drive home. The pain in her heart speared through her whole body. And she was cold. Even though it was summertime, she was suddenly freezing, shivering hard enough to make her bones rattle. She turned on the car's heater and soon had it blasting at her like a furnace but the chill wouldn't go away.

Eventually she pulled herself together enough to start the car again and head out into the street. Somehow she managed to get herself home and into the house. She didn't think she had any tears left, but by the time she reached her bedroom, her eyes were flooded again.

I knew it. I just knew it.

Becoming involved with Marc, addicted to him, was one of the biggest mistakes of her life. She wanted excitement and she'd gotten it, but along the way, she'd left her brain in cold storage. If she'd thought it out, she'd accepted from the beginning she was out of his league. Maybe she should savor that one night with him and never gone back to the club. But her heart and her hormones conspired against her to defeat common sense. And this was what she got.

She threw herself onto the bed and just let them flow,

questioning if it was possible to die from too much crying. Or too much heartache.

ॐ

Marc was beside himself. He couldn't remember the last time he'd been so upset. He didn't even feel the scrapes on his skin from where he'd fallen on the asphalt. He couldn't believe she'd just driven off without even giving him a chance to explain.

Shit. How the fuck had this happened?

"Hey, Marc. Marco Polo."

Marc whirled to face Rick. "Don't ever call me that stupid fucking name again or I'll have to really hurt you."

"Whoa." Rick pulled to a stop and held up his hands. "What's going on, buddy? What's the deal here?"

"You know what the fucking deal is. I've been screwed. Damn that bitch Lacey. She's been after me since the first time she saw us play."

"But you never hung out with her. Hooked up." Rick frowned. "Did you?"

"Of course not." He was sick with rage and heartache. "She's a piece of trash. When I find out who gave her the pass for tonight I'll tear him a new one. She's chased away the best thing to come into my life."

Rick frowned. "Are you talking about ML? Or whatever the hell her name is? Jesus, Marc, the broad won't even tell you her name. I don't even know why you brought her tonight. How can you get so twisted up about someone who hides who she is? That's nuts."

Marc grabbed Rick by the shirt and got right in his face. "Don't you dare call her a broad, you asshole."

"Wait. Wait a minute." Rick grabbed his wrists and tried to yank them away. "Is there more going on here than I know about? I know she's been eating up your brain, though who the hell knows why. There are plenty of other women where she came from."

"She's not just any woman. I've been trying to tell you." His words were as brittle as chips of ice. "This is my Music Lady. She's special. Very special. I told you how I felt, for chrissake. And now I don't even have a clue how to find her."

"Listen." Rick's voice was apologetic. "We all thought Lacey was just being cute with you. Who the hell knew you had something serious going?"

"Lacey knew," Marc spat out. "She's seen her at the club a few times. This was just her nasty way of getting back at me for turning her down."

"Okay. All right." Rick eased himself from Marc's grip. "I'll take the heat for not taking your situation more seriously, pass the word to everyone to lay off and help you figure out how to find her. But right now, can we go inside? Butch is waiting to talk to us again. Things went really well tonight. You'll be pleased."

He threw his arm around Marc's shoulder and began leading him toward the door.

He shrugged off Rick's hand and moved toward the facility with long, angry strides.

Damn you, Lacey. And damn me for being caught off guard by her.

Rage exploded again as he remembered the uncomfortable feel of her and his efforts to peel her away from his body.

"I want to know who brought that bitch, Lacey, tonight," Marc growled over his shoulder.

"You can lay that one on Danny, but please let it go for the moment." Rick caught up to him as they reached the door.

Marc froze. "*Danny's* seeing her?"

"No. He's with her sister, Shelley. And Shelley begged him to get a pass for Lacey. Marc, if I'd had any idea what she had in mind, or where you and ML stood—"

Marc held up his hand. "Stop." He sucked in a deep breath, control threatening to desert him. He had business to take care of. "We'll work it out later. But before I go back inside there, I want the women out. All of them. If someone has a problem with that, they can take it up with me."

He was still vibrating with rage when they re-entered the facility and headed toward the dressing room. Leaning against the wall with his hands shoved in his pockets, he waited while Rick cleared the room. He didn't move until Lacey stormed past him with two other women. Like quicksilver, he reached out and grabbed her arm.

"That was a rotten thing to do, Lacey." He had to restrain himself from actually doing her bodily harm.

"Why?" she sneered. "Because it offended Little Miss Nobody?" Lacey tossed her thick mane of hair over her shoulder. "She's not your style and you know it."

"You have no idea what my style is, but I can assure you, you're not it." He gritted his teeth. "You've tried that game before and I wasn't buying it then, either." He was aware everyone had stopped at the door to watch their little tableau play out, but he didn't care. "I'm going to tell you something for your own good." His voice was pitched low and uninflected but not even an idiot could mistake the fury bubbling beneath it. "Don't come around me again. Don't come around this band. Don't even show up where we're performing. Because I promise you, if you do, I will make your life a living hell."

"You think you're such hot shit," she sneered. "You don't know what you're missing out on."

"Yes, I do. And I don't play around with used goods." He pushed her away. "Now get out of here."

She stamped along the floor in the wake of the others, twitching her ass as if Marc would in any way find her movement appealing.

"Come on." Rick clapped him on the shoulder. "We've got important business to discuss. Good business. Let's get the band taken care of. Tomorrow we'll see if there's a way to find your Music Lady."

Chapter Fifteen

*E*mma couldn't ever remember feeling as bad as she did. She cried enough tears for ten people, her eyes and throat raw and painful. She was thankful she was alone so no one had to see her misery or force her to interact with them. She managed to call the human resources number at work and leave a message on the machine she was taking a sick day. Maybe two. The sun was coming up by the time she pulled off her clothes and threw them on the floor. For some perverse reason, she dug out the Lightnin' T-shirt Marc had given her and slipped it on, his scent invading her body, and then she crawled into bed. Still cold, she hauled the covers up tightly and tucked them beneath her chin, wondering if she'd ever be warm again, and curled up into a fetal ball.

This is the worst birthday I've ever had in my life.

She'd looked forward to it with such expectations. Tonight she would have told Marc what her name was, all about herself, and they'd have a big celebration for her birthday and the success of the concert appearance.

Yeah, right. How dumb could I be?

She was convinced she wouldn't be able to sleep but eventually sheer exhaustion claimed her.

The telephone woke her, dragging her up from what felt like

a vat of cotton balls but she chose to let it ring. There wasn't anyone she wanted to talk to. Certainly not her folks, who would be calling to see how her birthday went. The phone rang at least six more times until Emma managed to stumble out of bed and unplug it from the wall. If it rang in the kitchen, at least, it wouldn't be so loud.

Emma drifted back to sleep only to be disturbed by someone ringing her doorbell and banging on the front door. When even pulling the pillows over her head didn't blot out the sound, she pushed herself out of bed and staggered down the hallway to the front door.

This better not be dipshit Andrew. It would be just like him to show upon my birthday with flowers and chocolates and think he could make nice with me.

But when she peered through the peephole, what she saw was even worse.

Annie. In full attack mode.

Oh, hell.

"I know you're in there," Annie called. "You better open the door or I'll get someone to break it down."

She sighed, brushed the hair out of her eyes, unlocked the door, and pulled it open.

"Enter at your own risk," she muttered and headed back to her bedroom.

"Holy shit!" Annie trailed after her. "You look like hell. Worse than that. What happened? I thought last night was the big celebration?"

"Yeah. Some celebration." She crawled back into bed and yanked the covers up over her head.

"Emma? Honey?" Her friend sat down on the edge of the bed and gently tugged the quilt and sheet down, resisting Emma's efforts to hold onto them. "Jesus. What happened?"

That was all it took for the tears to start again. As she buried her face in the pillow, Annie's soft hand stroking her hair, she wondered how she even had any moisture in her eyes left. She was sure she'd cried enough for an entire family yet still the waterworks came and came.

"I didn't want you to see me like this," she said, her voice muffled by the pillow.

"Oh, sweetheart, if not me, then who? Can you tell me what happened? Did Marc turn out to be a rat bastard after all?"

She just nodded, unable to form the words.

"Emma, Emma, Emma." Annie's sigh was so heavy Emma could practically feel it. "I am just so very sorry."

"Not your fault," she mumbled. "My own stupidity."

"Turn over and let me get a look at you."

Emma just shook her head.

"Come on, now. You're making yourself sick like this."

"I'm not sure I ever want to get out of bed again."

Another sigh, then Annie brushed the tangled hair away from her face. "I know. Been there, done that. But trust an old hand at this. Hiding under the covers won't do you any good."

"Will, too," she said stubbornly.

Annie laughed softly. "I know it seems that way but it won't."

"I think I'll burn the clothes I wore last night. And this stupid T-shirt, too. How pathetic am I that I actually put it on and slept in it?"

"No clothes burning. I'm giving you an order. Hold on. I'll be right back."

When Annie returned she had a warm washcloth, which she used to bathe Emma's face. She then went back to the bathroom again and this time, returned with an ice cold cloth. Emma shrieked when Annie placed it over her eyes.

"Just for a couple of minutes, to help with the swelling. I've got some of those little sterile tears vials in my purse. I use them when my eyes get dry during the day. In a minute we'll rinse out those awful red eyes with one. Then I want you to get up and take a good hot shower and wash your hair. No, don't give me any lip," she went on when Emma moaned. "While you're doing that, I'll put on some coffee. Then I want to hear the whole story. Every gruesome detail."

Emma wanted to pull the covers back over her head and

bury herself until the pain went away. If it ever did. But Annie was relentless. Somehow she found herself standing under a hot spray letting it beat down on her, hoping maybe the some of the memories from the night before would wash away. Finally, clean and dressed in T-shirt and jeans, hair pulled back in a ponytail, she sat at her breakfast room table with a steaming cup of coffee in front of her and Annie in her face.

"Okay, chickadee. Give. And don't leave out one single thing."

Reliving it was as bad as going through it the first time. Maybe worse, because now the pain was sharper. More intense. But Annie dragged it all out of her, every excruciating, hurtful, humiliating detail. She was exhausted when she finished, ready to dive back into bed and hide.

"So you see?" Emma took a sip of the coffee, now cooled off, and made a face. "I was right all along. I was just a novelty to him. A new toy. No matter what he said." She looked across at her friend. "Right? You agree with me, don't you?" When Annie didn't answer her she repeated, "Right?"

Annie heaved another long sigh. "I was so afraid of something like this."

Emma's eyes widened. "What? You knew he was just fooling around with me? Why didn't you say something? Why did you encourage me?"

Her friend shook her head. "No. That's not it at all."

"Not it? Then what? I don't understand."

Annie got up, emptied the cold coffee from both of their cups and refilled them with fresh hot liquid.

"We've known each other for ten years now, right?"

Emma nodded, frowning. What was Annie getting at?

"We've spent a lot of time together but never really socialized. I mean gone out on double dates or gotten together with the guys we were dating. Right?"

"Yes, but—"

"There's probably a good reason. You had a very well-ordered life and dated very stable guys. I, on the other hand, took a lot of walks on the wild side so our men had absolutely nothing in common."

"I guess I never thought about it that way." She pushed her tangled hair out of her face. "Maybe you're right and I'm just now able to see it. So, what's the point you're trying to make here? That I'm out of my element?" She snorted. "Tell me something I don't know."

"The point is I know a little bit more about the music scene, the rock scene, than you do. I've been to clubs, followed the blogs, all that stuff. And I know what goes on there. Hell, my friend Jodi Lynn dated a guitar player for about six months, and I hung out with her at some of their gigs."

"So? None of this is making me feel any better."

"Then listen to me." Annie took a healthy swallow of her coffee, flinched as it burned her tongue. "Groupies are a hazard of the trade. They're like viruses, popping up everywhere and there doesn't seem to be a cure."

Emma snorted. "No kidding."

"The point is, my little innocent, they are amoral and aggressive. Whoever brought the redhead to the concert last night, you know it wasn't Marc. And you don't know if he made the moves on her or the other way around. What did he say when you asked him about it?"

"I didn't," Emma mumbled.

"What? What's that you said? Speak up."

"I said, I didn't ask him."

Annie flopped back in her chair. "Well, why the hell not? You mean you just turned tail and ran out of there? Boom?" She sat up and took Emma's hand in hers. "Honey, you're establishing a pattern here. Do you see it?"

Emma frowned. "No. What do you mean?"

"I love you like a sister. You know that. Right? I don't think anyone was as excited as me to see you decide to savor life a little more. I was your cheering section."

"And?"

"And one thing hasn't changed. When you hit a wall, your

first tendency is to run away."

Emma was instantly defensive. "That's not true. I don't either."

"Yes. You do. When you'd had enough of Andrew instead of sitting down with him, telling him how you felt and breaking it off the way you probably should have, you ran out of his house without giving him an explanation and then resented the fact he wanted you to give him one."

"I guess you're right. But at the time it seemed the only thing I could do. Just get up and run. Before he tried to talk me out of anything."

"No buts. Listen. Maybe you could have saved yourself a lot of aggravation if you'd just laid it out for him and then taken a hike. Not to mention avoiding the issue of the breakup with your folks."

"They'd still have objected." Emma took a swallow of her coffee, now cold, and made a face.

"Maybe," Annie agreed. "But at least you would have gotten it out there and not been on the defensive."

"So what does that have to do with Marc?"

"You did the same thing with him," her friend pointed out. "Instead of waiting to see if there was an explanation, you just turned and ran."

"Hey. I thought you were on my side."

"I am. I'm just pointing out the truth, as hard as it might be for you to accept it."

"Anyway, I didn't need an explanation for this. If you'd seen the two of them together, you wouldn't have had to ask any questions. The answers were obvious."

Annie shook her head. "Nope. Don't believe it. I do believe you saw what you described, but try this on for size. What if *she* went after *him?* What if he was doing his best to peel her off of his body? Groupies are predators and they like nothing better than invading someone else's territory. And didn't you tell me he told you more than once he wasn't interested in her and never had been?"

Emma just stared into her coffee cup.

"Pay attention. From everything you've told me about Marc, he doesn't seem like the type of guy to swim in those waters. He's fixing up his house. He talks about his family. He's been willing to put up with you even though you refused to tell him your name. Does that sound like a guy lusting after groupies? Honey, he could have tossed you out any time but he didn't. Think about it."

Emma glanced out the big window looking over the backyard. Was Annie right? Had she just jumped to a conclusion because it was what she expected? She'd told herself all along the joy ride would be over soon. Had she deliberately misread what she'd seen?

Was she a coward who ran from confrontation? Maybe the reason she refused to tell Marc her name was because all along she'd been taking a moment in time to step into a life she could never have. Maybe believing underneath it all that she really couldn't change. Or just playing a game with Marc all along, only he didn't know it. Or she'd just set herself up for failure....

She wasn't seeing a very pretty picture of herself.

"I'm sure Marc feels like shit today," Annie went on. "Especially since he probably expected you to at least give him the courtesy of an explanation. Think how hurt *he* must be?"

"I don't want to think about how he feels." Emma knew she sounded like a petulant child but she couldn't seem to help herself.

"Yes. You do." Annie reached over and touched her arm. "Honey, I know how badly you're hurting, but don't you think you at least owe him the chance to explain? Then if he turns out to be a rotten bastard, I'll personally help you kick his ass clear across the country."

Emma gave a weak laugh. "Sounds good to me."

"So, not to get off track here but how was the concert?"

"Oh, Annie, it was fantastic." For a moment, all the pain and hurt subsided and she was back at the Amphitheatre, caught up in the enchantment of the night. The excitement. The vibrancy of the music. And Marc, totally absorbed in what he was doing, at one with his magical bass guitar.

"God, Annie, you should have seen them. They were unbelievable. And Butch Meredith went out to talk to them even before they walked off stage."

"That's fabulous. He's made superstars out of Deep Blue River. Honey, this could be the big break every band works for."

"I know." She sighed. "And I'm really glad for them. I just wish...."

"Want to see if any of the blogs have picked up the word yet?" Annie grinned.

"Oh, Annie, I don't think I'm up for anything right now."

"Sure you are." Annie rose and tugged Emma up from her chair. "Underneath it all you're dying of curiosity. Right?"

"Dying of something," she agreed. "Are you sure I can't just go back to bed?"

"Not for one minute. Where's your laptop?"

"In my room."

"Then let's get it."

Reluctantly, very much aware of her bruised heart and drained body, Emma trudged to her bedroom and grabbed her laptop case. Before she even realized what was going on, she was sitting cross-legged on the bed with Annie and her friend's fingers were flying over the keyboard.

"All right," Annie crowed suddenly. "There it is. Look." She turned the computer at an angle so Emma could get a better look.

The heading on the screen read *Music Musings Around the City*. Emma squinted at the words.

"*The formal announcement has yet to be made but informed sources have told Musings hot local band Lightnin' is about to hit their breakout moment. After a stellar performance last night as the opening act for Deep Blue River, rumor has it they are about to sign a contract with River's manager, Butch Meredith. We hear a concert tour and a CD are in the immediate future. Stay tuned.*"

"Ohmigod!" As badly hurt as she was, Emma still felt a surge of excitement for Marc and the others. *But that means he'll be leaving. How will I ever get to see him?*

"Indeed." Annie began scrolling through other pages. "Man, it's all over the Web. Those guys must be in the stratosphere. Listen." She turned to Emma. "You have to get in touch with Marc and congratulate him. And at least give him the chance to make this right."

Emma nibbled on a thumbnail. "I just don't know, Annie."

"Sometimes I could just smack you." Annie blew out a breath of disgust. "You have to give him a chance, honey. You told me there was something strong between you. Don't throw it away because you don't have the courage to face him. Or are you afraid of what he offers?" She cocked her head. "Are you scared of becoming Music Lady for real? Having something solid with him? Emma, this is your chance. Your big opportunity. Hey, maybe you can even pull out those notebooks you've been scribbling in for years and try your hand at writing the way you want to."

"I'll...think about it." She looked at her bedside clock.

Annie eyes took on a thoughtful look. "Here's another option for you. Keeping your name secret was to give you an out if this fell apart. So you could go back to your old life. No harm, no foul. Is that what you want to do, Emma? Go back to the way things were? Was the new life too much for you?"

Emma looked at her horrified. "Hell, no. That's like a living death."

A tiny smile curved Annie's lips. "Then you aren't left with a whole lot of options, are you?"

Silence settled over them while Annie waited patiently and Emma churned everything in her mind. She glanced at the bedside clock. "Hey. How come you're not at work?"

Annie worked as a paralegal for one of the partners in a large law firm in the city.

"When I couldn't get hold of you, I told my boss I had an emergency. He's a really good guy and I don't do this very often.

How come *you're* not at work?"

"I left a message for human resources saying I was taking a couple of sick days." No way could she have shown up at work. She could hardly go an hour without a few tears leaking form her eyes and her head felt the size of a house. Not to mention the damage to her heart. But now that she'd had this talk with Annie....

"Then let's make good use of them." Her friend swung her legs off the bed and put the laptop on the nightstand. "You need to get out of this house. Right now."

"No. No, no, no." The temporary surge of excitement for the band had faded, and Emma wanted to dive under the covers again.

"Yes. Yes, yes, yes." Annie yanked the quilt and sheet down to the foot of the bed. "Come on. We'll have lunch and margaritas at Hot Salsa and then find you another great new outfit. For when you go talk to Marc."

"No more new outfits." Emma shook her head. "And I don't want to go to Hot Salsa or anyplace else."

"Tough. You're going." Her friend paused. "Or shall I call your mother and tell her you're sick and need her?"

Emma leaped off the bed. "Forget that. Let's get going."

"You need to snap out of this. We have a lot of work to do."

Rick sat next to Marc on the back porch, watching his friend through narrowed eyes.

"I'll be fine by tomorrow. Just go away for today. Okay?"

"Not okay. You're a mess."

Marc knew it but at the moment he didn't care. His heart ached so badly he was afraid it was permanently damaged, and he didn't need Rick trying to piece it back together for him. He just wanted to wallow in his own misery. If he didn't realize what a disaster it would turn out to be, he'd have started drinking when he got home the night before. Alcohol was a great anesthetic, but not Marc's style. Never had been. He'd seen too many others fall into that trap.

"I'll be fine by tomorrow. We don't have anything going today, right?"

"Right. I just don't think you should be alone. Hey, why don't you go over to your folks' house?"

Marc raked his fingers through his hair. "Maybe later. Right now I don't feel like seeing anyone. Including you."

He'd considered talking to his mother but the more he went over everything in his mind the more he felt like a fool. He was probably right to doubt ML, to have reservations about a woman who refused to tell him her name. He hated the ugly thought creeping in that he was the one doing all the giving, all the accommodating. So maybe this was all for the best. His brain got the message, only it didn't migrate to his heart.

Rick stretched his long legs out in front of him. "Maybe it's for the best, guy. I mean, she wouldn't even tell you who she is."

"That has nothing to do with it," he snapped. That was one subject he had no intention of discussing with anyone. He had a hard enough time wrestling with it himself.

"Hey." Rick held up his hands. "Don't bite my head off. If it worked for you, then fine."

Marc rubbed his unshaven jaw. "I know you can't understand this but she's very special. She had some kind of trust issues. Maybe because the whole rock club scene was new to her. I'm sure she had misconceptions like a lot of people, and that bitch Lacey just solidified them." He snorted. "You can tell Danny and Shelley thanks for helping to fuck up my life."

"They feel real bad about the whole thing, Marc. Shelley and Lacey had a big fight about it last night. But Lacey's been after you for a long time, and her sister was just trying to do her a favor. Nobody realized you were so serious about your mystery woman."

"Maybe I didn't even realize it myself until she ran off. Jesus, it's like my heart's been ripped out." He shoved his fingers through his hair. "I was trying to let her know how I feel but still keep it low-key. Not frighten her off. But she means so much to me, and now I'll probably never get the chance to tell her. Make a life with her."

And that was no lie. If nothing else had come out of this disaster, it had forced him to accept the fact the he was in love with her. He'd do anything to find her, let her know what was in his heart and pray his hardest it was in hers, too.

Actually he wanted to crawl into a hole and hide, but he had obligations to the band he couldn't ignore. Especially now when the things they'd worked so hard for were within reach. He'd looked forward to sharing everything with his Music Lady, but now....

"All right." Rick pushed himself out of the chair. "I'll leave you to your misery. But we're all having breakfast with Butch tomorrow morning to hammer out the details of the management contract. He's also got the dates for the tour, and he's talked to the record people. So put on your best and brightest smile. And brain."

"Don't worry. I'll be on my game."

After Rick had left, Marc wandered around the house. He couldn't remember ever feeling this bad. This lost. This totally bereft. He'd found the woman he believed to be his soul mate, the woman he could love forever, and now everything was fucked up. In his bedroom, he stretched out on the bed, pulling the pillow against him so he could inhale ML's scent, wishing she was there with him. And how stupid was that? The chance he'd ever see her again was almost nonexistent and the pain of such knowledge nearly drove him to his knees.

He'd replayed the scene in the dressing room more times than he'd seen reruns of old television shows. He'd been thoroughly jazzed, just like the others, when Butch had come onto the stage to talk to them, walked them out into the wings and told him he wanted to put them under contract. Dozens of bands had tried to get him to take them on, but he'd focused only on Deep Blue River until he'd established them at the top. Then it was a mob scene to see who he'd sign next. And Lightnin' had won the lottery.

Marc wanted to share this with ML. Let her know how connected he felt to her. What he saw in the future for them. Beg her for her name if begging was what it took and show her they could have something solid together. Finding the one right person in this business wasn't easy. It took someone who could put up with the crazy hours and the uncertainties endemic to it. But he also knew you couldn't pick the time and place when the one right person walked into your life.

For him it had been ML, the moment he saw her at Aftershock. He wanted her to be part of his success with her. His excitement. Take her home with him, open the bottle of wine and get her to talk to him about her trust issues. Hopefully begin the foundation of a life together.

Those were his thoughts when he walked off the stage with the band at the Amphitheatre. He'd glanced back once over his shoulder and seen ML slide off the equipment crate where she'd been sitting, and expected her to head for the dressing room. Several of the women the other band members had brought were already there but not ML. That damn Lacey jumped up, plastering herself all over him, and tried playing tonsil hockey the minute ML walked through the door.

By the time he shoved Lacey aside and raced out to the parking lot, ML was already heading to her car and not interested in listening to him. If he'd ever thought she'd trust him, that had gone right down the drain. The look of betrayal on her face and the pain in her voice were burned into his brain.

Marc thought again about taking Rick's suggestion and seeing if his mother had any advice for him, but he wasn't ready yet to drag the whole mess out for her to see.

Unable to sit still, he dug his acoustic guitar out of the closet and headed back to the porch. Maybe he'd do something productive with his pain and put it into a song.

Chapter Sixteen

The week was pure hell for Marc. Days were filled with business meetings, rehearsals and starting the two-week gig at The Rock Den. They had one more two-week commitment, but Butch had managed to get them out of everything else. Deep Blue River would be hitting the road in six weeks with Lightnin' as their opening act. Ten dates in three states. Butch had used the tape of *On the Edge of the Woods* to get them a quick record contract with the guys who had been at the concert. A single, pushed out, down, and dirty to get airplay with the concert tour with a full album to follow if the first results were good.

"Labels aren't committing to too much in front these days," Butch told them.

But they were good with that. They knew they had a good product.

They worked their asses off rehearsing, talking business, getting ready for the tour, signing contracts. Playing the club at night. Marc was glad for the long hours. He could fall into bed exhausted and try to sleep without seeing Music Lady's face every time he closed his eyes.

But when he did, he'd get up and work on his song. A song filled with pain, agony, and love.

Music playing, hips swaying, dance for me, Music Lady.

And he could see her at Aftershock, moving to the beat of the songs, tentative the first time but gradually losing herself in the rhythm. Swept up in it. Letting it all go.

Body moving, hot and grooving, Music Lady.

He saw her in his bed, like an unleashed tiger, wild and passionate and giving.

Sweet and sexy, that's her style. Make her stay a while. Music Lady.

Then he'd have to stop, because the agony of loss was enough to bring him to his knees. Maybe if he finished it, he could get the band to play it. It wouldn't take more than one rehearsal. He had to find her, even if he had to hang out in the stupid grocery store for the rest of his life, something he did every day between rehearsal and work. The tour might interrupt it but he wouldn't give up. Sooner or later she'd have to come back there. It was the only link he had right now and he hung onto it.

"So exactly how am I supposed to find him?"

As usual Emma and Annie were at Hot Salsa, sucking up the margaritas during happy hour. This was the third night in a row, and Emma was beginning to look forward to the numbing effects of the alcohol. She always got the last drink to go, carrying it home with her so she could crawl into bed. Pathetically, she'd worn the Lightnin' T-shirt every night, pulling it on the moment she got home, inhaling his scent that clung to it. Then the pain would surface again, she'd chug down her to-go margarita and try to fall asleep, praying she didn't keep seeing Marc's face in her dreams.

The only good thing about the entire week was Andrew had gotten the message at last and left her alone. And the dinner with her parents had gone very well. They still tended to look at her as if someone had snatched their daughter and left a stranger in her place but they understood her changes were permanent and the old Emma was gone for good.

"As you keep reminding us," her mother said, "you're thirty. You have to make your own decisions. We love you, Emma. We just want you to know, whatever happens we will always be here for you."

That had made her cry happy tears.

After ripping herself inside out for five days, she'd come to the realization Annie was right. She'd reacted without thinking. Run away like...like...like the old Emma. There had to be an explanation and the new Emma owed Marc the opportunity to give her one. Otherwise she wasn't any different than the woman who had ran out of Andrew's house as if her tail were on fire. If she didn't like what Marc said she could walk away.

But now the question was how to go about it. She knew where he lived but she couldn't bring herself to go to his house. She only had so much courage. What if he slammed the door in her face? At least a club was neutral territory. She knew they weren't at Aftershock anymore, which presented a problem.

"Actually that's going to be a lot easier than you think," Annie told her.

"What do you mean?"

"Honey, Lightnin's a hot topic right now. You can hardly hit a blog without seeing something about them." She lifted her tote, reached inside, and pulled out a folded sheet of paper. "I printed this out for you today, hoping you might get around to shaking your brain into place."

Emma opened the sheet of paper and scanned it.

Music Musings Around the City

Hotter than hot rock band Lightnin', appropriately named for the electricity in their music, will be the opening act for superstars Deep Blue River on a ten city tour starting the end of this month. Meanwhile local fans can get a last glimpse of them until the end of next week at rockin' new club The Rock Den. But get there early. The lines are longer than those at a Deep Blue River box office.

She looked at Annie. "I'll never get in. Look what it says about the lines." She refolded the sheet and set it down on the pub table. "And I can't see myself hanging around at the back door like one of the groupies I so despise."

"Fortunately," Annie winked, "you have friends in high places."

Emma frowned. "I do?"

"Uh huh. My cousin is the bartender and he'll put our names on the list. So we *can* go to the back door but a nice man will let us in."

Her stomach turned upside down. "So...I'm really going to do this?"

"Listen to me. Do you care about this guy?"

Emma nodded. "More than I realized. More than I ever thought I could. If I learned nothing else this whole miserable week I learned that."

"Then you need to do this or you'll hate yourself for the rest of your life."

She rubbed her forehead. "Can you see me bringing him home to my folks? They'll pass out in shock."

"Or just maybe they'll see the same thing in him you do. So what's it gonna be? Fish or cut bait?"

Emma took a long swallow of her drink and stared at Annie. "Fish. I'm going to fish."

The blog had been right. The line to The Rock Den stretched down the sidewalk and around the corner, but Annie just headed to the parking lot in back. She'd insisted on driving both of them, leaving Emma with no option but to work things out with Marc. And Emma had offered up every silent prayer she'd ever heard, including a few incantations.

This was her chance to find out if Marc was right and they had something real. If he could forgive her for being such a coward, hiding her identity from him and running away the first time the going got tough. If she understood nothing else during her hours of self-examination, it was that she loved Marc and wanted to make a life with him. Whatever shape it took. Now if she could just get him to listen to her....

"I don't know if I can do this." She wiped her sweaty palms on her new jeans. "I mean, come on, Annie. What if he just ignores me?"

"If it's that bad, we'll just leave and I'll drive you home."

"You promise?"

"Word of honor." She winked. "Pinky swear."

Emma blew out a breath. "Okay, then. Let's go. I guess."

Her legs were trembling as they approached the back door, and Annie pressed the buzzer. The door opened and music blasted out at them at a very high decibel. Her friend shouted their names to the guy in jeans and a long-sleeved T-shirt, and he checked his list.

"Oh, yeah." He grinned and shouted back. "Ron's cousin. Sure. Come on in. But I warn you, it's packed."

"That's okay," Annie told him. "We're used to it."

Emma couldn't make herself move, but Annie grabbed her hand and pulled her into the club.

The Rock Den was larger than Aftershock but no less jammed. Again Emma realized there were very few booths, mostly a huge dance floor crowded with people watching the band and moving to the music.

"I don't think we can get to the bar for a drink," Annie yelled in her ear.

"That's okay. I couldn't swallow anyway."

They were right at the edge of the stage and her gaze was focused on Marc, caught up as usual in his music, doing a bass solo that reverberated through her entire body. She'd wondered if her feelings for him would have lessened, if the humiliation and pain would have blotted everything away. But the moment she saw him, she was struck with an emotion so strong it stole her breath.

Around her, people stamped their feet and gyrated, the energy so high octane it was almost visible. Emma blocked out the rest of the band, watching only Marc until the song ended. The applause was deafening.

She saw Rick's gaze land on her, his eyes widened, and he nudged Marc. The minute he spotted her, the familiar heat and electricity rushed through her with a force that made her weak. They stared at each other for a long time, while she tried desperately to read the expression on his face, but the shifting lights made it nearly impossible. Then Rick nudged him again, Marc whispered something to him, and he nodded and spoke to the other two members of the band.

In the next instant, a wailing intro flowed out from the lead guitar, almost insubstantial in the air without the other instruments. Emma waited for Danny, the lead singer to step up to the microphone, but instead it was Marc who moved forward to the mic on the stand in front of him. His deep bass voice blended perfectly with the mournful sound of the guitar. He looked straight at her, his arm outstretched, his hand pointing in her direction.

"There she is, Music Lady..."

One long underscoring note on the bass.

"All I want, all I need. Music Lady..."

Another long, resonating note.

Emma felt as if her entire body had turned inside out and chills raced through her. Music Lady! He was singing about her and the words were pure poetry, about a love like no other. Strong. Forever. A forever love. He was singing a love song for *her!*

Ohmigod!

She clutched Annie's hand, squeezing it.

"...And lives in my heart forever, Music Ladyyyyyy."

Her own heart cracked and swelled, packed with all the emotion she had guarded so carefully. The words poured out to her so powerfully they reached every corner of her being.

Then the tap, tap, tap percussive staccato of the drums, the harmony from the lead singer and finally the full-bodied bottom of the bass. As the full crashing sound of the song exploded, Marc's body began to move with it as he usually did. The song reminded Emma of Eric Clapton's original version of *Layla* in its heavy sound and power and intensity. She stood completely immobile the entire time the song played, enraptured, until the final notes blasted out into the air and died away. When it was finished she was weak, unsure if she could keep standing. The applause was deafening and sustained. People whistled and shouted.

Vaguely she heard Rick say, "Thank you. We'll be back in a few."

Annie was shaking her arm to get her attention, pulling her back to earth. "Here comes Marc."

And then he was there. Right in front of her. The heat in his gaze burned into her, searing her soul. People were trying to talk to him, sliding curious glances at her at the same time, but he ignored them all.

"You came."

She nodded, staring up at him. "I did."

"We need to get out of here."

"Hi!" Annie interjected. "I'm Annie. Remember me?"

"Yeah, sure." But he didn't stop staring at Emma's face.

"Uh, just so you know, I drove her," Annie told him. "She doesn't have her car with her so if I leave, she's got no ride home."

"I got it covered," Marc said, already moving Emma toward the back door.

Emma was hit with a sudden case of nerves.

What's going to happen? What will he say? Will he listen to me? Will he—shut up, Emma. You came here to do something. Give it a chance. Let him know you've finished growing up and you want a life with him. In his world.

The guy with the clipboard smiled at them and swung the door open. "Fifteen minutes," he reminded Marc.

"Got it."

Marc had a firm grip on her elbow as he walked them to the farthest corner of the lot, away from the smokers and the direct beam of the parking lot lights. When they stopped, he turned her to face him, pulled her into his arms, and kissed her as if he'd never stop. His tongue was a living flame, sweeping every surface, sliding across her own small one, sucking it into his mouth. His fingers threaded through her hair as his hands cupped her head, moving it this way and that to give himself a better angle. When he pressed his body against hers, she could feel the hard thickness of his erection even through two layers of clothing.

They stopped only to drag air into oxygen-deprived lungs but he never let go of her, fingers curved around her skull and holding it so he could look directly into her eyes.

She tried to read his face but he was doing a good job of keeping it blank. Damn!

At last he spoke. "I didn't think I'd ever see you again."

"I wasn't sure I *wanted* to see you again."

"I figured." He brushed his thumbs along her cheekbones. "What changed your mind?"

She swallowed, her mouth suddenly dry. "My friend Annie told me I'd probably break both legs jumping to conclusions, that I needed to quit running away from things and should have given you a chance to explain."

That special Marc smile curved his lips. "Remind me to send Annie a dozen roses."

"She also said if I cared for you, I needed to talk to you."

His dark irises were like lasers boring into her. "And do you? Care for me, Music Lady?"

"Y-Yes." She wet her lips. "I-I do. Guitar Man."

"Good. Because I care for you, too." He looked at her as if he wanted to see every thought running around in her head. "I love you, ML. I want a life with you. A home. Kids." He grinned. "Breakfast. You stole my heart and I never want it back."

Relief swept through her. She hadn't blown it after all. But she sure as hell had probably run out of chances. "I'll do my best to take good care of it." Her voice was shaky. "You wrote the song for me." She hardly believed it.

"My heart was breaking." His expression was pained. "I had to do something. I made the band rehearse it so if you ever showed up we could play it."

Her heart was beating so hard she could hear it hammering against her ribs. "I love it."

"I love *you*." He kissed her again, long and deeply, as if he'd never get enough of the taste of her. "If you believe nothing else, believe that. Take a leap of faith, ML."

This was it. Fish or cut bait. She wanted what he was offering more than she wanted her next heartbeat. And she hoped that he could accept the blending of her two personalities—Emma and ML.

Do it, Emma. It's now or never.

She let out a slow breath. "Okay."

"But before anything else I want to clear up last Sunday night. Don't say anything until I finish. Okay?"

Emma nodded, shoving her hands in the pockets of her jeans.

Pacing back and forth in front of her, raking his hands through his hair every so often, he told her everything, going all the way back to the first time he'd met Lacey and how she'd put the moves on him. And his rejection of her.

"I'm no saint," he said. "I've certainly been with other women. But I've always stayed away from groupies like Lacey. They just aren't my style. I'm not sure if she actually wanted to be with me Sunday night or if she just saw a way to get back at me by hurting you." He came to a stop in front of Emma and looked hard into her eyes. "So. Do you believe me? Please?"

She took her hands from her pockets and wound her arms around his neck. "After listening to that song you wrote, how could I not? No one could write those words and sing them the way you did without meaning them." She lifted on her toes and brushed her mouth over his. "Besides, Annie pointed out to me exactly how stupid I was being. That if I cared for you and had half a brain, I had to at least listen to your explanation."

He chuckled softly. ""Maybe I should make that *two* dozen roses." His gaze locked with hers. "You'll come home with me?"

She laughed nervously. "Well, yes. I guess you're my ride. Besides, this isn't a very good place to talk."

"No, but then we'll have all night."

At the thought her entire body trembled.

The energy in the Jeep was so intense during the drive to Marc's house, Emma thought she could actually touch it. Emotional energy. Sexual energy. The power of it vibrated in the enclosed space. They didn't talk, didn't say a word to each other but every few moments, Marc reached over for her hand and squeezed it. Emma's body was a volatile cocktail of anxiety and sexual awareness.

I am so far out of my element here.

Then she thought, *but I don't have to be.*

When they reached Marc's home, he took her hand again as they walked up to the porch and he unlocked the door, pushing it open and tugging her through it. He flipped the switch, turning on the table lamp and a warm glow bathed the room. Emma stood there, tense, anxious again, until Marc turned her to face him. He studied her for so long all the doubts began creeping back.

"What?' she asked, wondering what was going through his mind.

"I thought I'd never see you again." His voice was thick with emotion. "I just want to look my fill."

Then he kissed her, slow and sweet, heated with the underlying passion but also packed with enormous emotion.

His arms tightened around her and he pulled her into his body. "I've never said this to you before tonight, but I need to say it again now. I don't even know your name or as much about you as I plan to but I love you, ML. I've never said that to anyone else. And I can wait for you to say it to me when you're ready."

Wasn't she ready now? She opened her mouth but somehow the words wouldn't come. She'd said them to Andrew but so matter-of-factly she wondered now why she'd bothered. This was so much more. This was...everything.

Suddenly she felt lighter than air, as if a burden she'd been lugging around had been lifted and tossed away. With Marc, she could face anyone or anything because he made her whole. His love was the nourishment that fed her.

"Not only do I love you. I adore you. My heart belongs to you, Guitar Man. So does my soul."

Heat darkened his eyes and he kissed her with intense passion that seared her to the soles of her feet. Every nerve fired, every pulse point throbbed, her sex dampened in anticipation of him and her breasts ached for his touch. She fit so well against his muscular body, the hard ridge of his cock pressing into her mound and the soft flesh of her tummy. Oh, God, she wanted him. Wanted him badly.

When he broke the kiss they were both breathless, dragging air into their lungs. Emma stroked his cheek, faint stubble just now rasping the skin.

"I read about the band on the Internet. I can't wait to hear all the details about what's happening. I'm really excited for you."

"Later. First I want to tell you again how much you mean to me. How special you are and always will be." He brushed his mouth against her. "Since I've been with you my music is stronger, my life is brighter. I look forward to getting up every day because the night might be one where you would come to the club." His body tensed. "Damn it, ML. I was so afraid it had all gone to hell, I was sick over it."

"Me, too." She nipped his jaw. "I don't think I've ever cried that much in my life." She raised her eyes to his. "I want you to understand I grew up with everything very rigidly defined for me. There were expectations, and I didn't dare not live up to them. Until...."

"Until?" he prompted.

"Until an old friend came through town and I realized how dull my life really was. I had a dead-end job and a dead-end boyfriend and the only people who were happy were him and my parents. I wanted more. That's how I ended up at Aftershock the first night." She shook her head. "That was the boldest thing I'd ever done. And it scared me. Can you understand that?"

He took her hands in his. "Yes, now that I know you better. You were driving on a highway with no roadmap."

"Exactly. Not telling you my name was my safety net. If it all fell apart I could run back to being who and what I was before and you'd never find me. I could pretend none of it ever happened."

"But it did happen." He lifted her hands and kissed her knuckle.

"Yes, it certainly did." She smiled at him. "I didn't know I'd meet the man who'd steal my heart and make my body sing. Who could teach me the wonders of making love with someone who really cares, and who loves giving pleasure as much as getting it."

"I always want to pleasure you." He trailed kisses across one cheek. "You're so beautiful, and you taste like heaven. When you're not with me I dream about kissing you, about holding your breasts in my hands. About drinking your essence and feeling myself inside you, all tight and wet and hot."

She shivered as desire coursed through her. "I...think of us naked in the shower." Heat crept up her cheeks. "You know I've never done that with anyone else."

"Yes, and I'm damn glad." His hands slipped down her back to cup her ass. "We'll take a lot of showers together from now on, Count on it."

"Marc?" She frowned.

"Yeah, baby?"

"I want you to meet my folks but they might not exactly be your cup of tea."

He laughed. "You mean I might not be theirs."

"Whatever."

"No matter. My family will love you. I can't wait to take you to Sunday brunch. In fact, how about this Sunday?"

"If...if you're sure."

"I've never been more sure of anything in my life. I love you. I want you with me forever."

Emma sighed and leaned her head against his shoulder. "Me, too."

"We'll talk about it after."

"After what?"

"After this."

He lifted her in his arms and carried her to the bedroom, pausing only to turn on the little bedside lamp.

This is so right. I belong here with him. I want this for the rest of my life.

He undressed her with exquisite care, his heart pounding as he exposed each area of her silken skin. Her breasts were heavy in his palms, her nipples taut as he brushed his thumbs over them. With his tongue he laved her taut buds, his teeth nipping them before he pulled them into his mouth. The taste of them was so delicious, like ripe berries, their flavor exploding as he gently nipped them. He could feast on them forever.

He knelt to remove her jeans and thong, his hands shaking with need and hunger and love, his mouth trailing moist kisses over her tummy and her thighs. He took a moment to caress her soft skin, touching the swells and valleys. Beneath his hands ML was trembling, too, and the scent of her musk drifted across his nose. The knowledge this woman would be in his bed for the rest of his life nearly made him come undone.

He lifted one foot, holding it in his hand as he pressed his mouth to her ankle, tasting her, feeling the pulse beneath his tongue. His thumbs traced the line of her calves, his mouth following until he reached her knee. He did the same thing with the other leg, taking his time. He'd waited so long to be able to make love to her without her doubts clouding the issue, he didn't want to rush. Instead, needing to savor every moment.

Marc caressed her thighs with his open palms, moving his hands up until he reached the seam where hip and thigh joined, framing her mound. He leaned his head forward slightly to run his tongue along her slit. She was shaking badly now, clutching his shoulders with her hands to steady herself, her nails digging into his muscles as he teased her clit and swirled her essence on his tongue.

"Oh, please." Her breathing hitched. "Please, Marc. I want you so badly."

"I want you, too, babe, but I want to make this special. I want you to know how much I love you with everything I do."

"I know. I just...can I touch you, too? Please?"

"In a while." If she touched him now, he'd go off like a rocket and it would be all over but the shouting.

He rose on legs far from steady and yanked his shirt over his head without bothering to undo the buttons. His gaze held hers as he toed off his shoes then pushed his pants and boxer briefs down his legs and tossed them to the side.

Her eyes on his cock were like twin lasers of unbearable heat. His shaft flexed under her gaze and a drop of fluid seeped from the slit, sifting on the soft skin. She brushed her thumb over the surface, catching the bead. When she licked it with a slow sweep of her tongue, Marc was sure he'd lose it then and there.

"Jesus, ML. Have pity here."

"I can't," she protested. "This week has been pure hell for me. I want to touch you and put my mouth on you everywhere. I'm so hungry for you I don't know if I'll be able to stop with one little taste."

"For the moment you might have to," he growled. "I can't wait to be inside you. I *have* to be inside you. Now."

In one swift movement, he yanked back the covers on the bed and nudged her backward until she was lying on the sheet. Lying down beside her, he moved his mouth over her again—the spot behind her ear that sent shivers through her, the line of her neck, the hollow of her throat where her pulse beat frantically.

Down over her beasts, her tummy, a swirl of tongue in her navel. Then the insides of her thighs, the touch making her quiver again.

When he used his thumbs to open the lips of her pussy, she arched up to him in silent urging. His tongue teased her clit before sliding along her slit and thrusting inside. She wrapped her legs around his neck to pull him in tighter, and his low laugh rumbled through her body. He could tell how ready for him she was.

"I love you," he murmured, rising over her, his mouth on hers as he shared her flavor. "You are everything to me."

"I love you, too. Even more."

"Mine." The word rumbled in his throat. His hands shook as he grabbed a condom and rolled it on then positioned himself, ready to enter her. "All mine."

"Yes." Her answer was a whisper. "Yours."

Very slowly, he pushed inside her, drawing it out so the thick length of his cock brushed every nerve in the sensitive tissues of her cunt.

"Ohhh," she sighed.

He held himself in place for a long time, watching her face, sending her messages with his eyes and his body. And then he began to move. Slowly first, then faster, one hand sliding between them to find her engorged clit. She felt so good gripping him with her tight, wet heat. He didn't want the ride to end, but his control, what there was left of it, was rapidly eroding.

In and out he moved, his thumb moving in rhythm with his hips, until she cried out in pleasure and need. Almost there. Almost...almost....

Now, now, now.

The words boomed in his head. And then they shattered, together, her body clamping down on him, his shaft pulsing inside the grip of her walls. They flew. That was the only description for what was happening. They soared and tumbled, cartwheeling in an explosion of fireworks as spasm after spasm rocked them both.

Then they were still, breath ragged, hearts thundering as their bodies attempted to recover. Marc kissed her cheeks, her forehead, her neck, before rolling to the side and taking her with him, their bodies still connected.

Music Lady pushed damp strands of hair from his forehead and looked up at him, her face still flushed, her eyelids heavy. She wet her lips, the sexy little sweep of her tongue that drove him wild.

"I have something to tell you. Well, a couple of somethings."

Her name? Finally? There's nothing holding her back now.

"What is it, ML?"

"Last Sunday was my birthday. I was...going to tell you my name. As kind of a celebration. Especially when the concert went so well."

Misery clenched his gut as memories of Sunday night stabbed him like sharp swords.

"Ah, babe." He rubbed his hand over his face.

"There really wasn't time before the concert and afterward...."

"Afterward it got ruined for you. Shit, shit, shit." He closed his eyes briefly. "I am so very sorry. I'd do anything to—"

"Shh." She pressed her fingers to his lips. "It's okay. Really. That's all over and done with. In the past." The look on her face told him she meant what she said. "We can still celebrate. Just a little late. This birthday and all the birthdays to come. Mine and yours. Anyway." She swallowed. "I just wanted you to know because I had planned to tell you some other things that night, too."

He lifted an eyebrow. "Yeah? Like what?"

"Well, one I've already told you, but I'll keep repeating it forever. I love you." She took a deep breath, letting it out slowly. "I won't lie. This started out as a joy ride, a heady thrill, a whole new world for me. But now...."

"Now?" he prompted, his body tense.

"Now I want the joy ride to last for the rest of my life."

His cock flexed inside her and the tension eased. "We may

have things to work through, you know," he said. "I want to be sure you know that. Like the tour and all the other things coming up."

"I know. I'm ready for whatever comes, Marc. Just as long as we're together."

"That's one thing that will never change."

"And I want to write."

"Yeah?" He lifted an eyebrow. "Write what? You know, I don't even have any idea what kind of work you do."

She made a face. "Boring. Just like the rest of my life used to be. I, um, edit textbooks."

Marc did his best not to laugh, knowing that would be a huge mistake. He just couldn't see his Music Lady sitting in a dreary office editing monotonous books day after day. Not when she was so full of life.

"So what is this secret dream of yours? What do you really want to do?"

She ducked her head, not looking at him as she spoke. "I want to write fiction. Romance novels. And try to get published."

"Then I think that's what you should do. Quit your job if you want to. I'll be making good money now, with more ahead of us."

"Really?" Now she looked up at him. "You mean it?"

"Of course I do. Everyone should be able to follow their dream."

"After all this time I want to chase mine."

"No problem, babe. I'll even give up my exercise room so you can have a home office." A thought struck him. "We are going to live here, right? I mean, I love this house. And we can always add on, but if..."

"Hush. Yes, of course. I'm only renting so moving isn't a problem. Besides, it would be a shame to leave this place after you've put so much work into it."

"I'll do anything, figure anything out, to make sure it works for us. I hope you know that. I just want you to be sure. About us."

"I am. More than sure. All the rest of the stuff? The tour? My folks? Just details. This, right here, is what counts the most."

Marc was afraid his heart would crack; it was so full. "Does this mean you'll stay and let me take you to breakfast?" he asked, smiling.

She laughed, a wonderful, musical sound. "I never go to breakfast with men who don't know my name."

Was this some kind of game? They were past that, right? "But—"

She touched his cheek. "So let me make the introduction. Hi. My name is Emma Blake."

A magical warmth traveled through him. "Hi, Emma. I'm Marc. Or you can call me Guitar Man. How do you feel about an invitation to breakfast?"

"I'd love to go to breakfast with you. When did you want to do that?"

He touched his mouth to hers. "How about for the rest for our lives? Forever. On a permanent joy ride?"

She smiled back. "I can get on board with that. Forever sounds just right."

~ABOUT THE AUTHOR~

Desiree Holt's writing is flavored with the rich experiences of her life, including a long stretch in the music business representing every kind of artist from country singer to heavy metal rock bands. For several years she also ran her own public relations agency handling any client that interested her, many of whom might recognize themselves in the pages of her stories. She is twice a finalist for an EPIC E-Book Award, a nominee for a Romantic Times Reviewers Choice Award, winner of the first 5 Heart Sweetheart of the Year Award at The Romance Studio as well as twice a CAPA Award for best BDSM book of the year, winner of two Holt Medallion Awards of Merit, and is published by five different houses. *Romance Junkies* said of her work: "Desiree Holt is the most amazing erotica author of our time and each story is more fulfilling then the last."

www.desireeholt.com

Immerse Yourself in Fantasy
with
Decadent Publishing

ജ

www.decadentpublishing.com

www.ingramcontent.com/pod-product-compliance
Lightning Source LLC
Chambersburg PA
CBHW031303170626
46807CB00001B/283